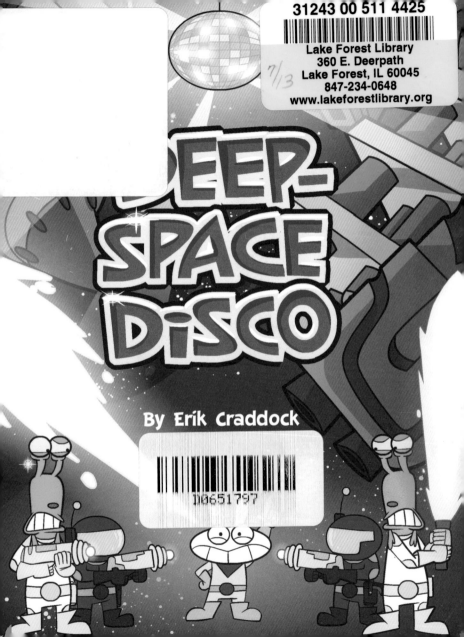

DEEP-SPACE DISCO

By Erik Craddock

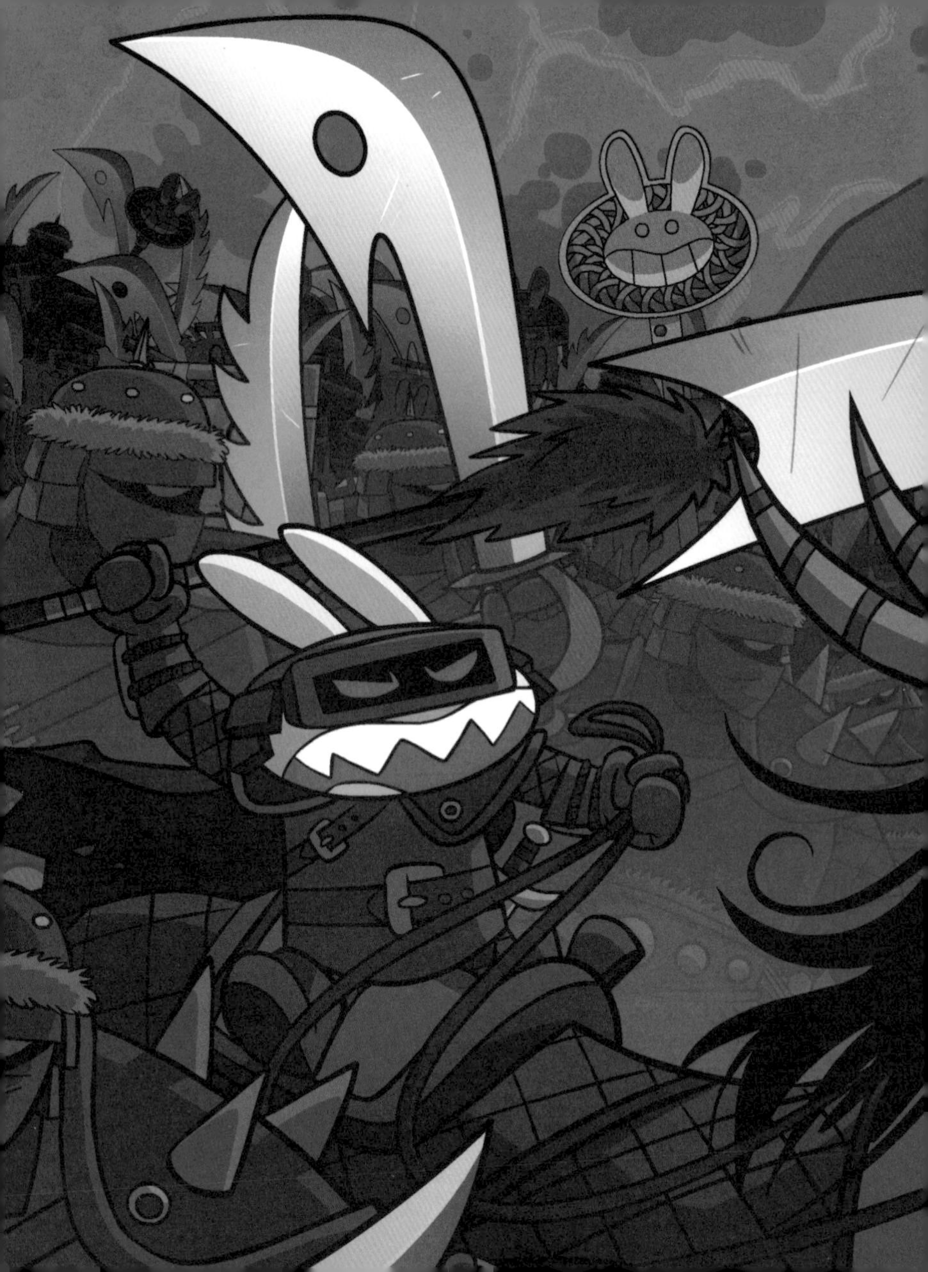

Published in the United States by Random House Children's Books, a division of Random House, Inc., New York. Random House and the colophon are registered trademarks of Random House, Inc.
Visit us on the Web! www.randomhouse.com/kids Educators and librarians, for a variety of teaching tools, visit us at www.randomhouse.com/teachers
www.stonerabbit.com

Library of Congress Cataloging-in-Publication Data
Craddock, Erik.
Deep-space disco / by Erik Craddock. — 1st ed.
p. cm. — (Stone Rabbit ; 3)
Summary: When an alien shape-shifter named Melvin the Plutarkian has Stone Rabbit tried for crimes Melvin committed and then wreaks havoc on Happy Glades, Stone Rabbit must find a way to get home and save his town and his friends.
ISBN 978-0-375-85876-5 (trade) — ISBN 978-0-375-95876-2 (lib. bdg.)
1. Graphic novels. [1. Graphic novels. 2. Rabbits—Fiction. 3. Extraterrestrial beings—Fiction. 4. Mistaken identity—Fiction. 5. Humorous stories.] I. Title.
PZ7.7.C73De 2009
[Fic]—dc22
2008040517

MANUFACTURED IN MALAYSIA
10 9 8 7 6 5 4
First Edition

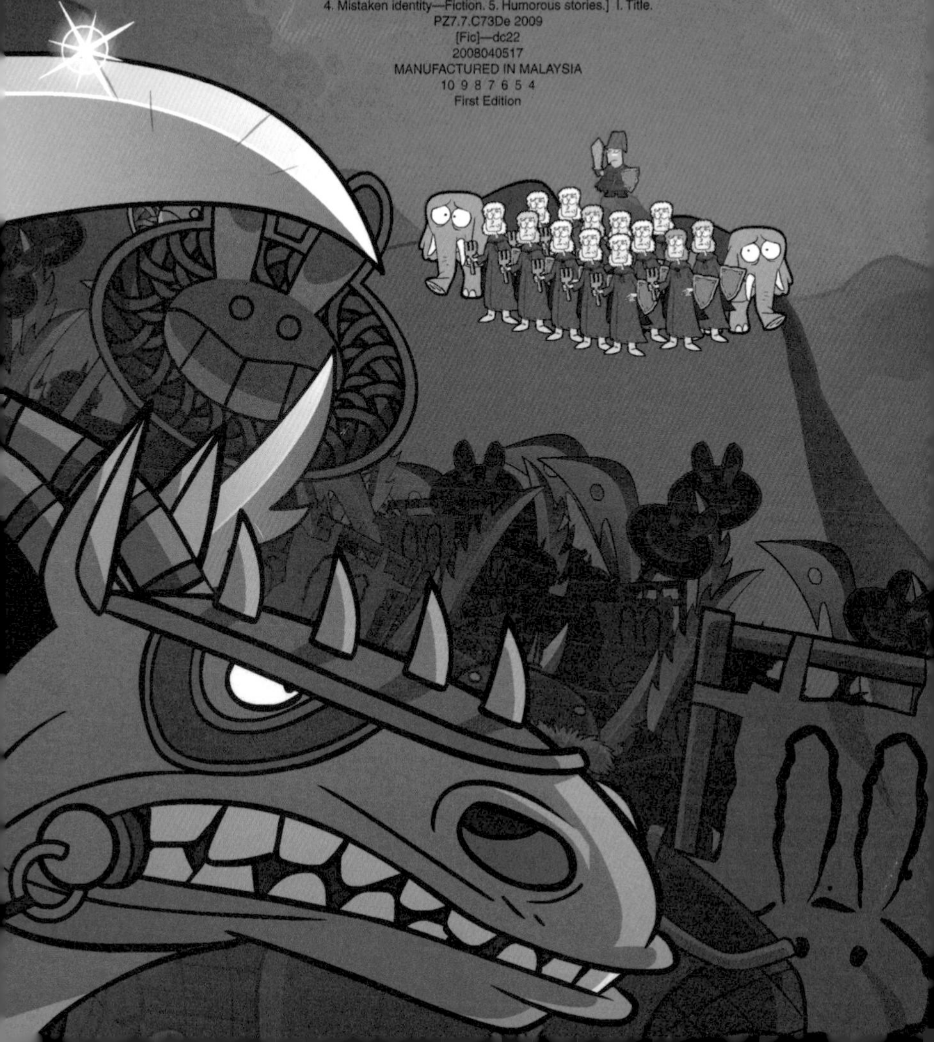

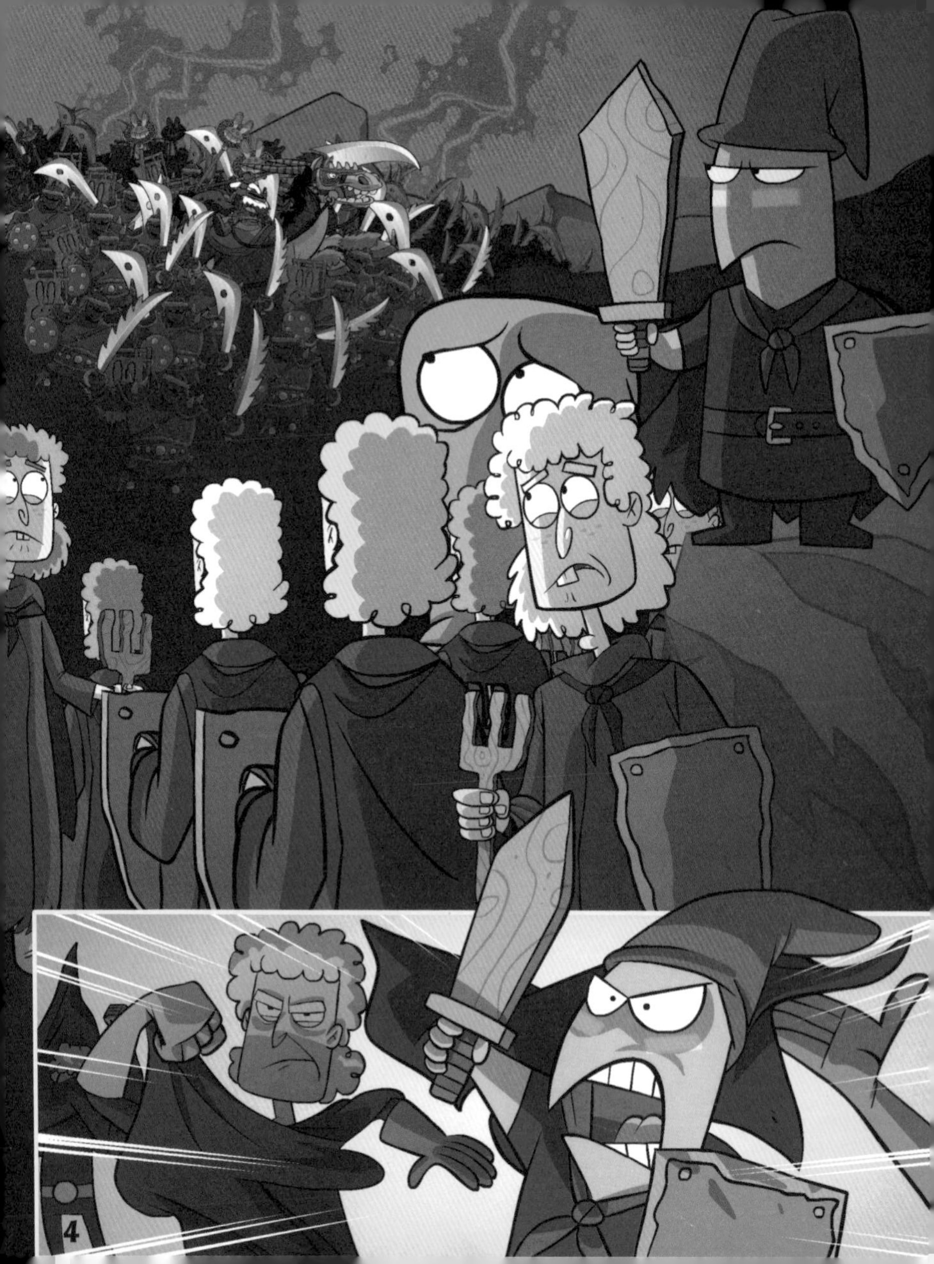

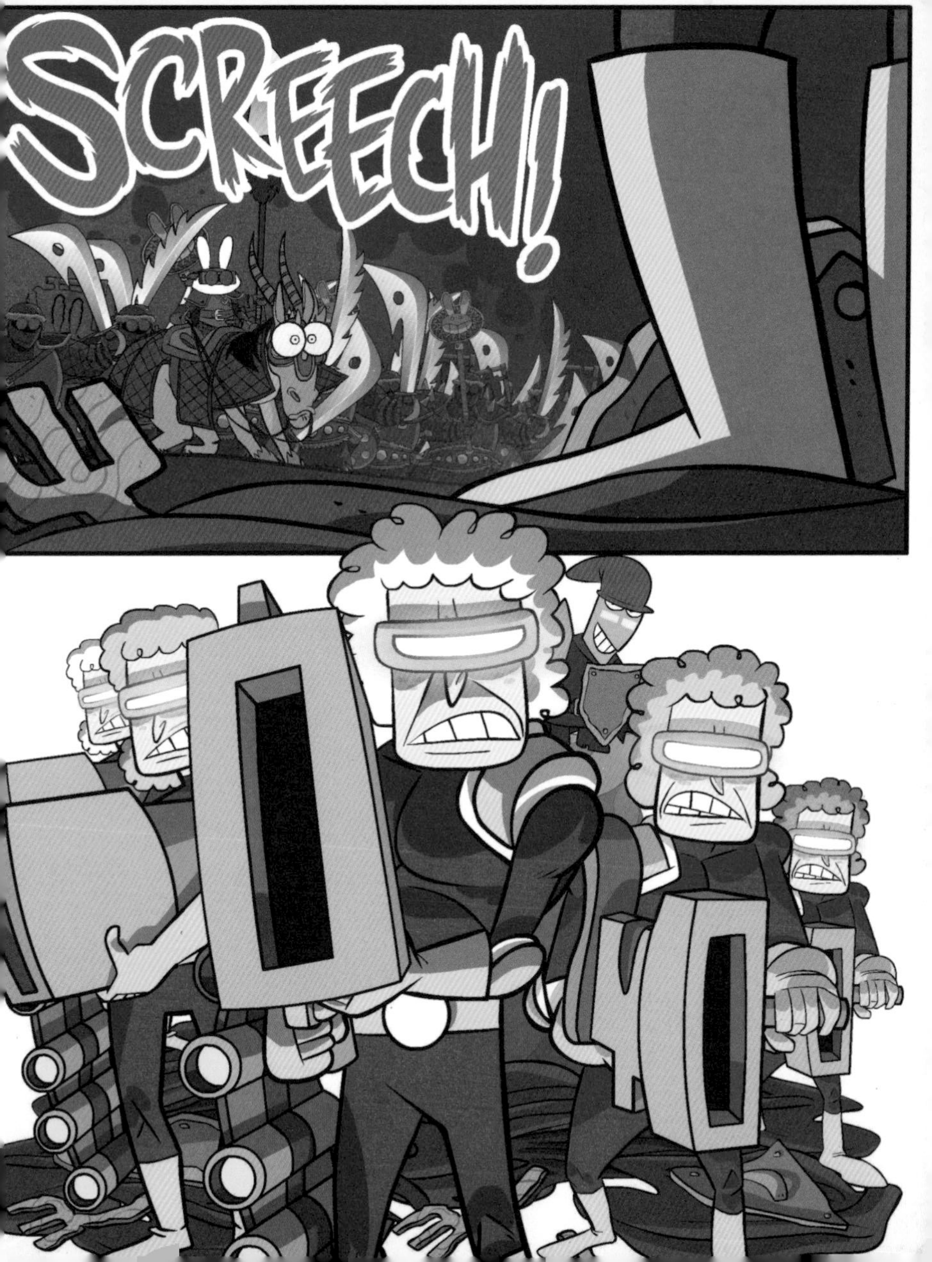
SCREECH!

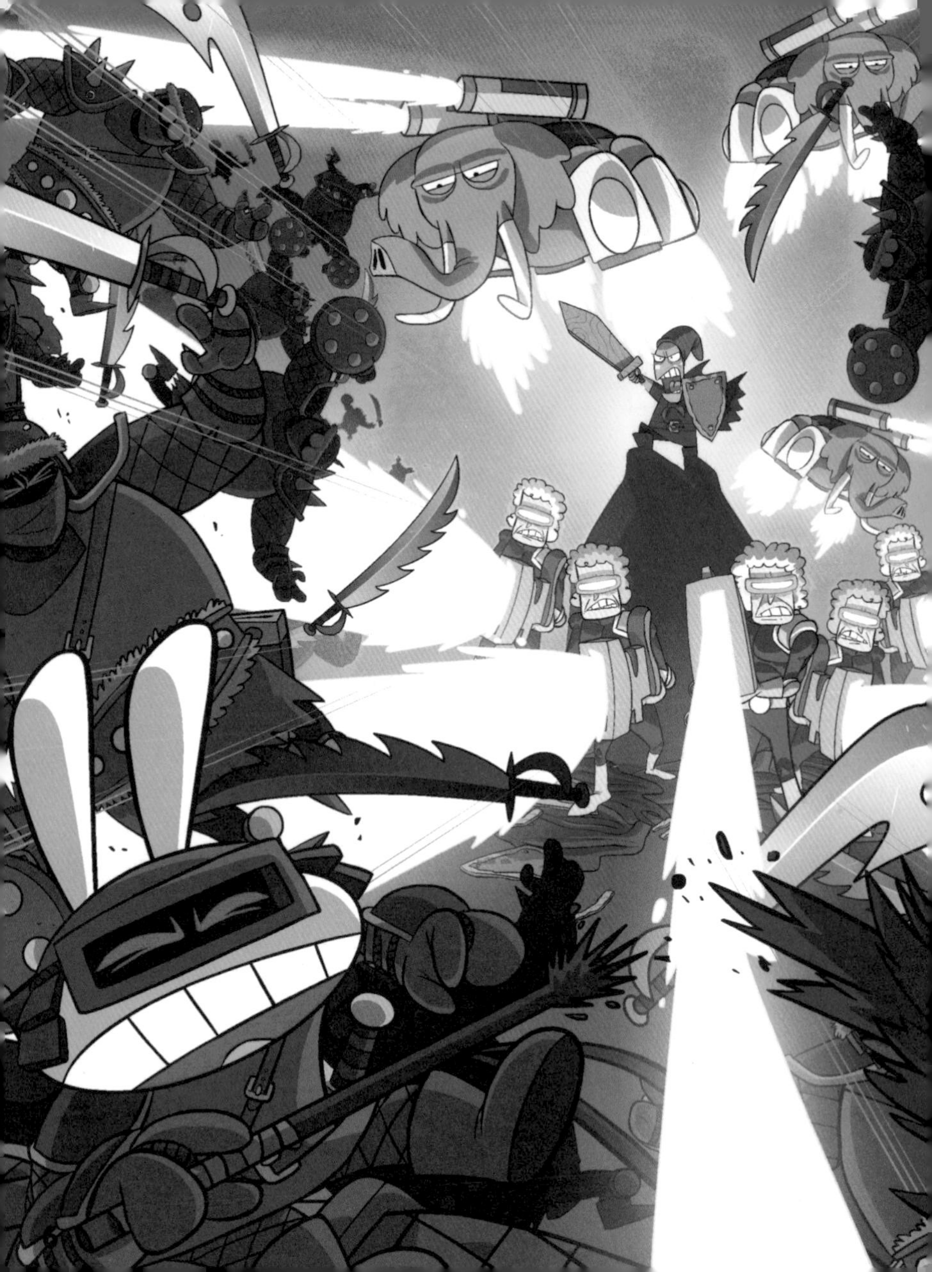

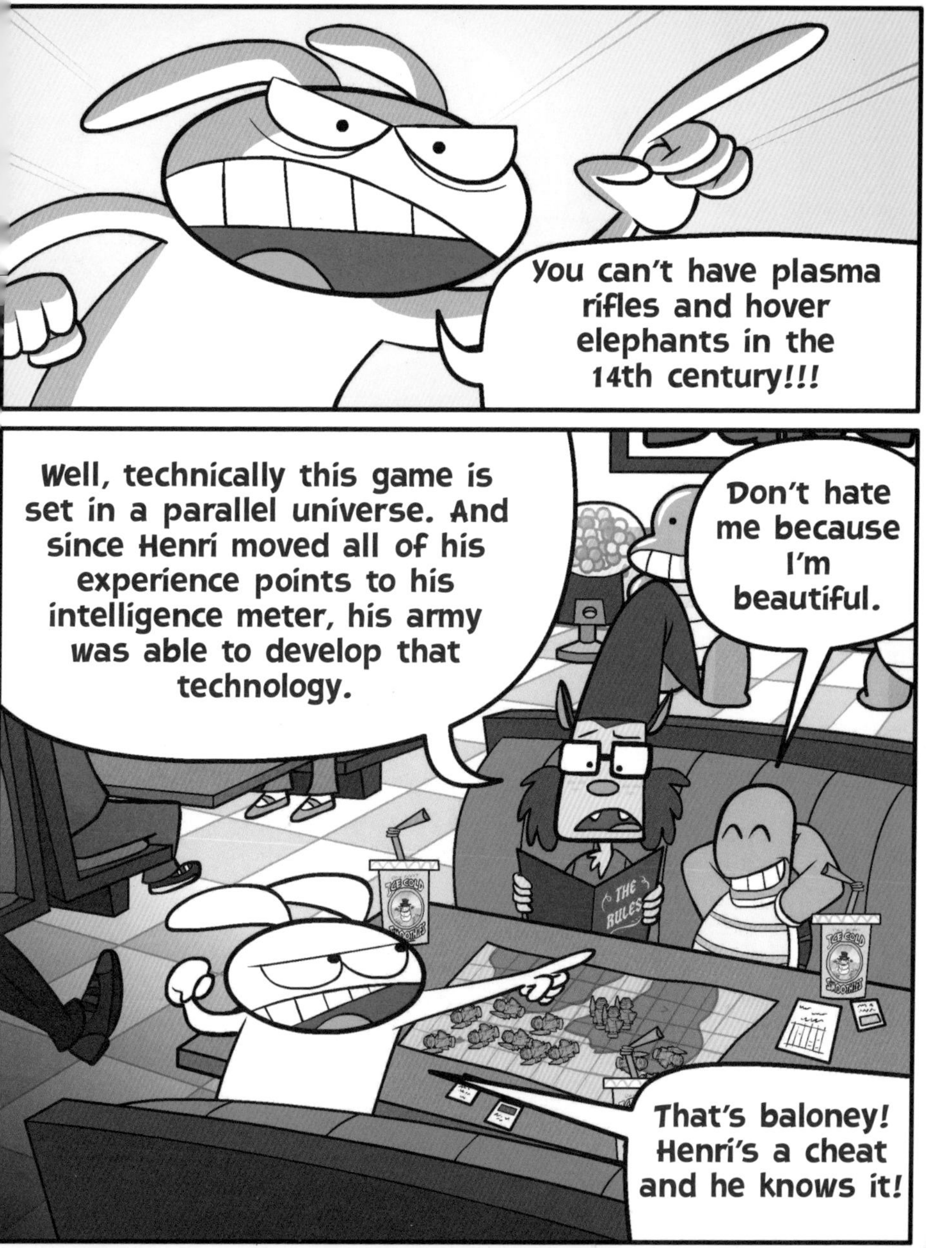
You can't have plasma rifles and hover elephants in the 14th century!!!
Well, technically this game is set in a parallel universe. And since Henri moved all of his experience points to his intelligence meter, his army was able to develop that technology.
Don't hate me because I'm beautiful.
THE RULES
That's baloney! Henri's a cheat and he knows it!

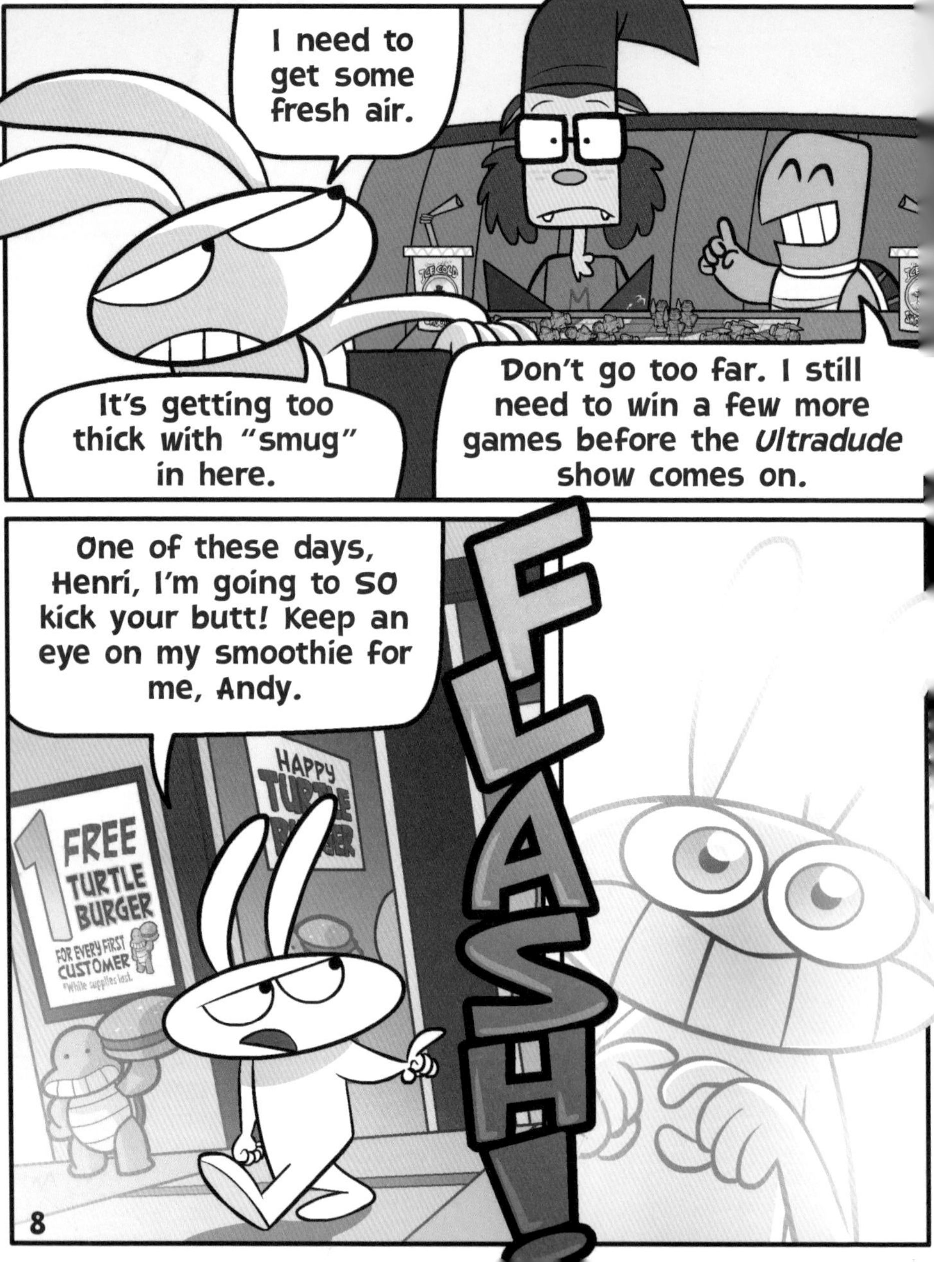
I need to get some fresh air.
It's getting too thick with "smug" in here.
Don't go too far. I still need to win a few more games before the *Ultradude* show comes on.
One of these days, Henri, I'm going to SO kick your butt! Keep an eye on my smoothie for me, Andy.
1 FREE TURTLE BURGER FOR EVERY FIRST CUSTOMER *While supplies last.
FLASH

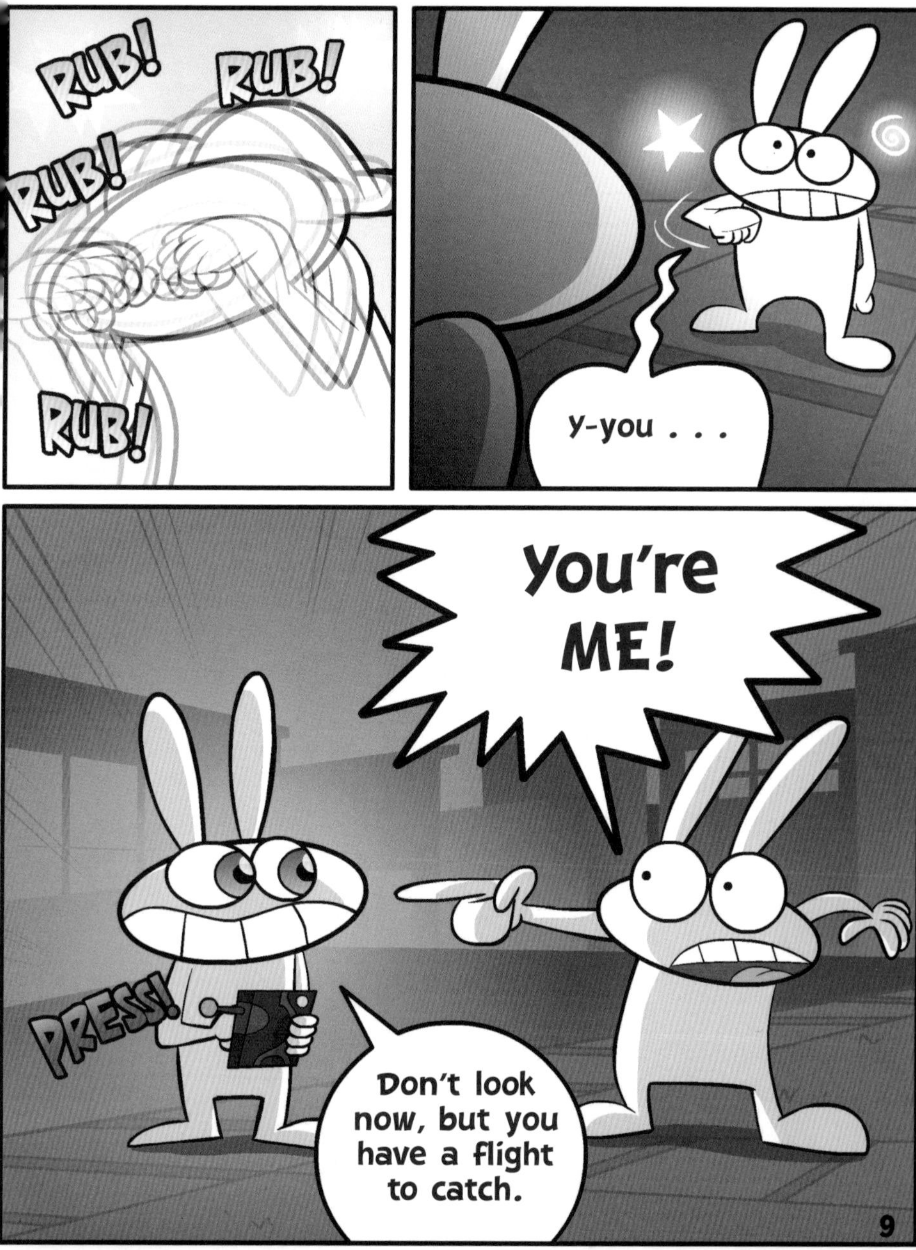
RUB!
RUB!
RUB!
RUB!
Y-you . . .
You're ME!
PRESS!
Don't look now, but you have a flight to catch.

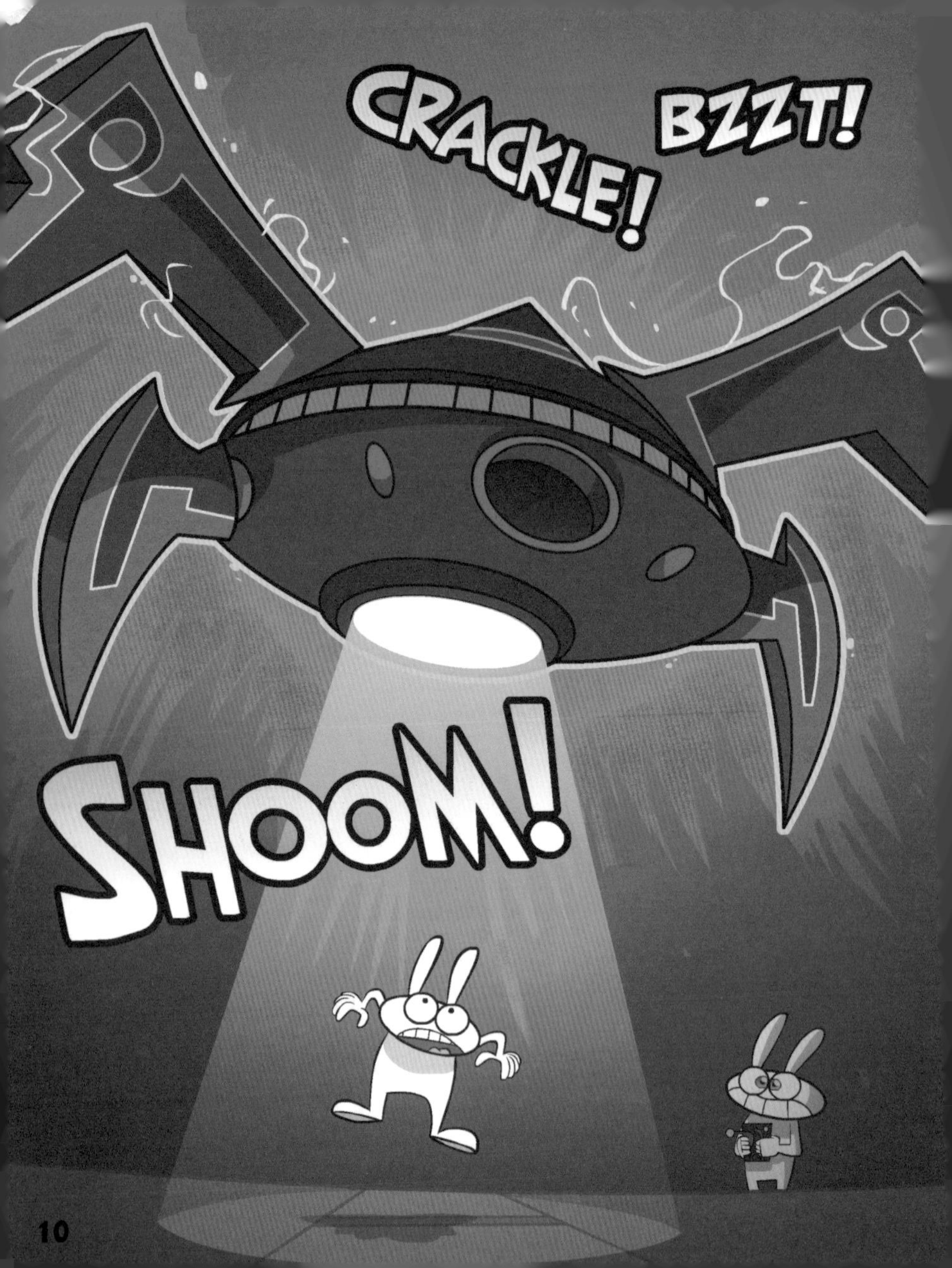
CRACKLE!
BZZT!
SHOOM!

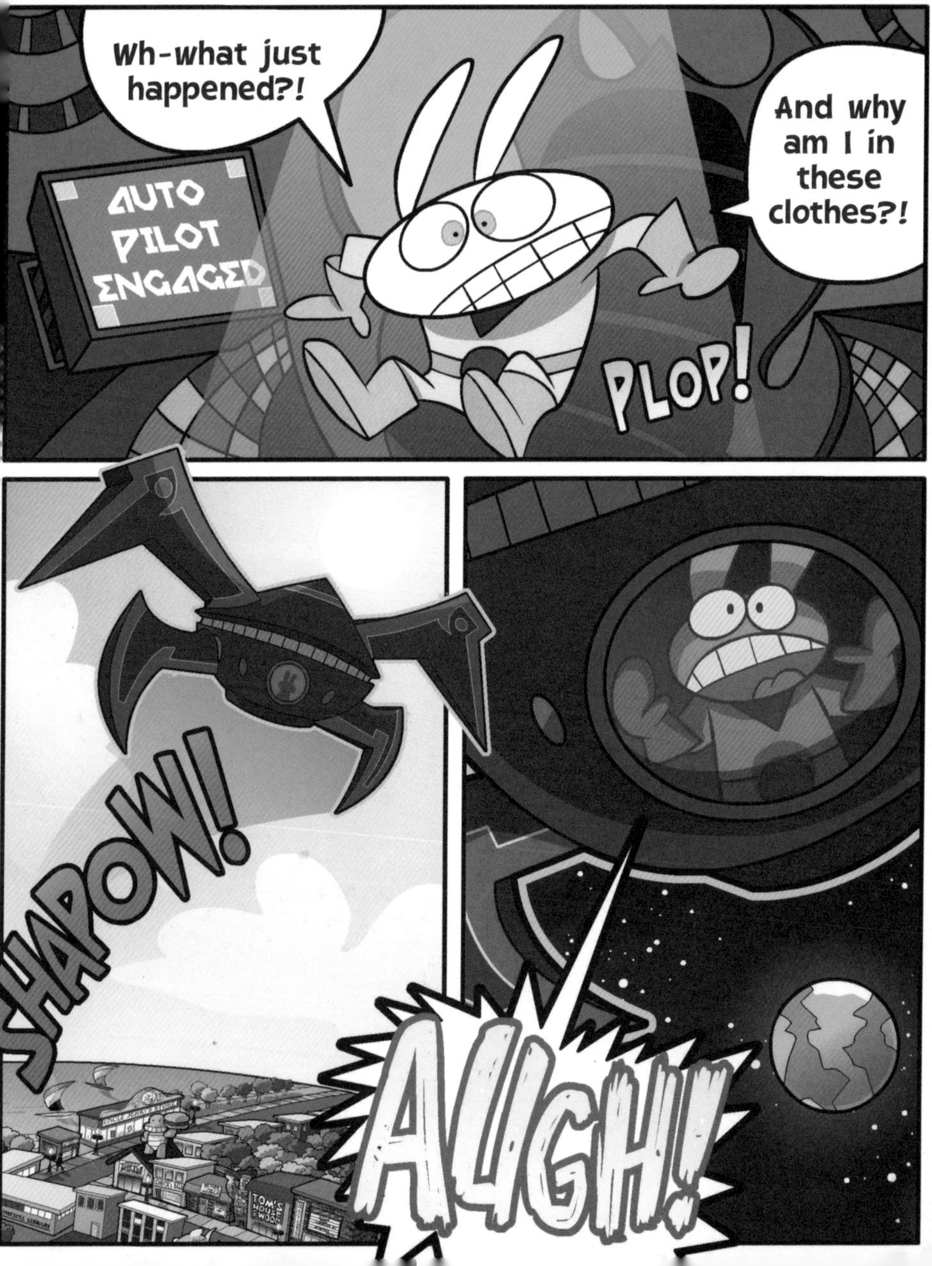
Wh-what just happened?!
AUTO PILOT ENGAGED
And why am I in these clothes?!
PLOP!
SHAPOW!
AUGH!

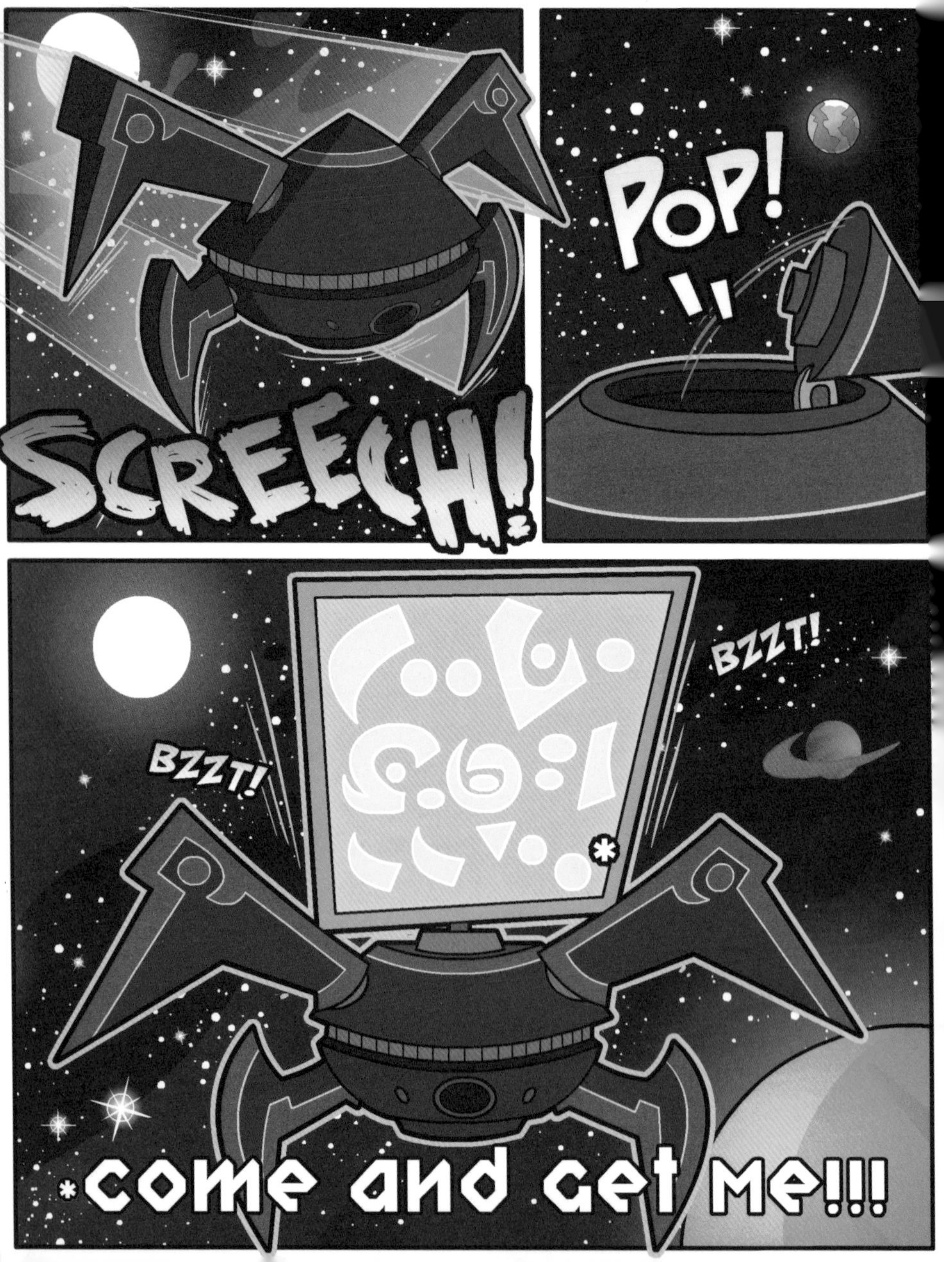
SCREECH!
POP!
BZZT!
BZZT!
*
*come and get me!!!

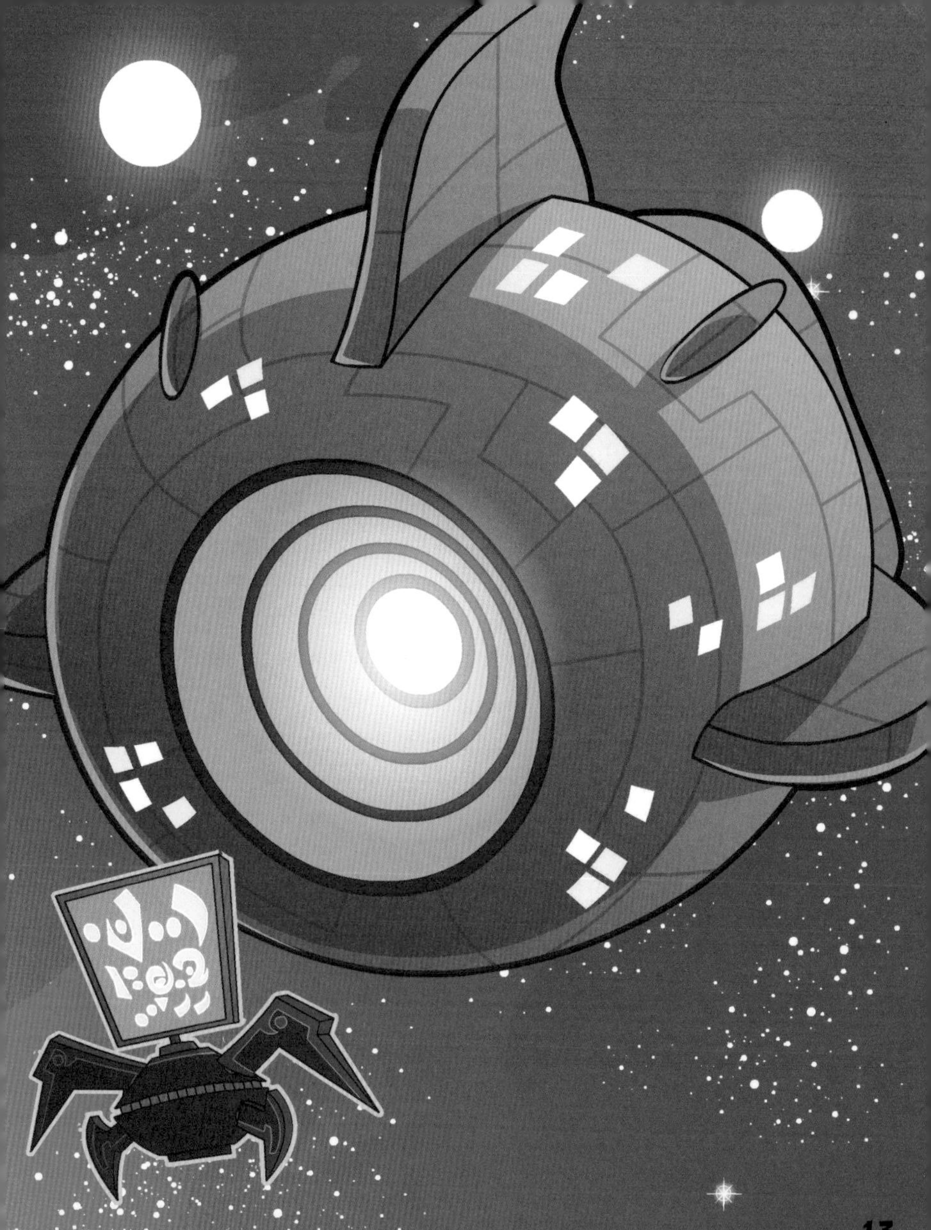

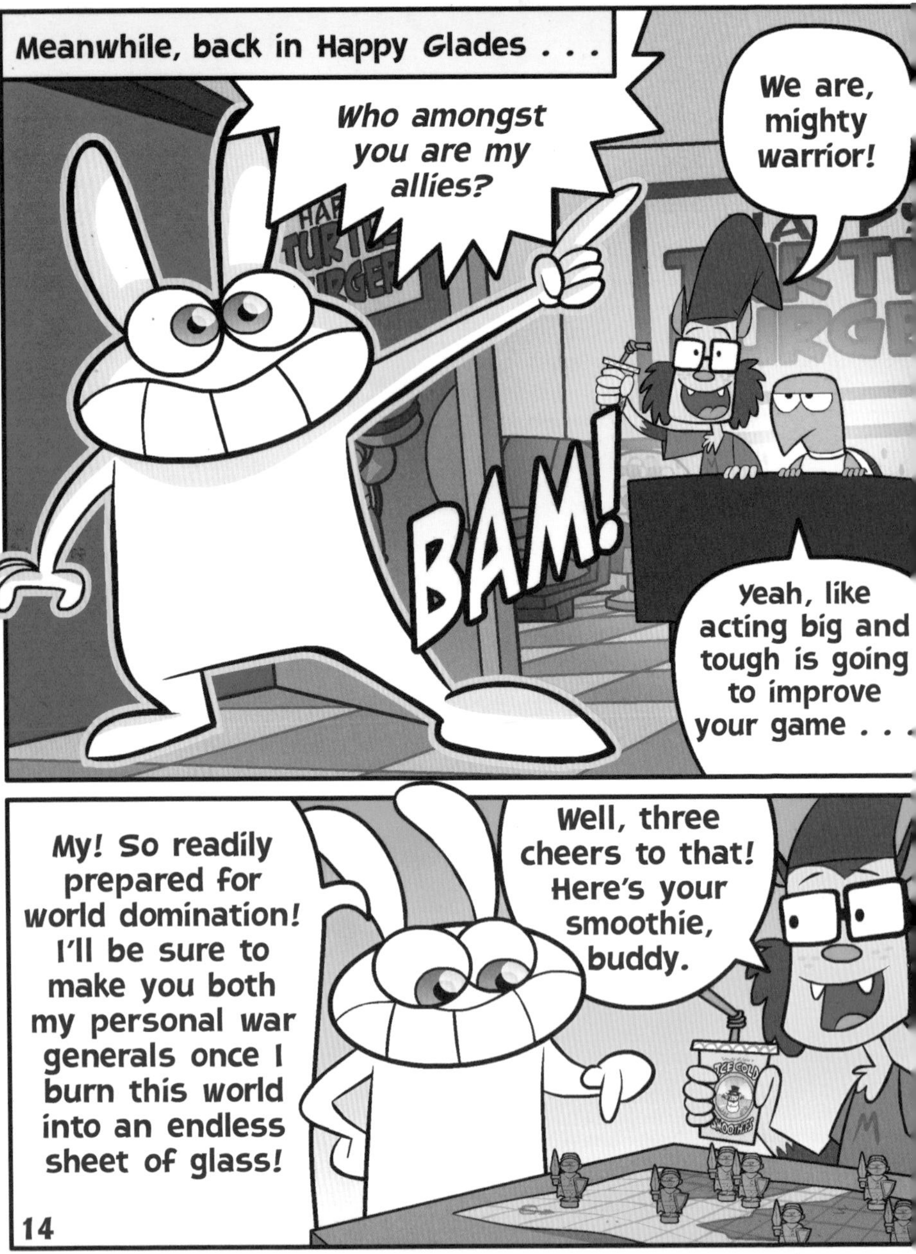
Meanwhile, back in Happy Glades . . .
Who amongst you are my allies?
We are, mighty warrior!
HAPPY TURTLE BURGER
BAM!
Yeah, like acting big and tough is going to improve your game . . .
My! So readily prepared for world domination! I'll be sure to make you both my personal war generals once I burn this world into an endless sheet of glass!
Well, three cheers to that! Here's your smoothie, buddy.
ICE COLD SMOOTHIES

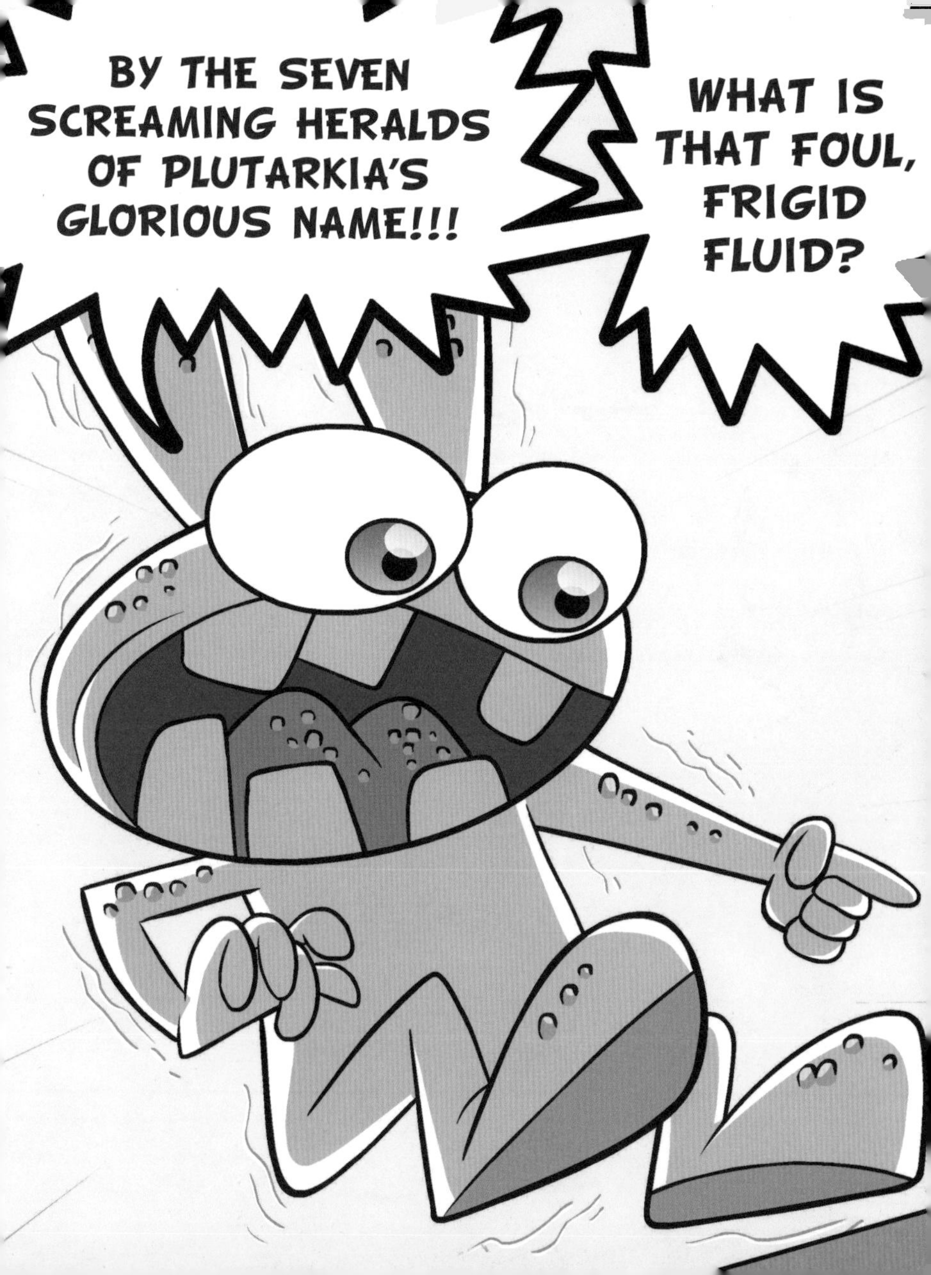
BY THE SEVEN SCREAMING HERALDS OF PLUTARKIA'S GLORIOUS NAME!!!
WHAT IS THAT FOUL, FRIGID FLUID?

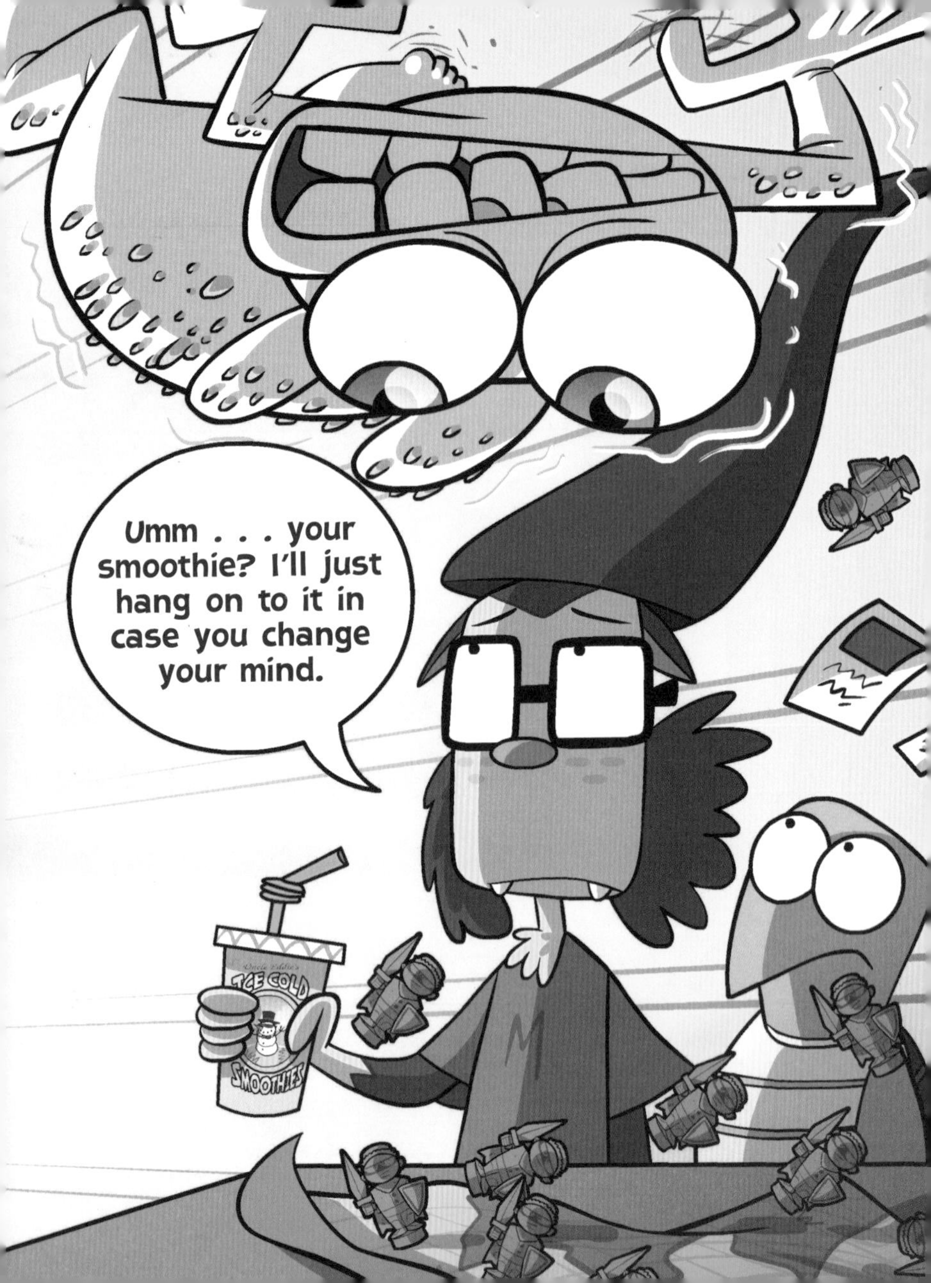
Umm . . . your smoothie? I'll just hang on to it in case you change your mind.
ICE COLD
SMOOTHIES

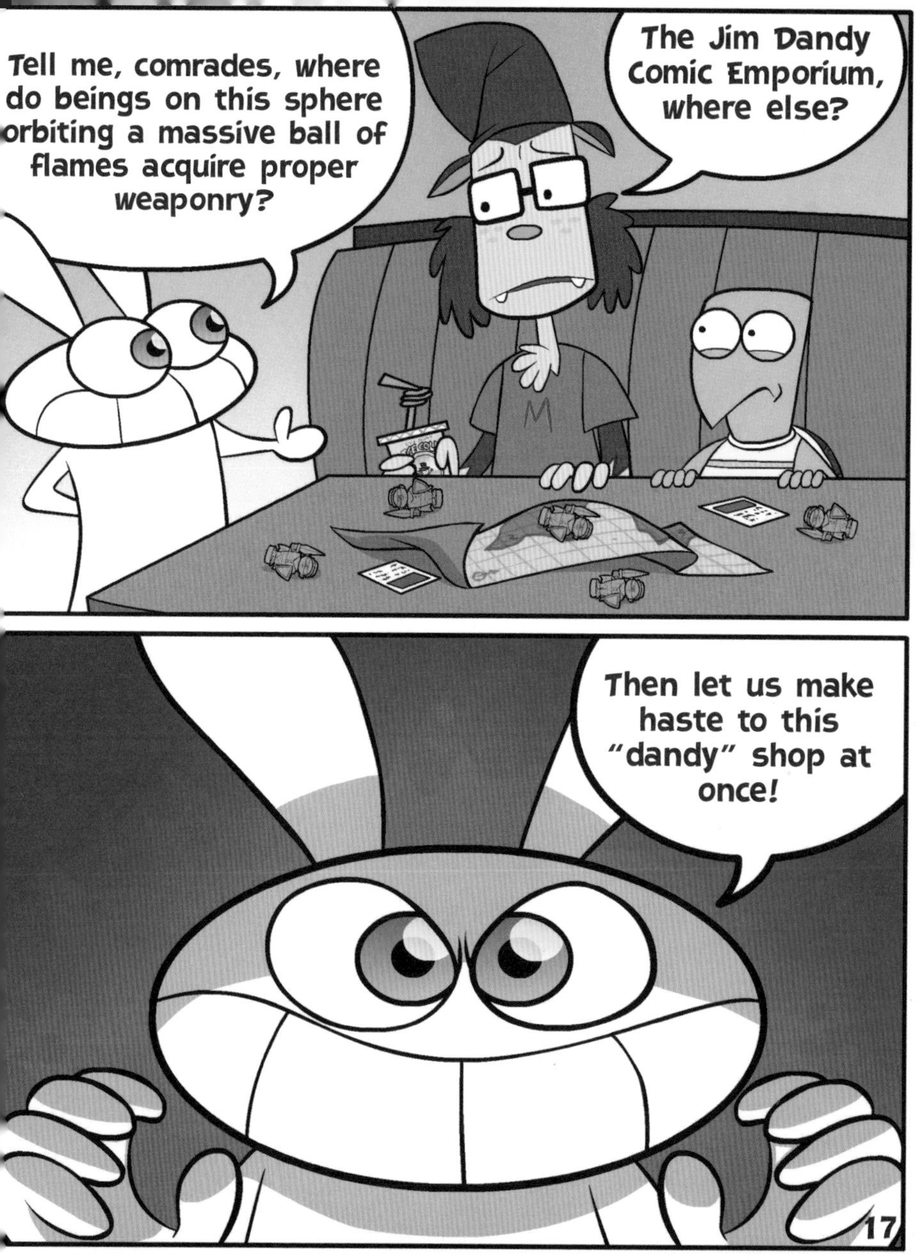
Tell me, comrades, where do beings on this sphere orbiting a massive ball of flames acquire proper weaponry?
The Jim Dandy Comic Emporium, where else?
Then let us make haste to this "dandy" shop at once!

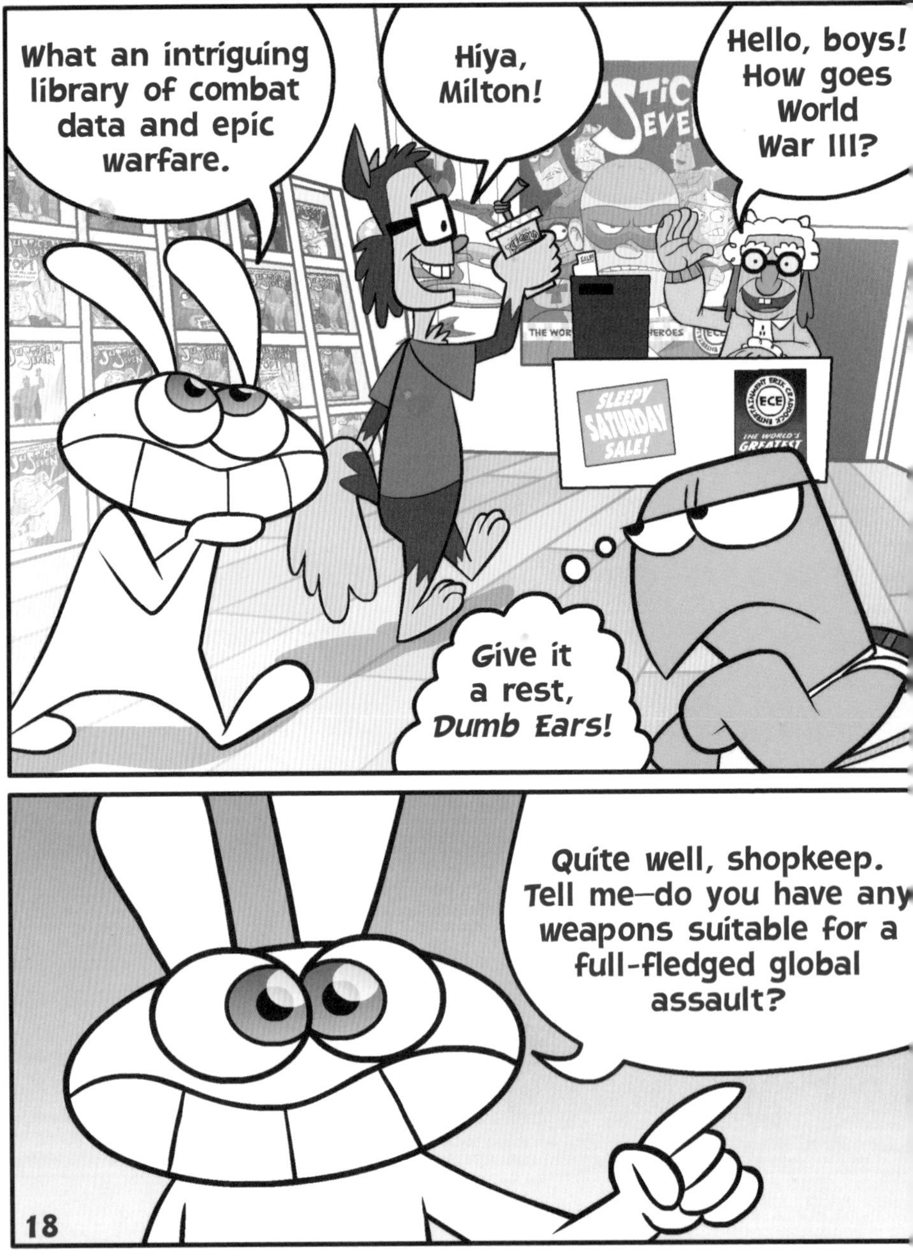
What an intriguing library of combat data and epic warfare.
Hiya, Milton!
Hello, boys! How goes World War III?
SLEEPY SATURDAY SALE!
Give it a rest, Dumb Ears!
Quite well, shopkeep. Tell me—do you have any weapons suitable for a full-fledged global assault?

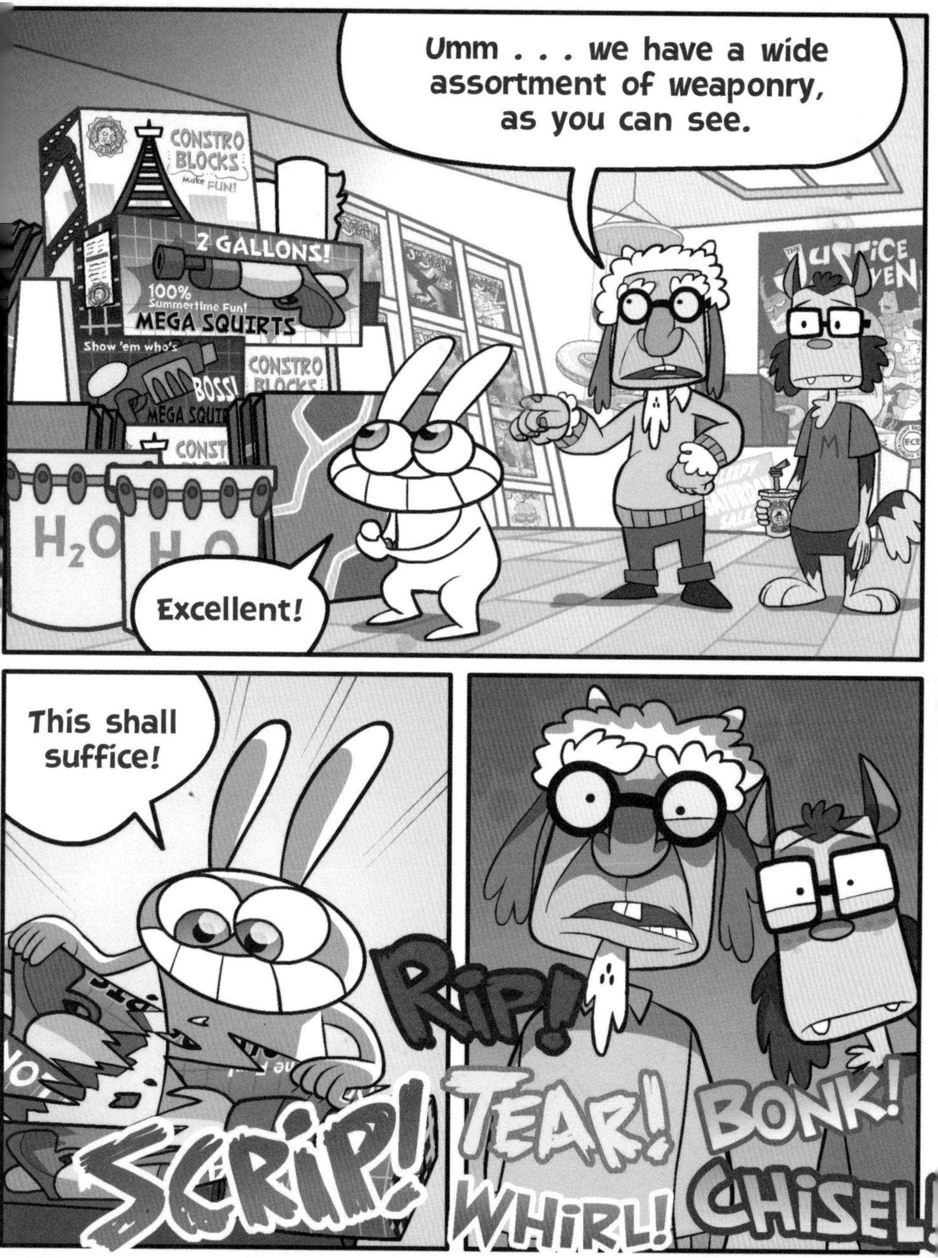
Umm . . . we have a wide assortment of weaponry, as you can see.
CONSTRO BLOCKS Make FUN!
2 GALLONS!
100% Summertime Fun!
MEGA SQUIRTS
Show 'em who's BOSS!
Excellent!
This shall suffice!
RIP!
SCRIP!
TEAR!
BONK!
WHIRL!
CHISEL!

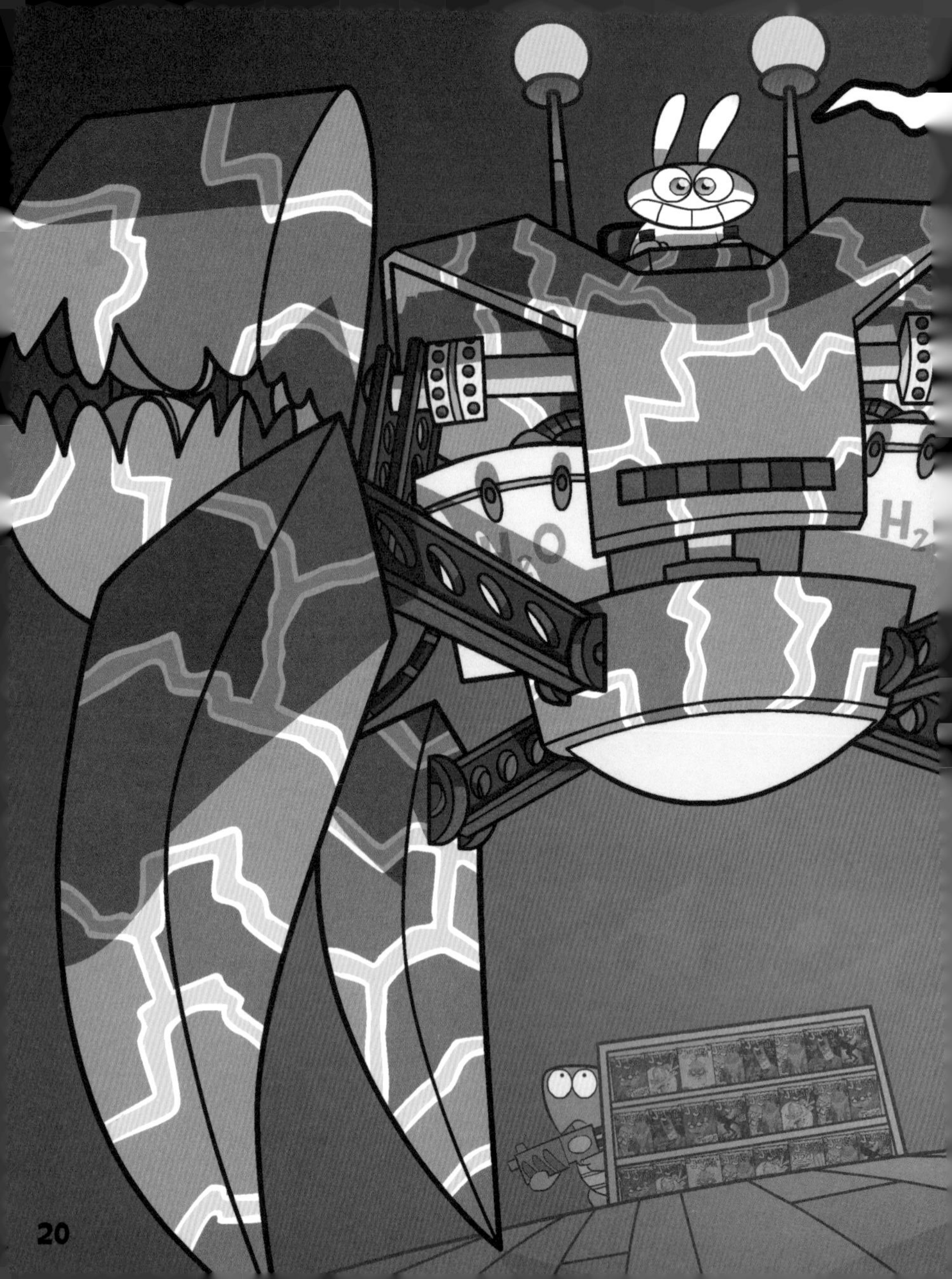

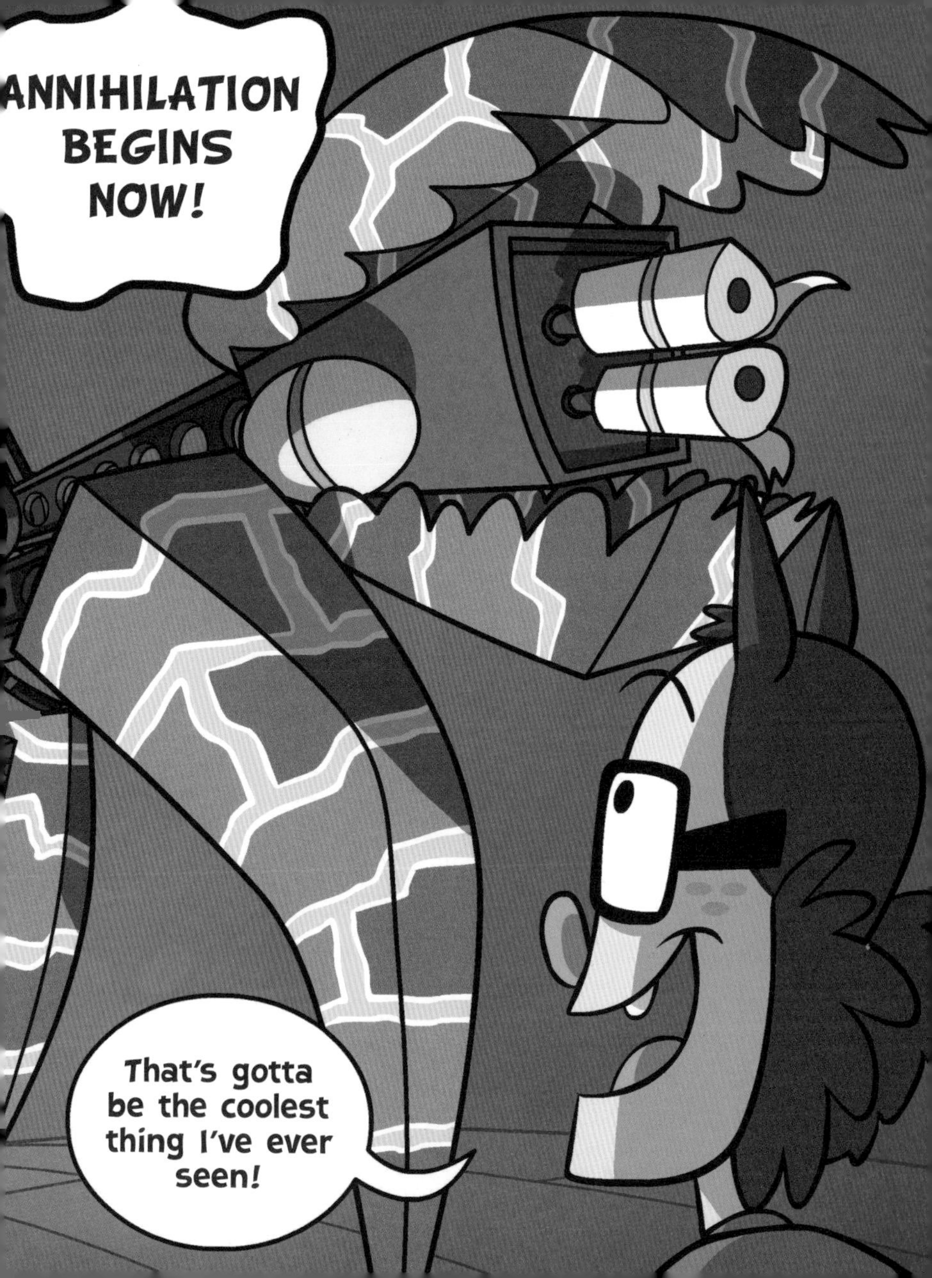
ANNIHILATION BEGINS NOW!
That's gotta be the coolest thing I've ever seen!

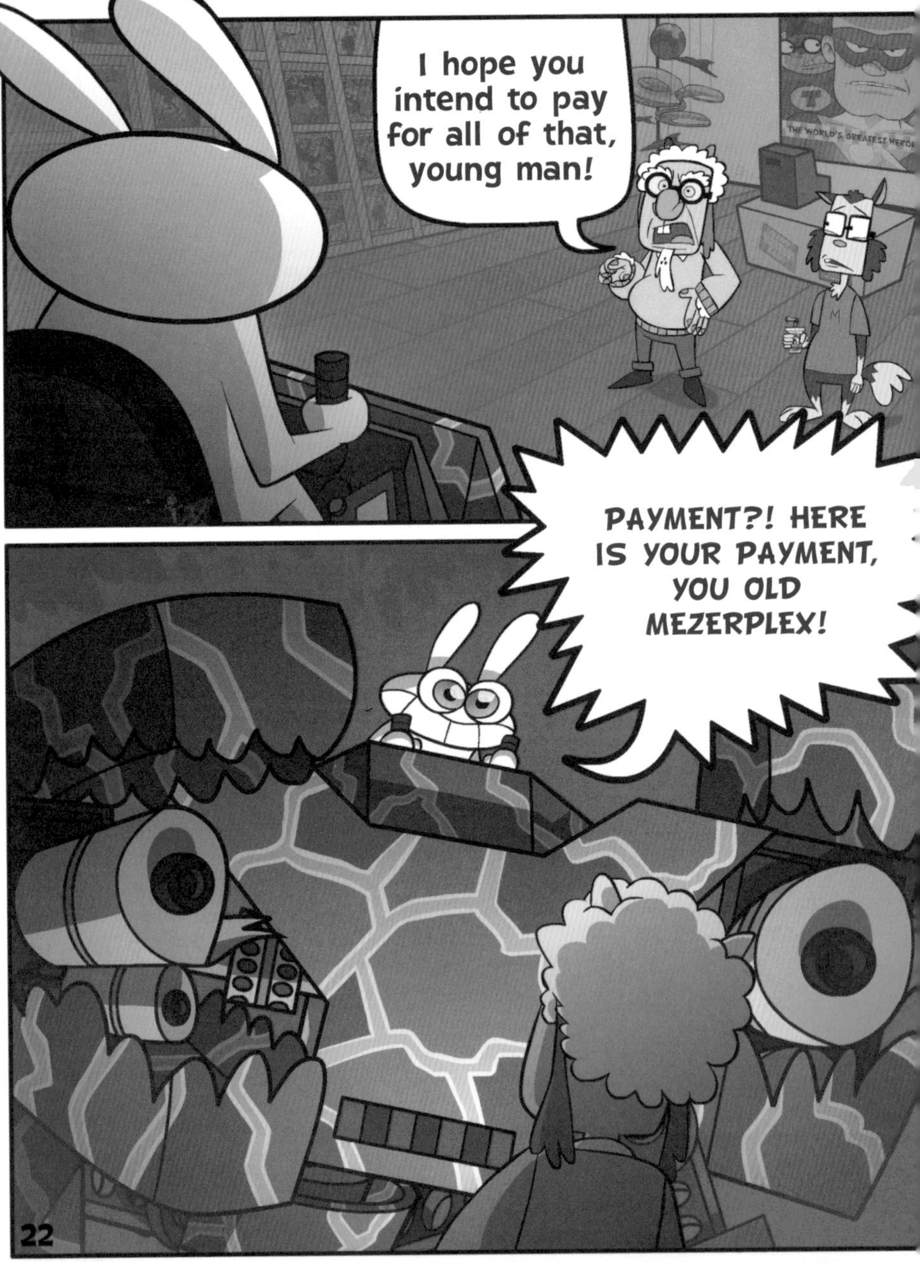
I hope you intend to pay for all of that, young man!
PAYMENT?! HERE IS YOUR PAYMENT, YOU OLD MEZERPLEX!

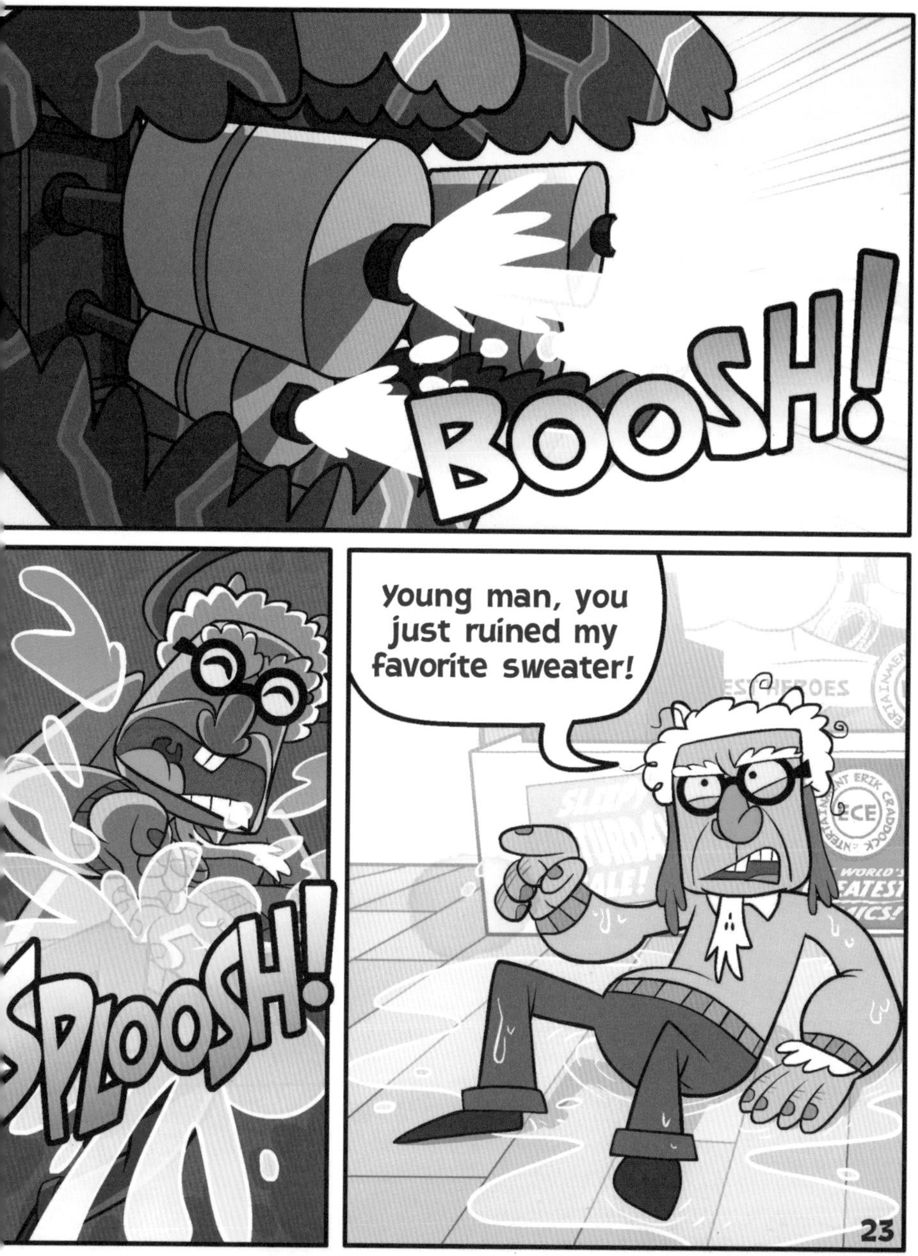
BOOSH!
SPLOOSH!
Young man, you just ruined my favorite sweater!

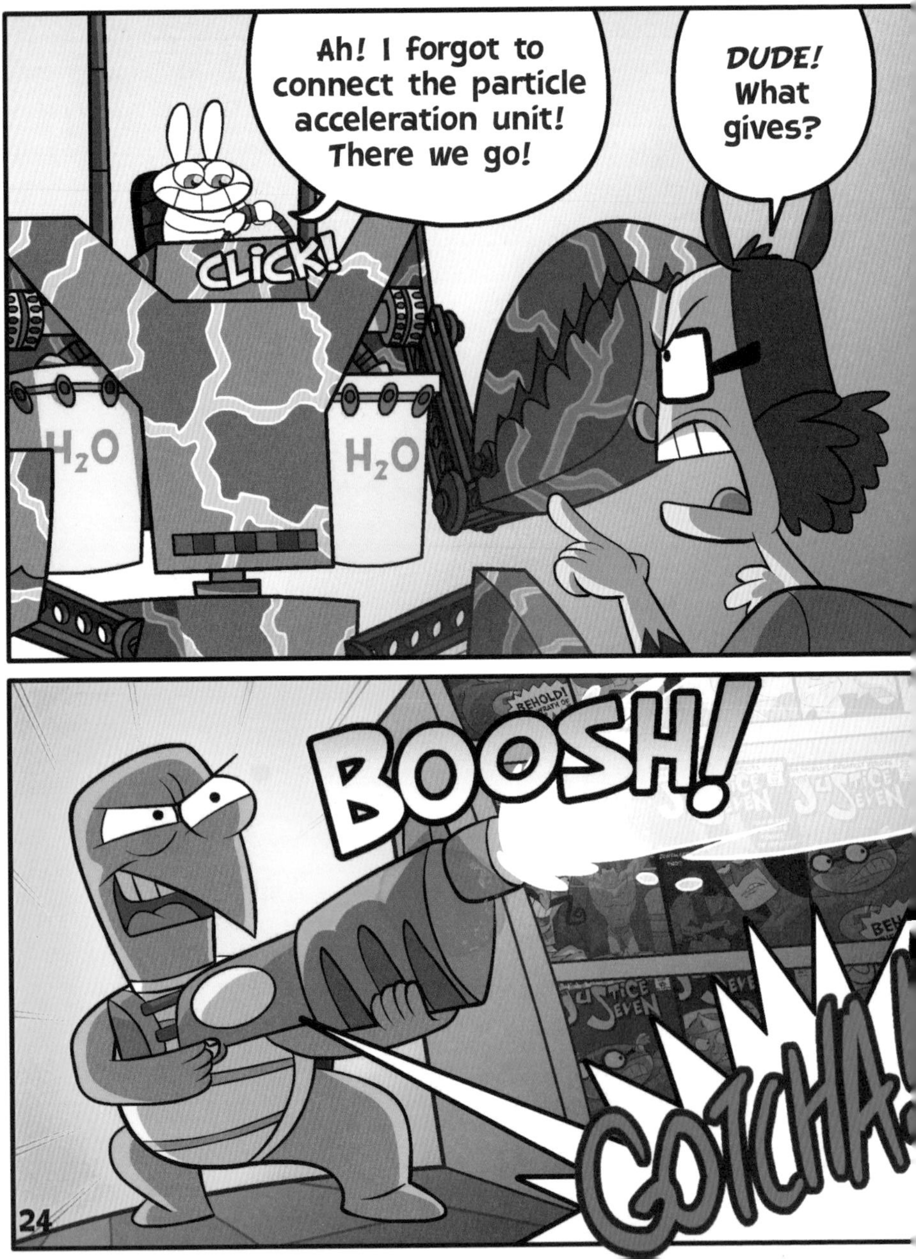
Ah! I forgot to connect the particle acceleration unit! There we go!
DUDE! What gives?
CLICK!
H2O
H2O
BEHOLD!
BOOSH!
JUSTICE SEVEN
JUSTICE SEVEN
JUSTICE SEVEN
GOTCHA

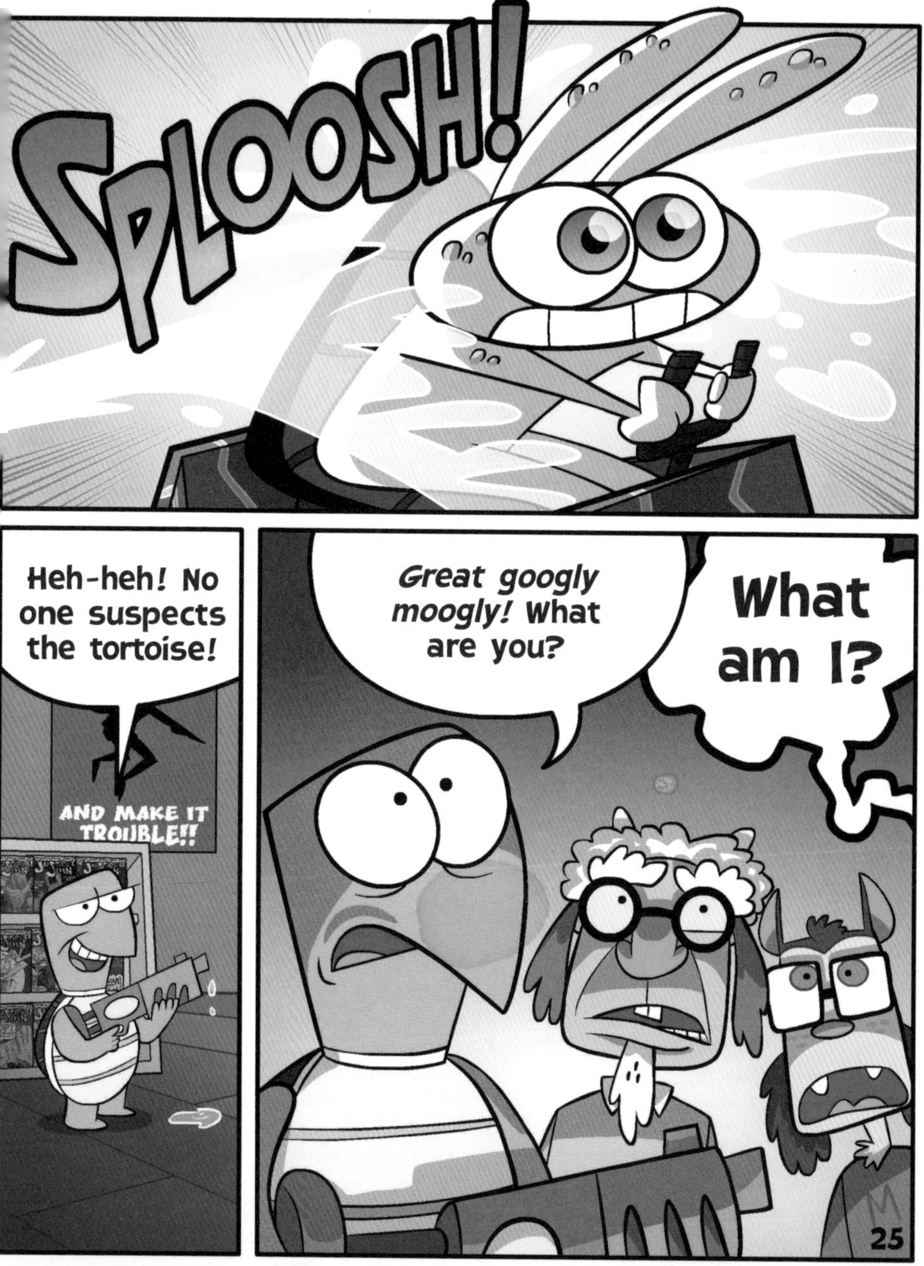
SPLOOSH!
Heh-heh! No one suspects the tortoise!
AND MAKE IT TROUBLE!!
Great googly moogly! What are you?
What am I?

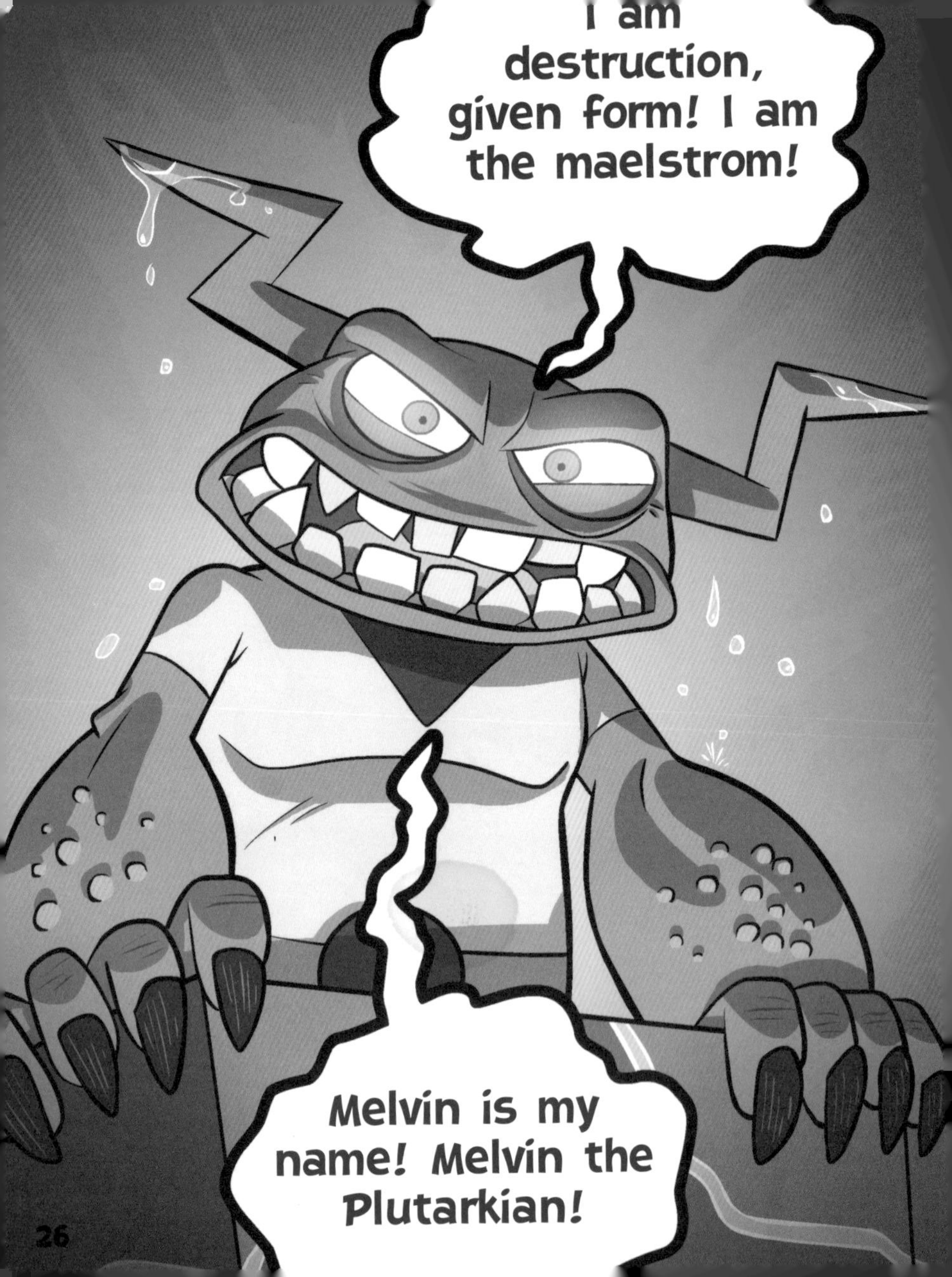
I am destruction, given form! I am the maelstrom!
Melvin is my name! Melvin the Plutarkian!

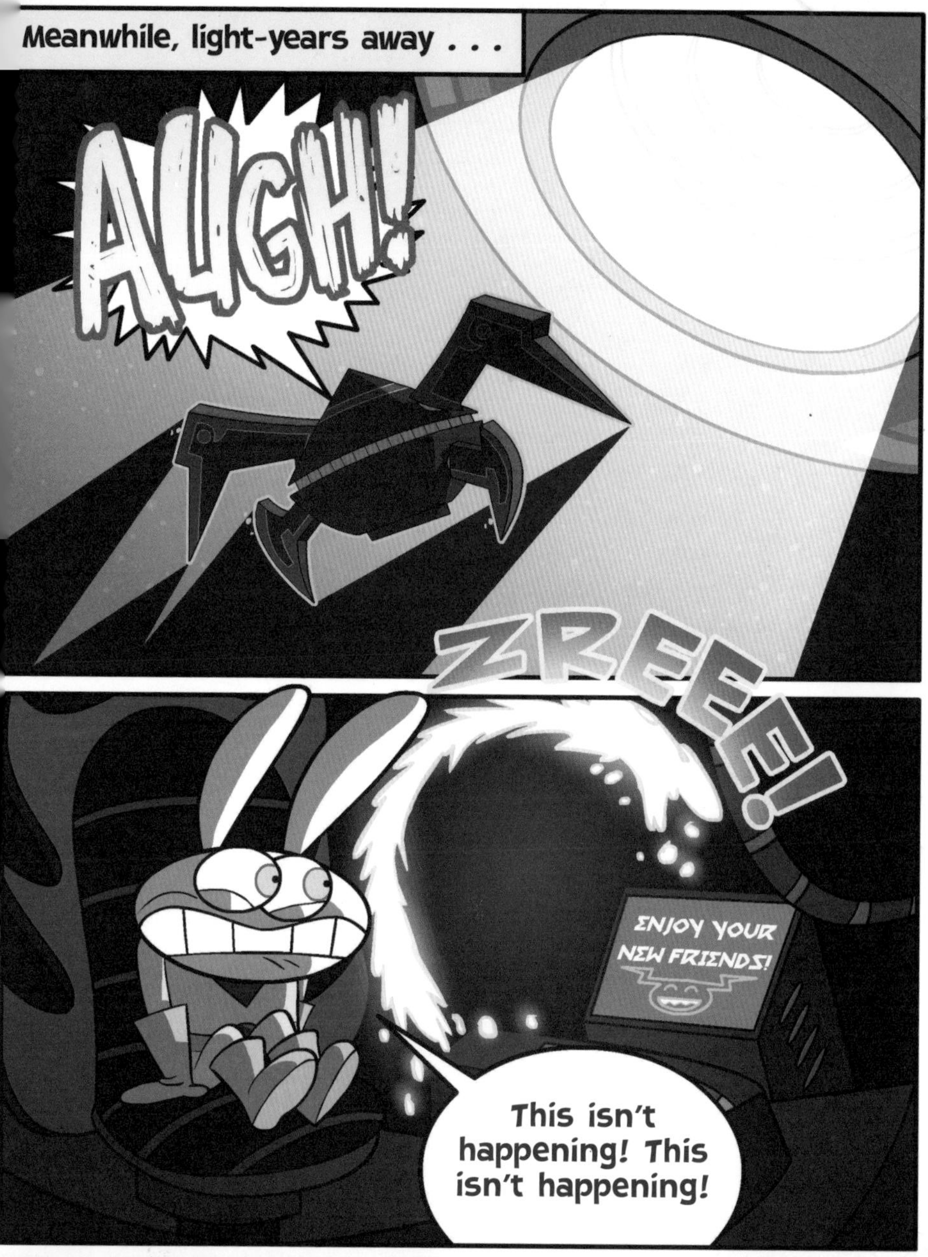
Meanwhile, light-years away . . .
AUGH!
ZREEEE!
ENJOY YOUR NEW FRIENDS!
This isn't happening! This isn't happening!

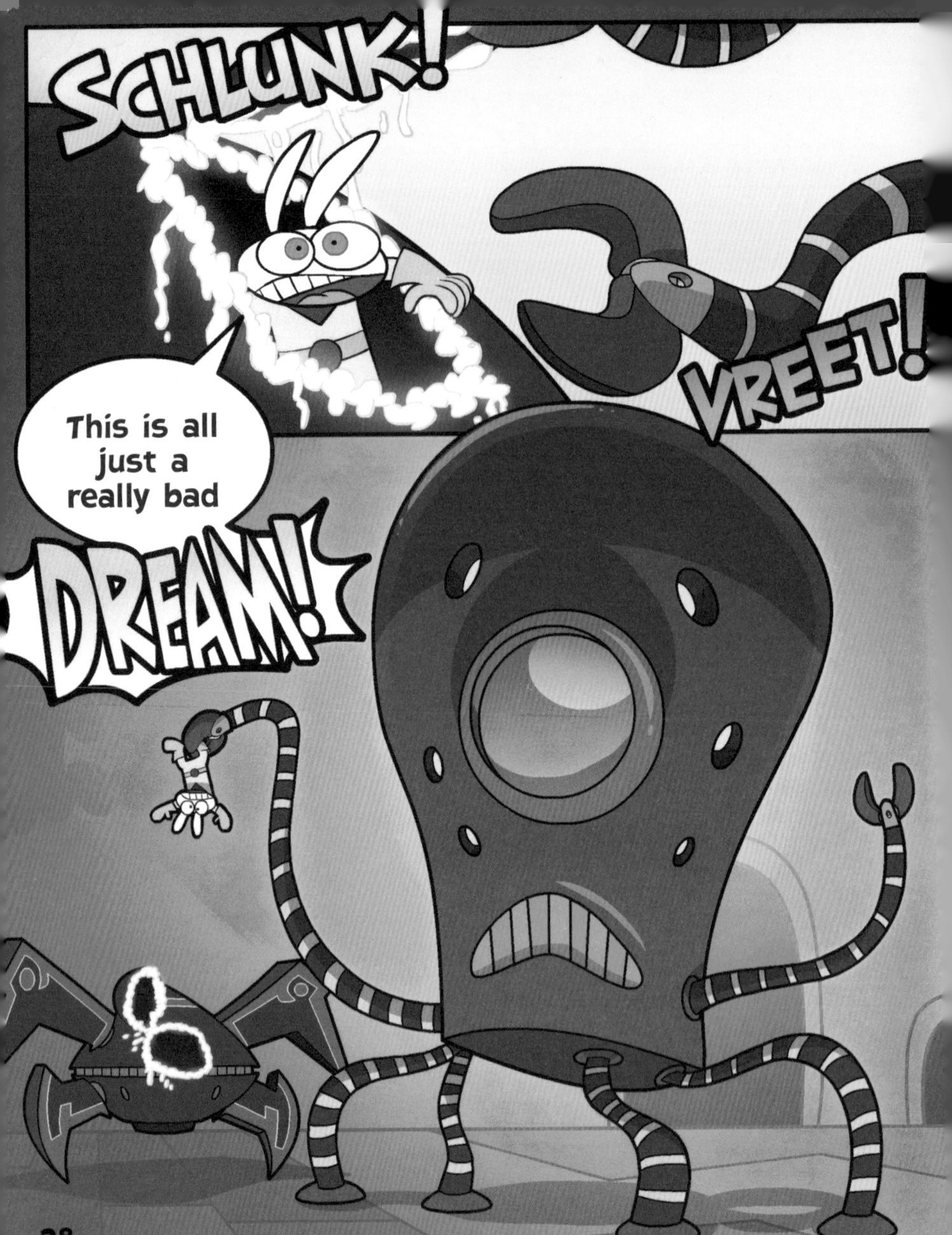
SCHLUNK!
VREET!
This is all just a really bad
DREAM!

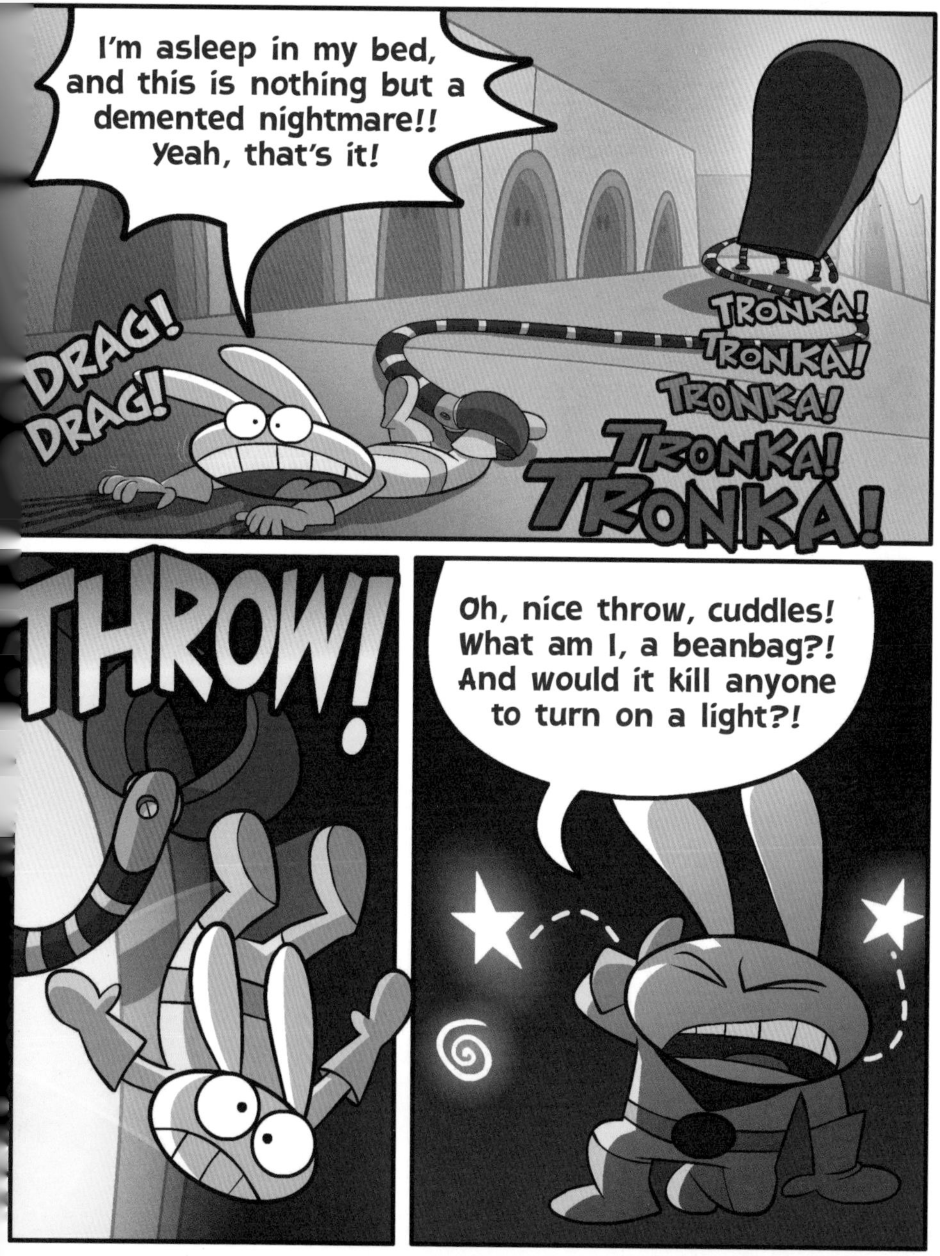
I'm asleep in my bed, and this is nothing but a demented nightmare!! Yeah, that's it!
DRAG! DRAG!
TRONKA! TRONKA! TRONKA! TRONKA! TRONKA!
THROW!
Oh, nice throw, cuddles! What am I, a beanbag?! And would it kill anyone to turn on a light?!

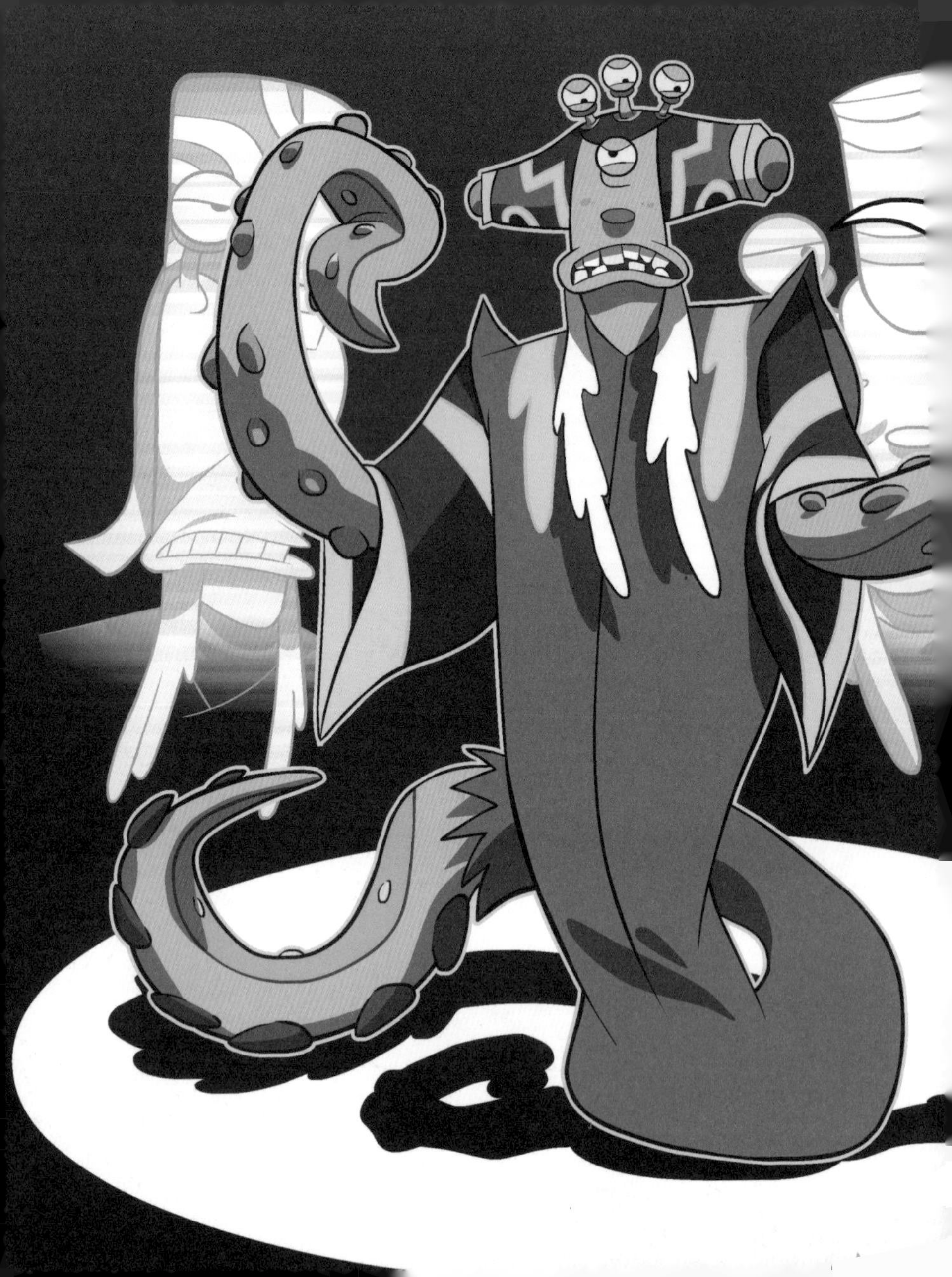

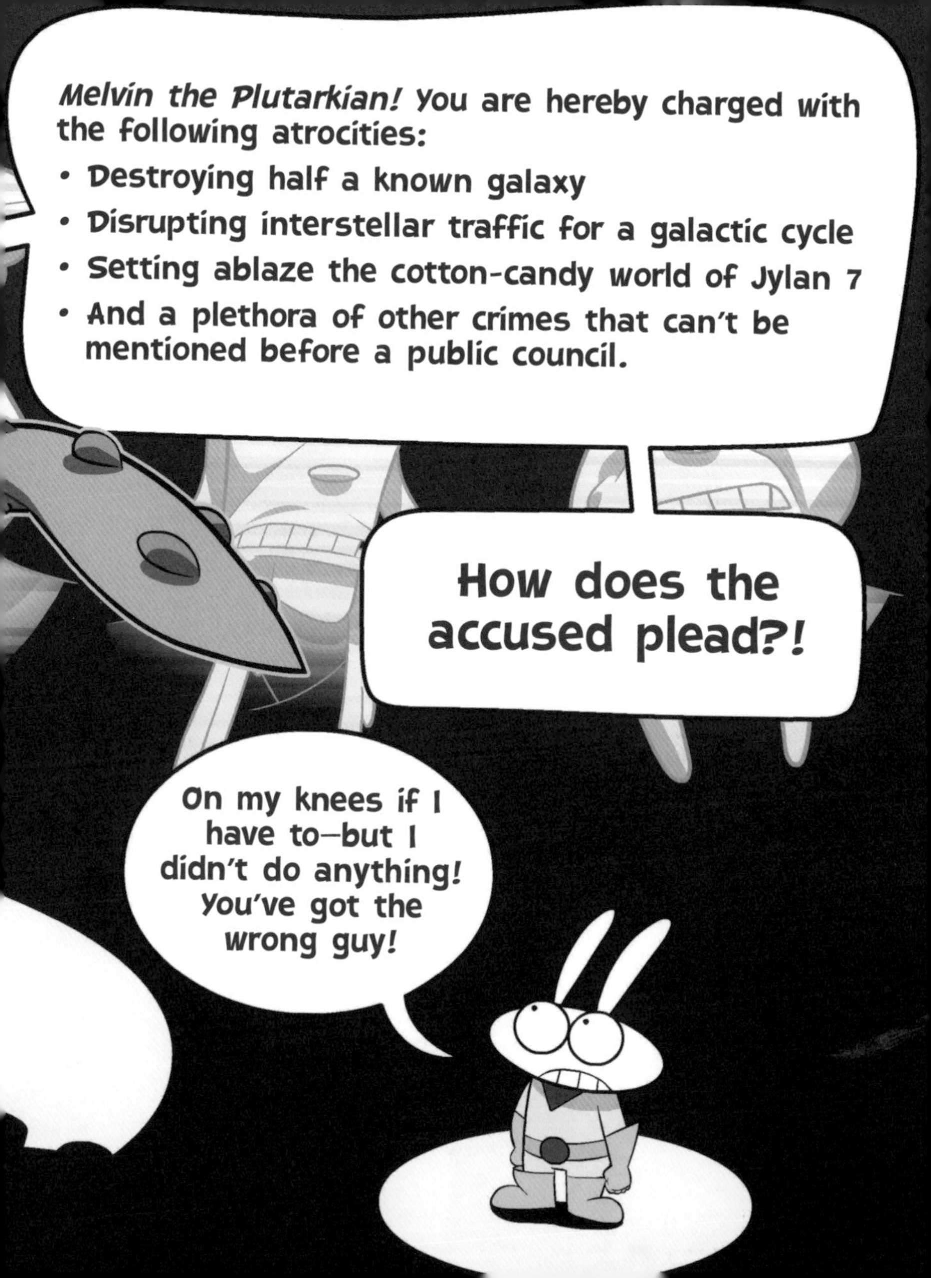

Melvin the Plutarkian! You are hereby charged with the following atrocities:
• Destroying half a known galaxy
• Disrupting interstellar traffic for a galactic cycle
• Setting ablaze the cotton-candy world of Jylan 7
• And a plethora of other crimes that can't be mentioned before a public council.
How does the accused plead?!
On my knees if I have to—but I didn't do anything! You've got the wrong guy!

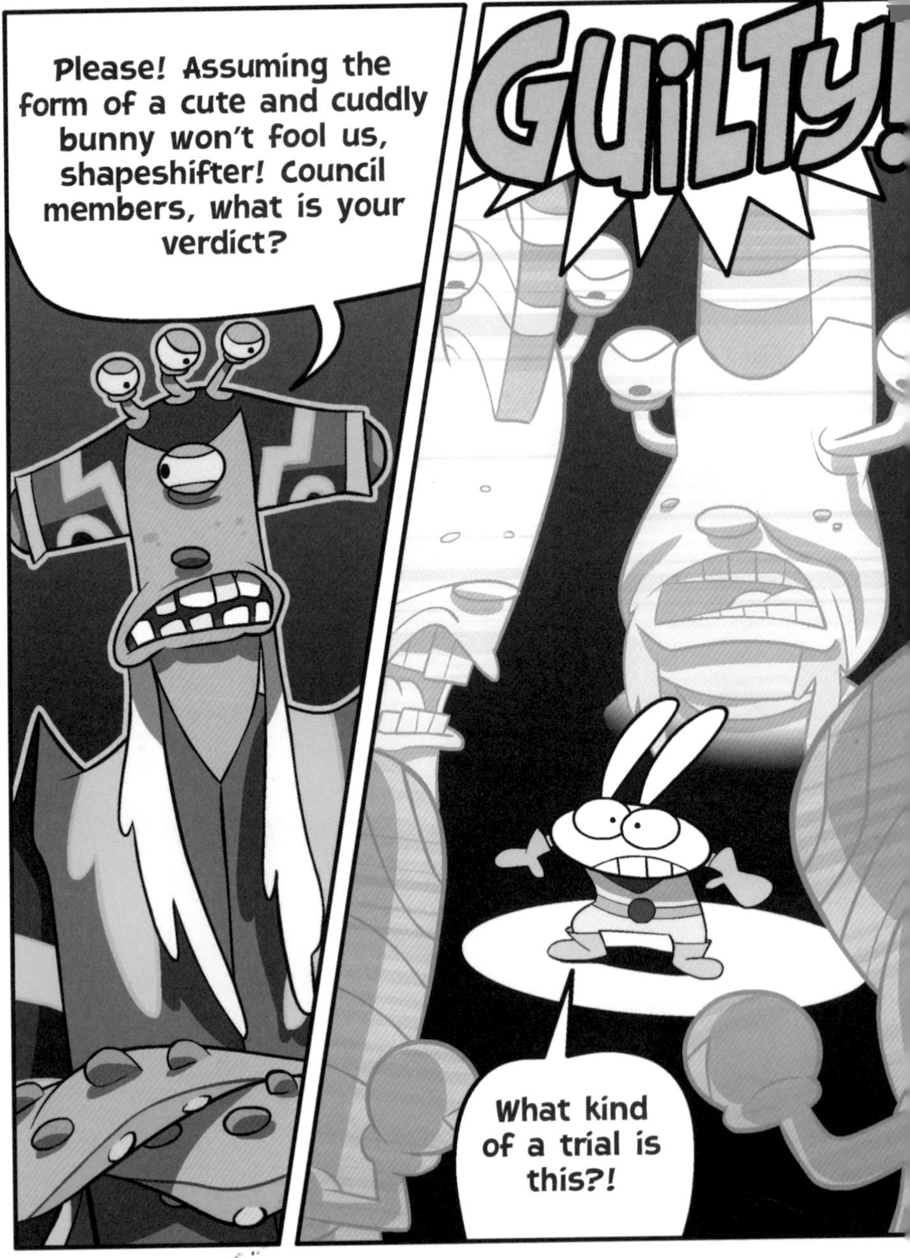
Please! Assuming the form of a cute and cuddly bunny won't fool us, shapeshifter! Council members, what is your verdict?
GUILTY!
What kind of a trial is this?!

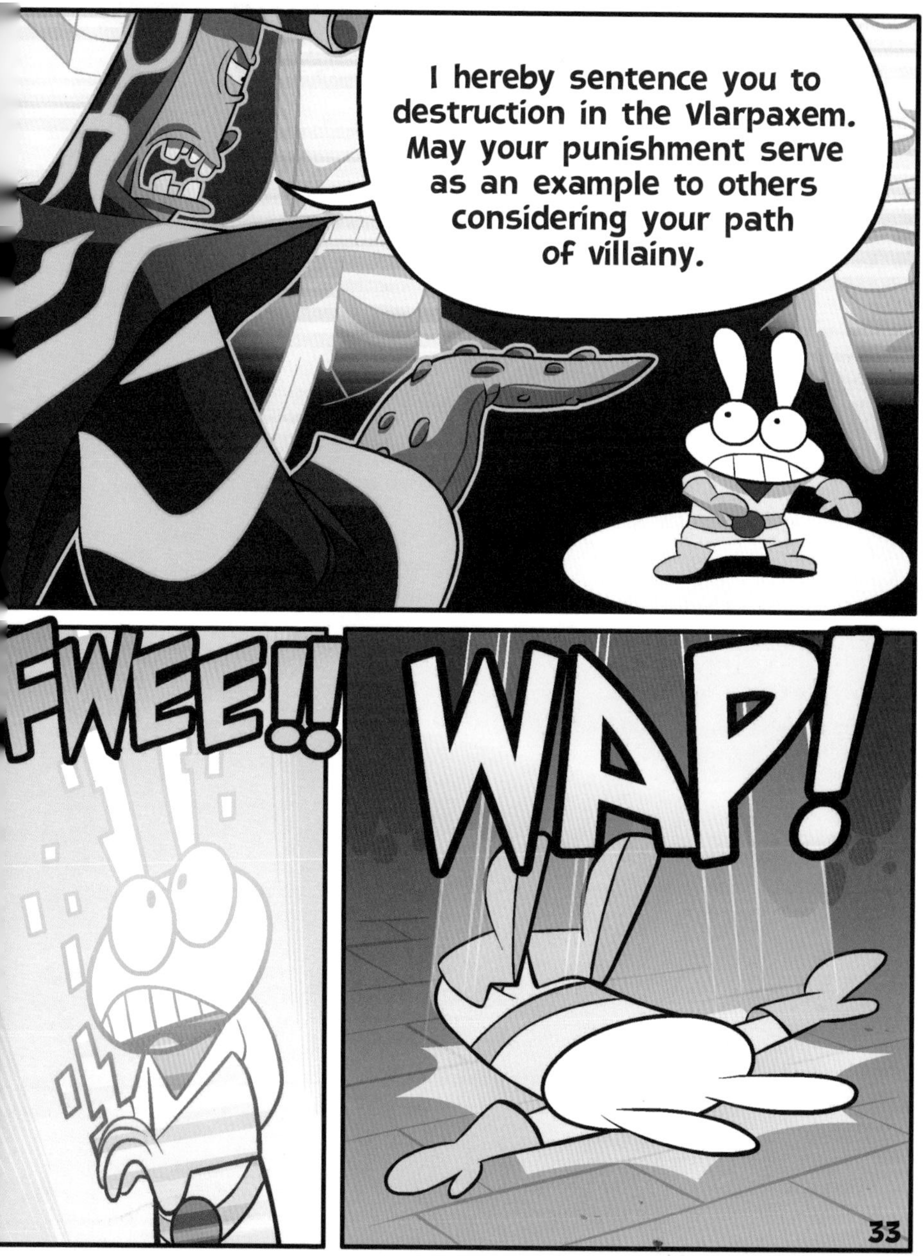
I hereby sentence you to destruction in the Vlarpaxem. May your punishment serve as an example to others considering your path of villainy.
FWEE!!
WAP!

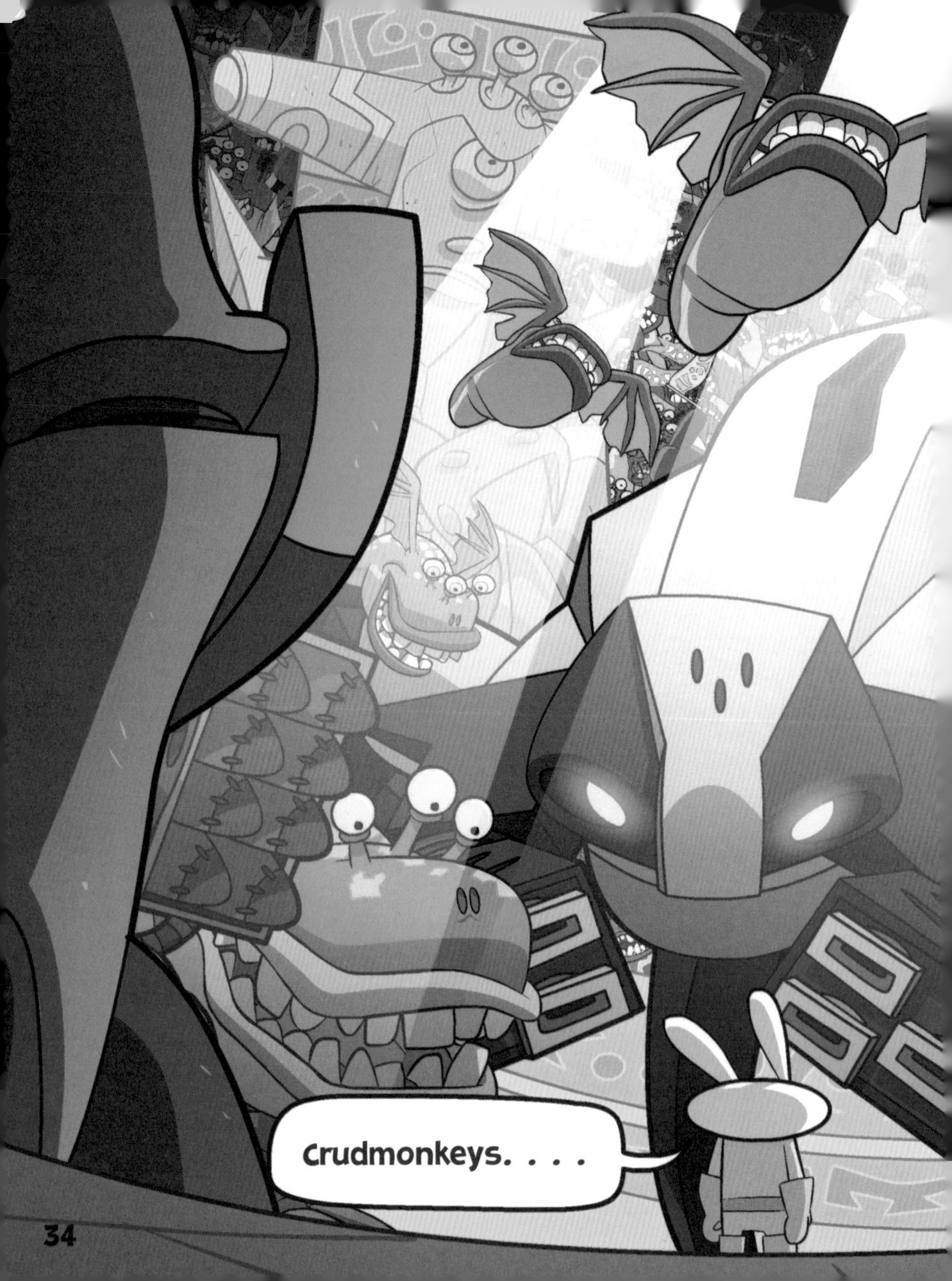
Crudmonkeys. . . .

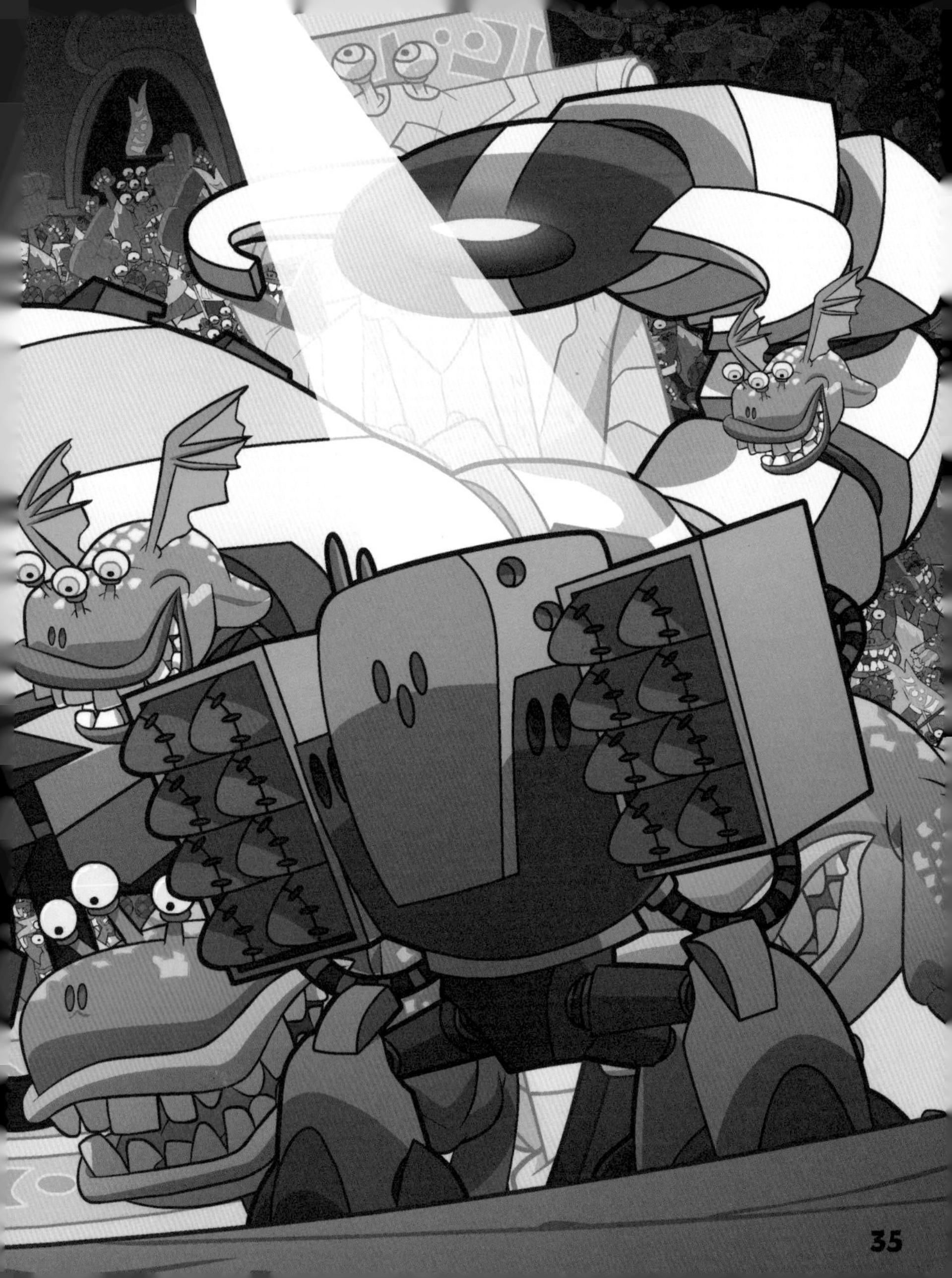

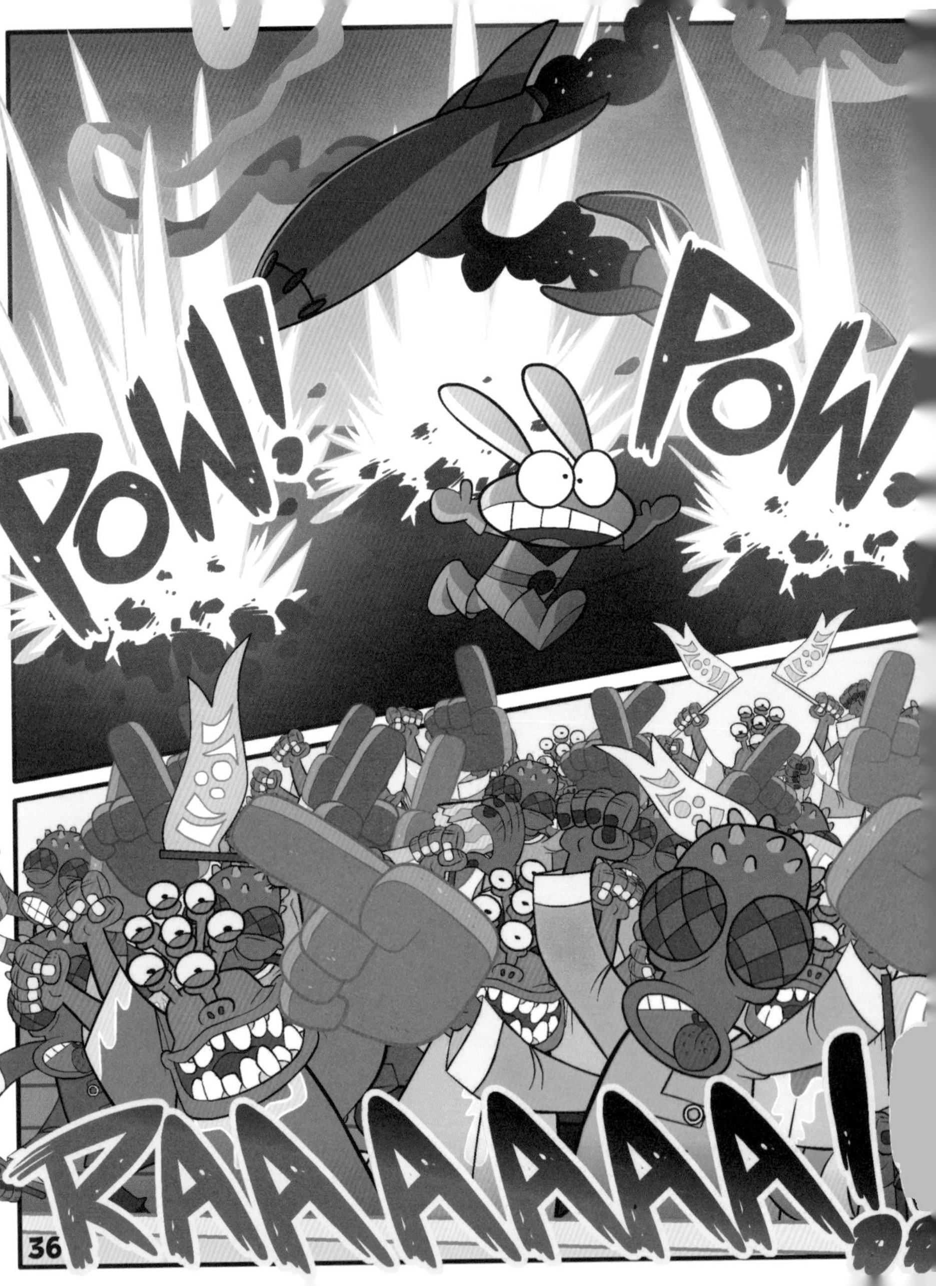
POW!
POW!
RAAAAAA!!

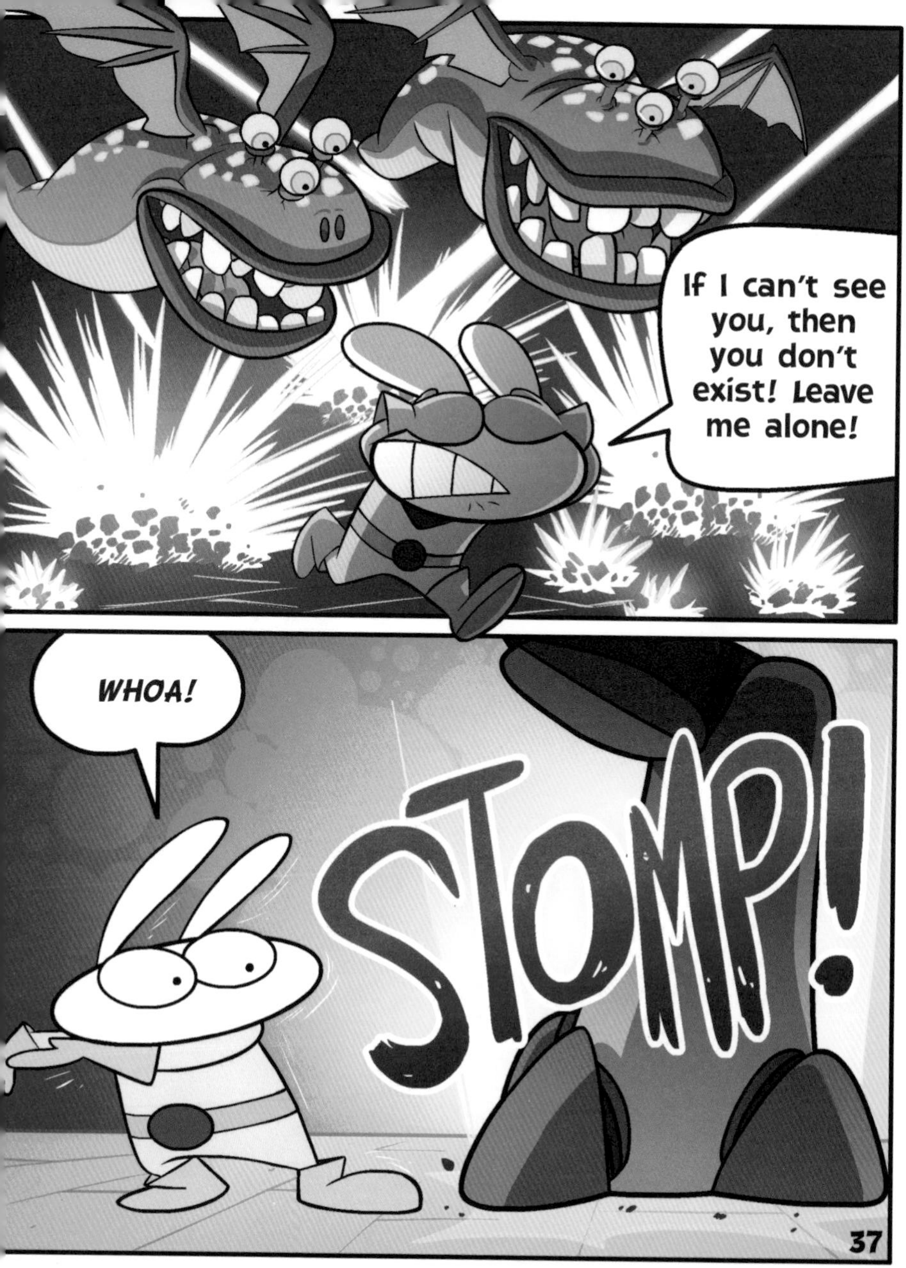
If I can't see you, then you don't exist! Leave me alone!
WHOA!
STOMP!

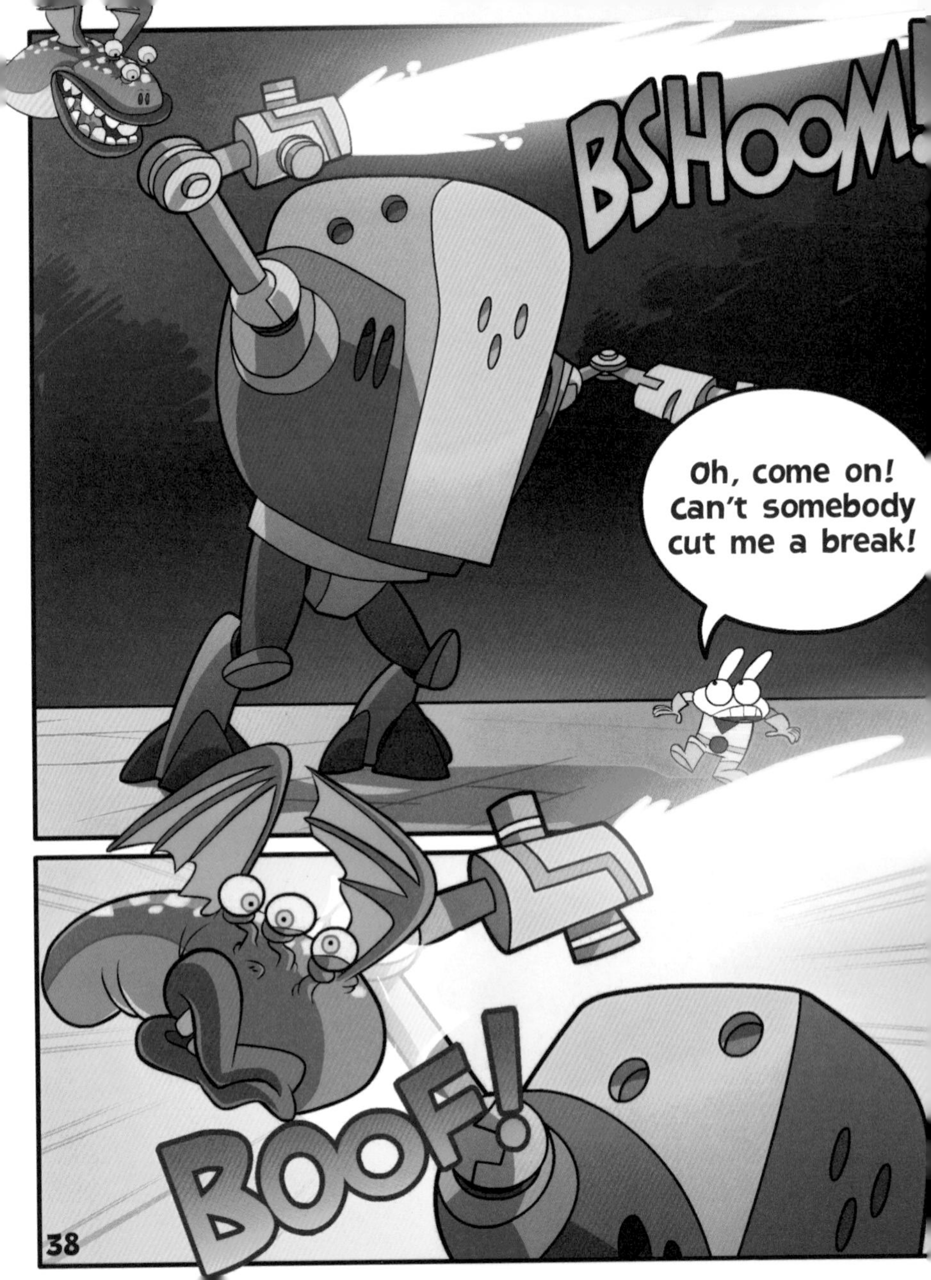
BSHOOM!
Oh, come on! Can't somebody cut me a break!
BOOF!

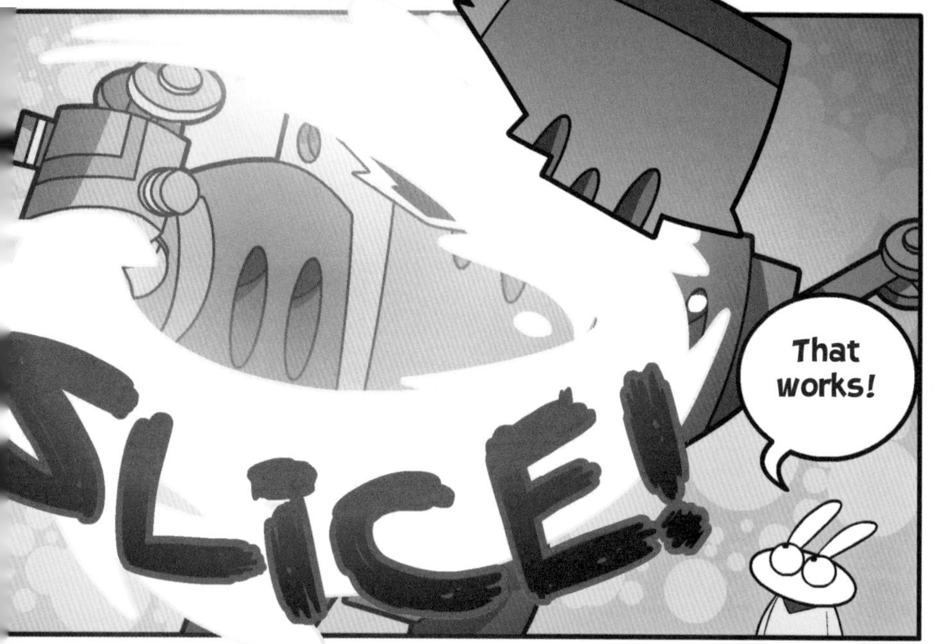
SLICE!
That works!

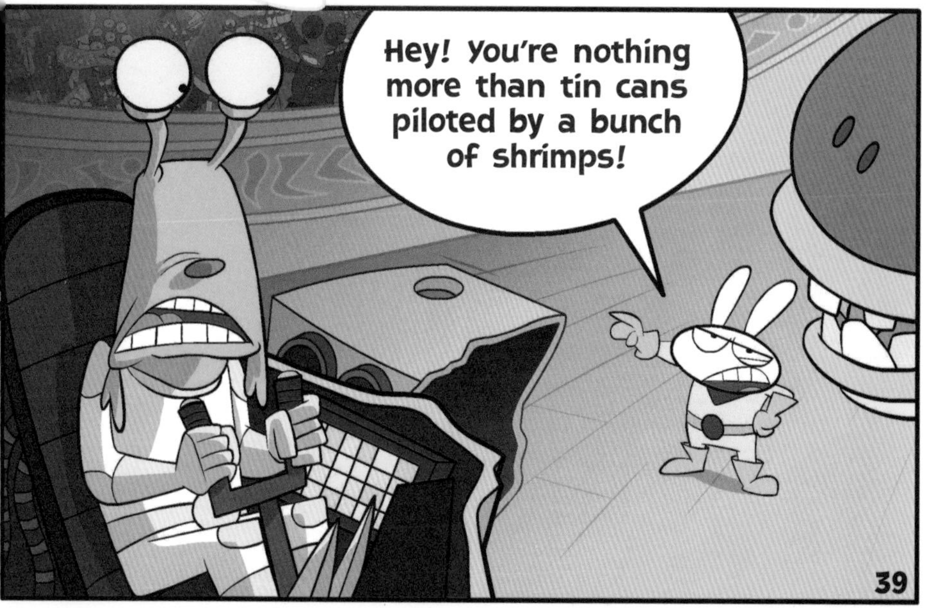
Hey! You're nothing more than tin cans piloted by a bunch of shrimps!

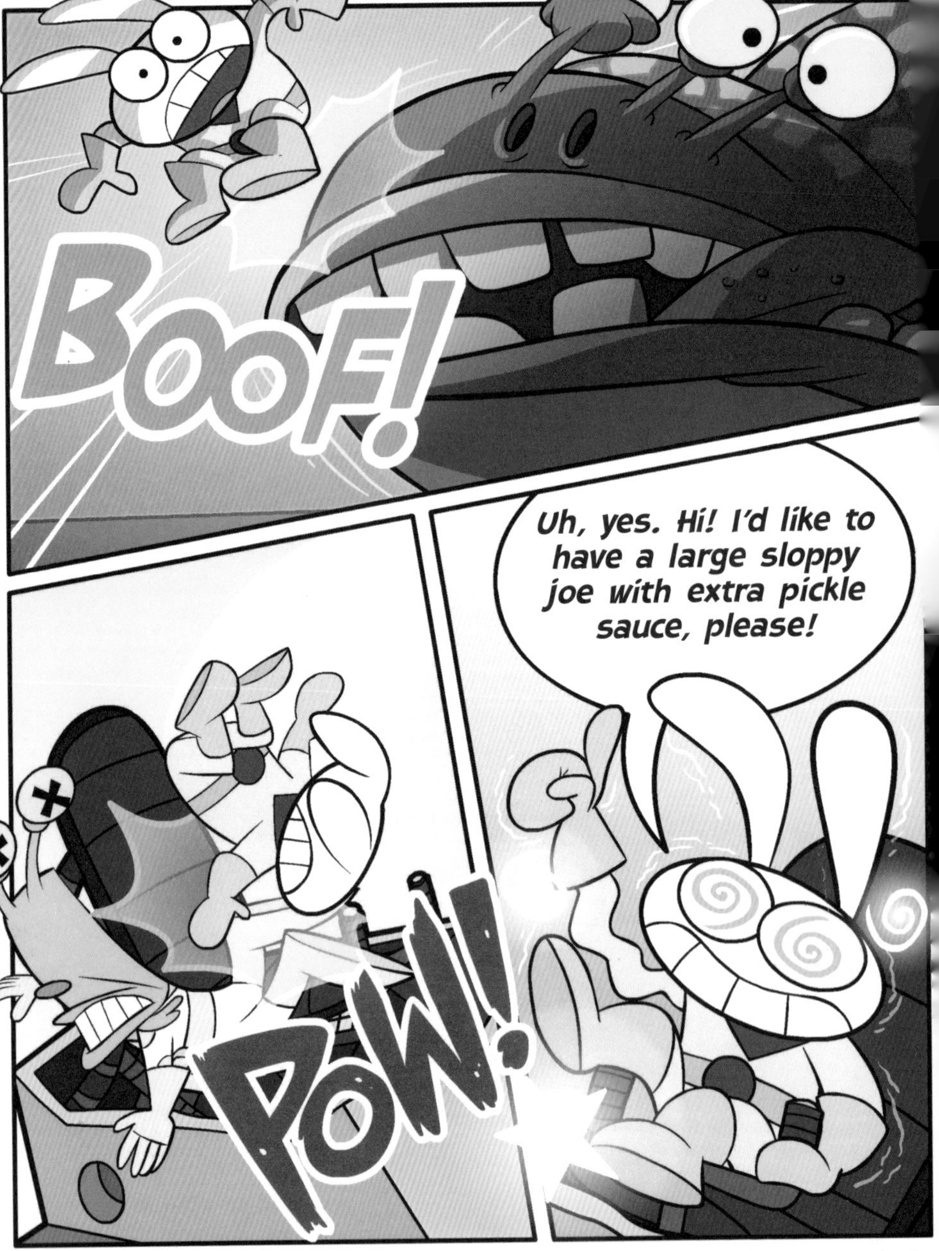
BOOF!
POW!
Uh, yes. Hi! I'd like to have a large sloppy joe with extra pickle sauce, please!

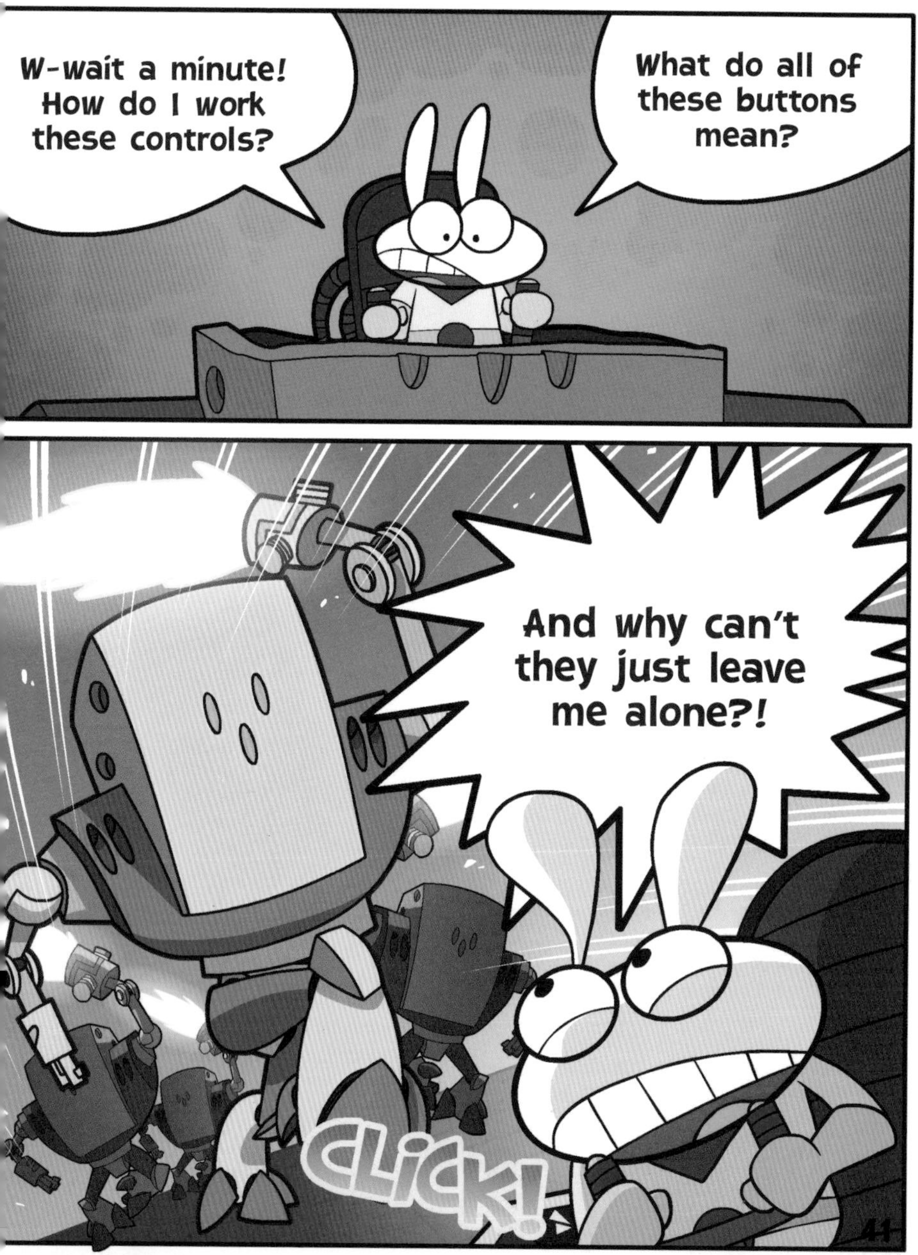
W-wait a minute! How do I work these controls?
What do all of these buttons mean?
And why can't they just leave me alone?!
CLICK!

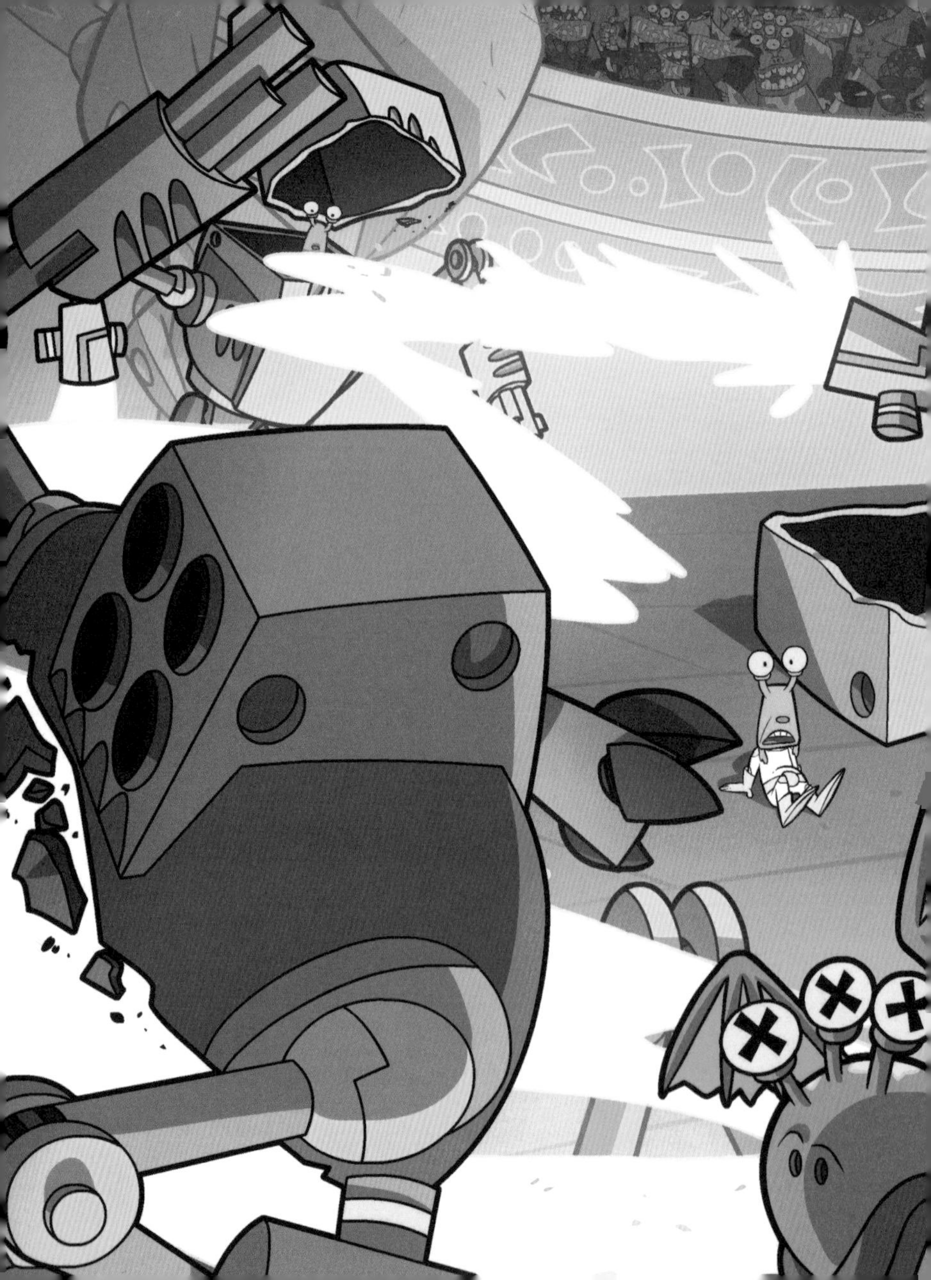

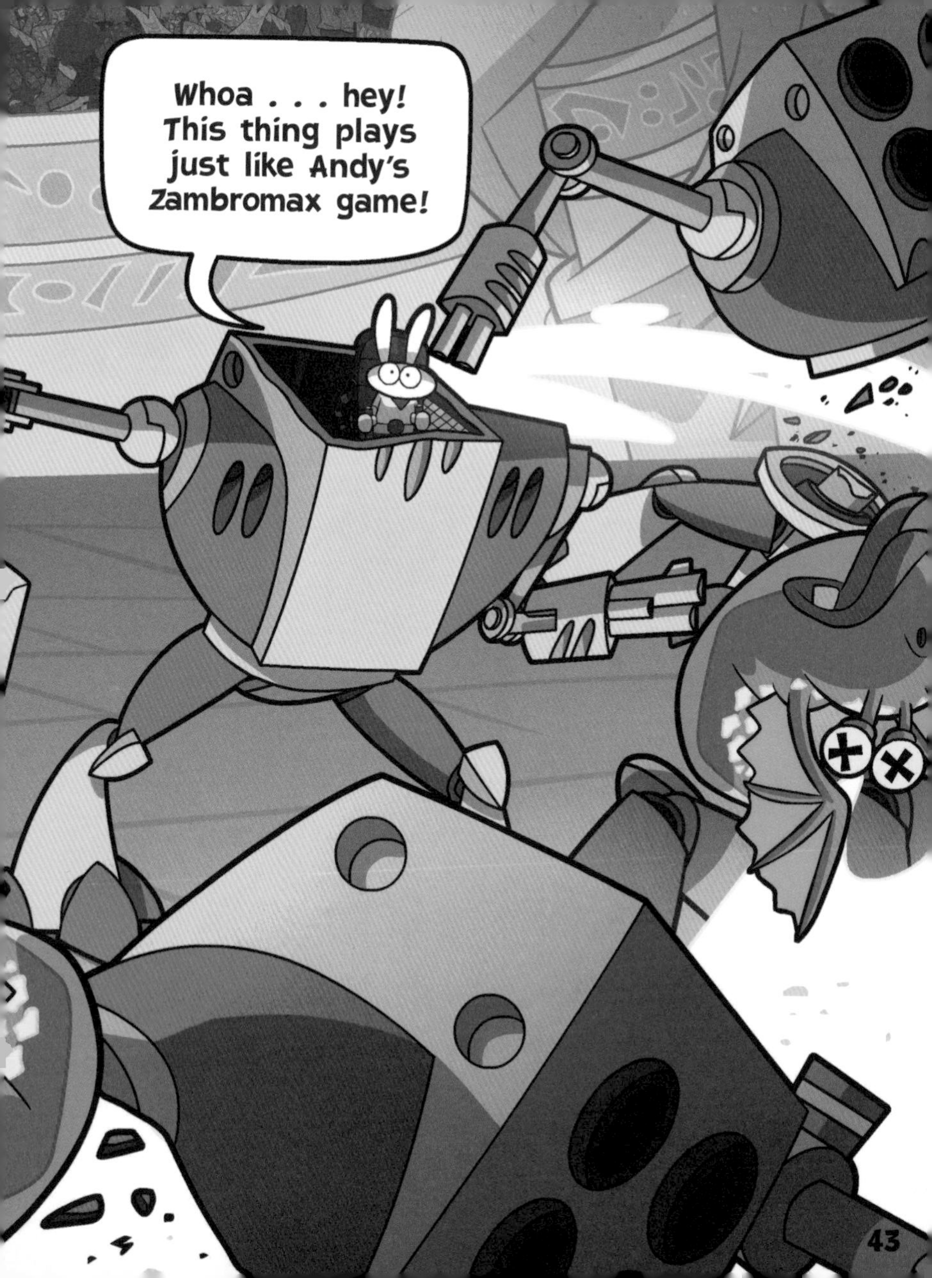
Whoa . . . hey! This thing plays just like Andy's Zambromax game!

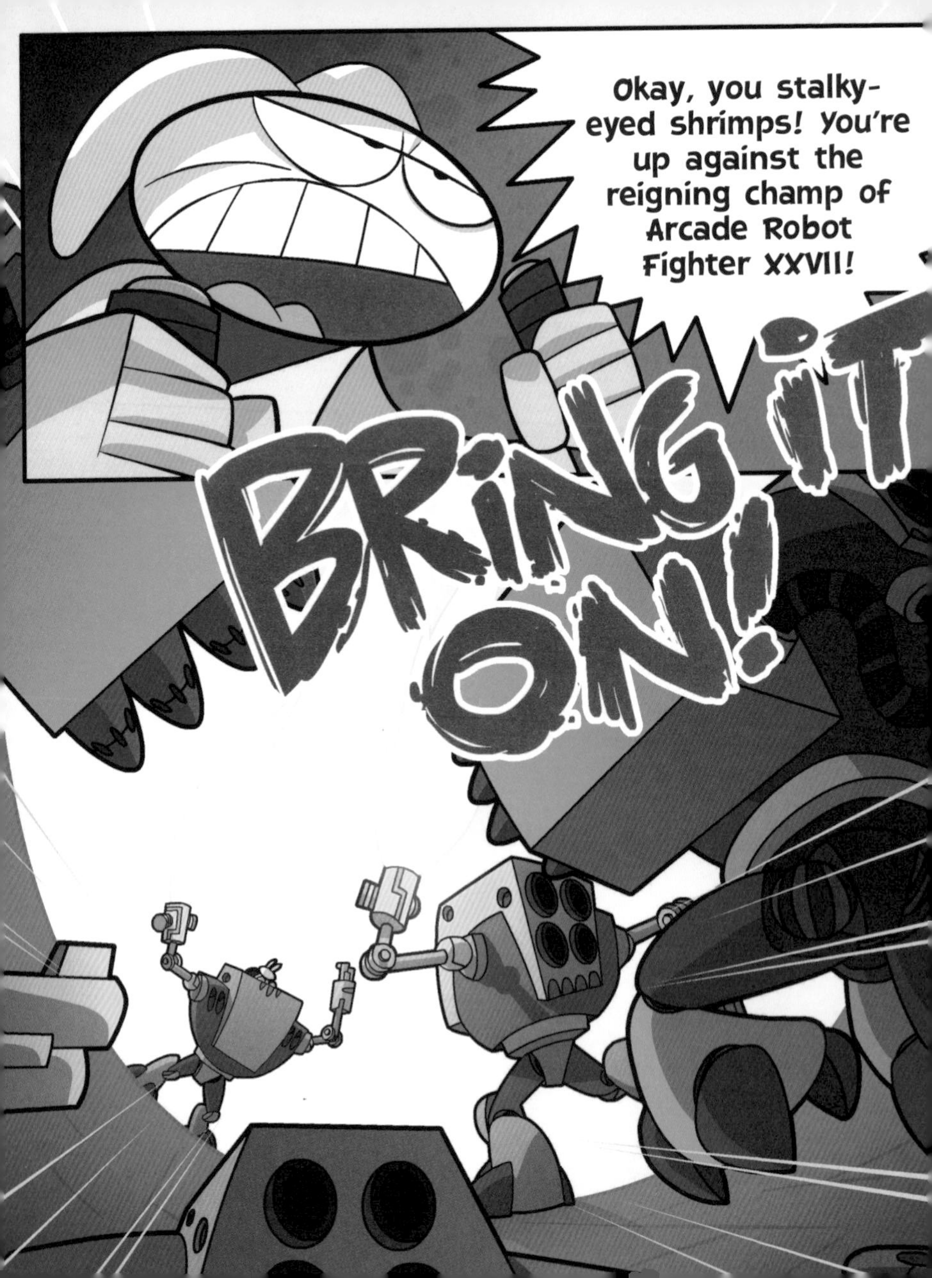
Okay, you stalky-eyed shrimps! You're up against the reigning champ of Arcade Robot Fighter XXVII!
BRING IT ON!!

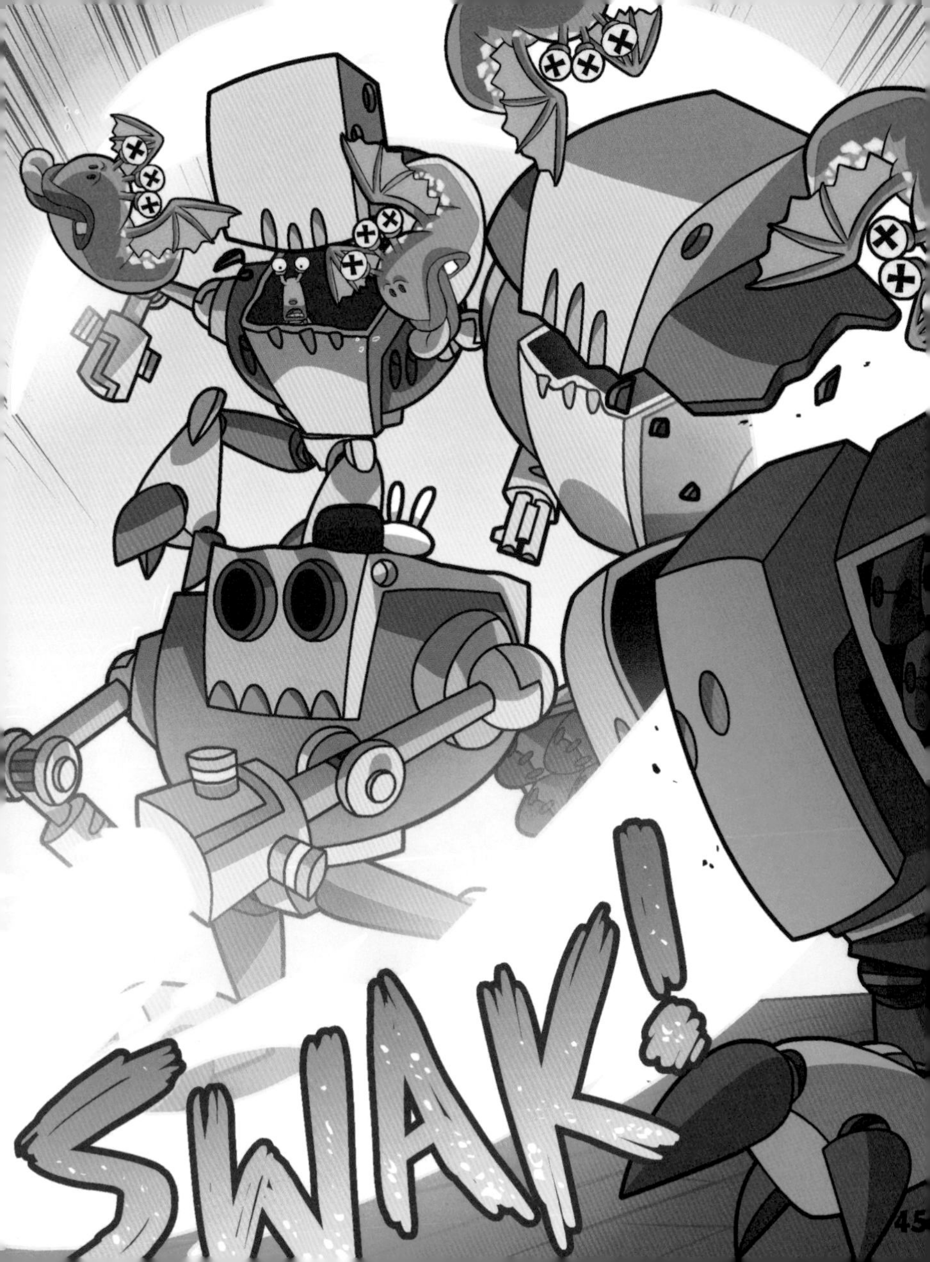
SWAK!

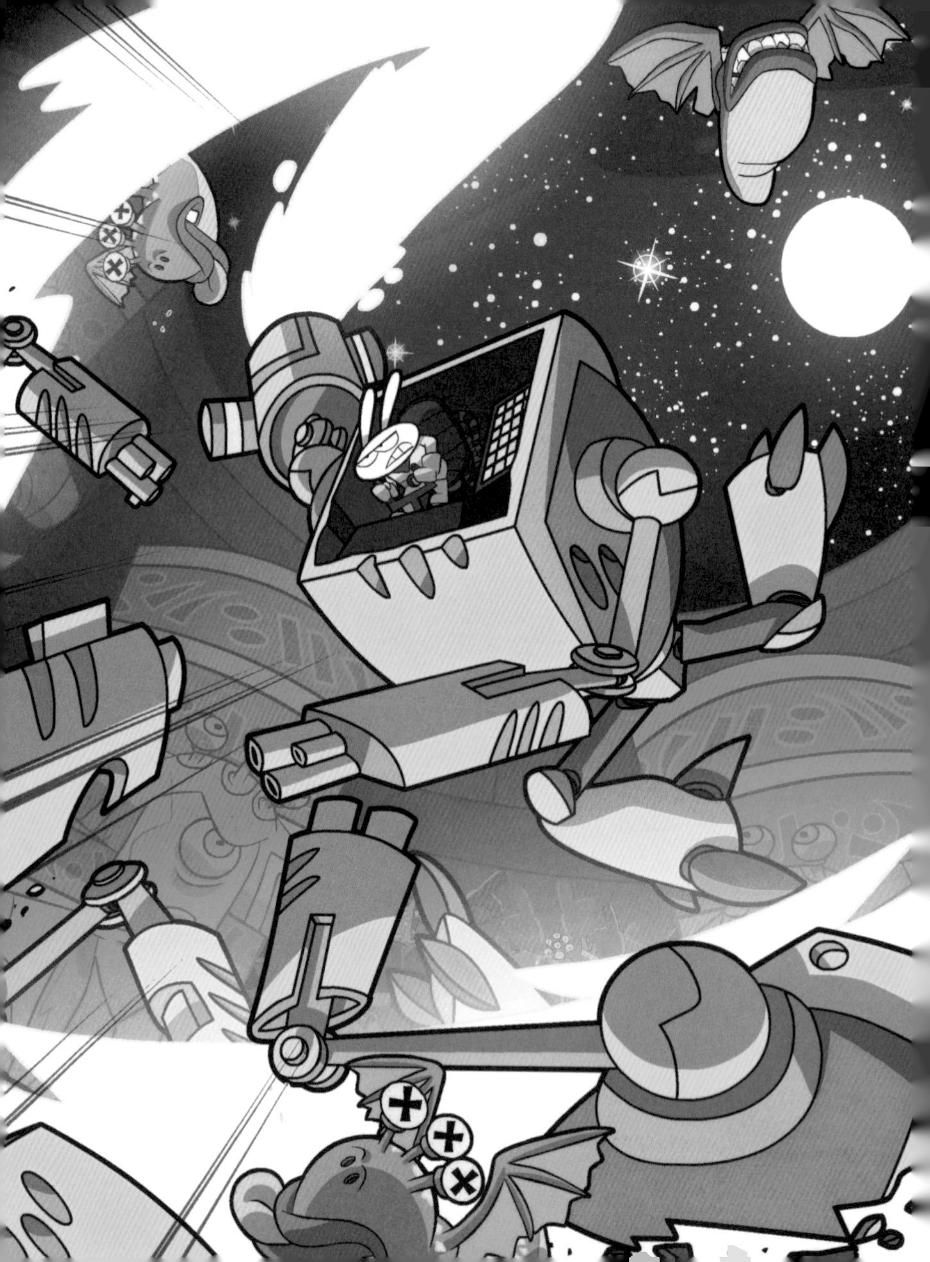

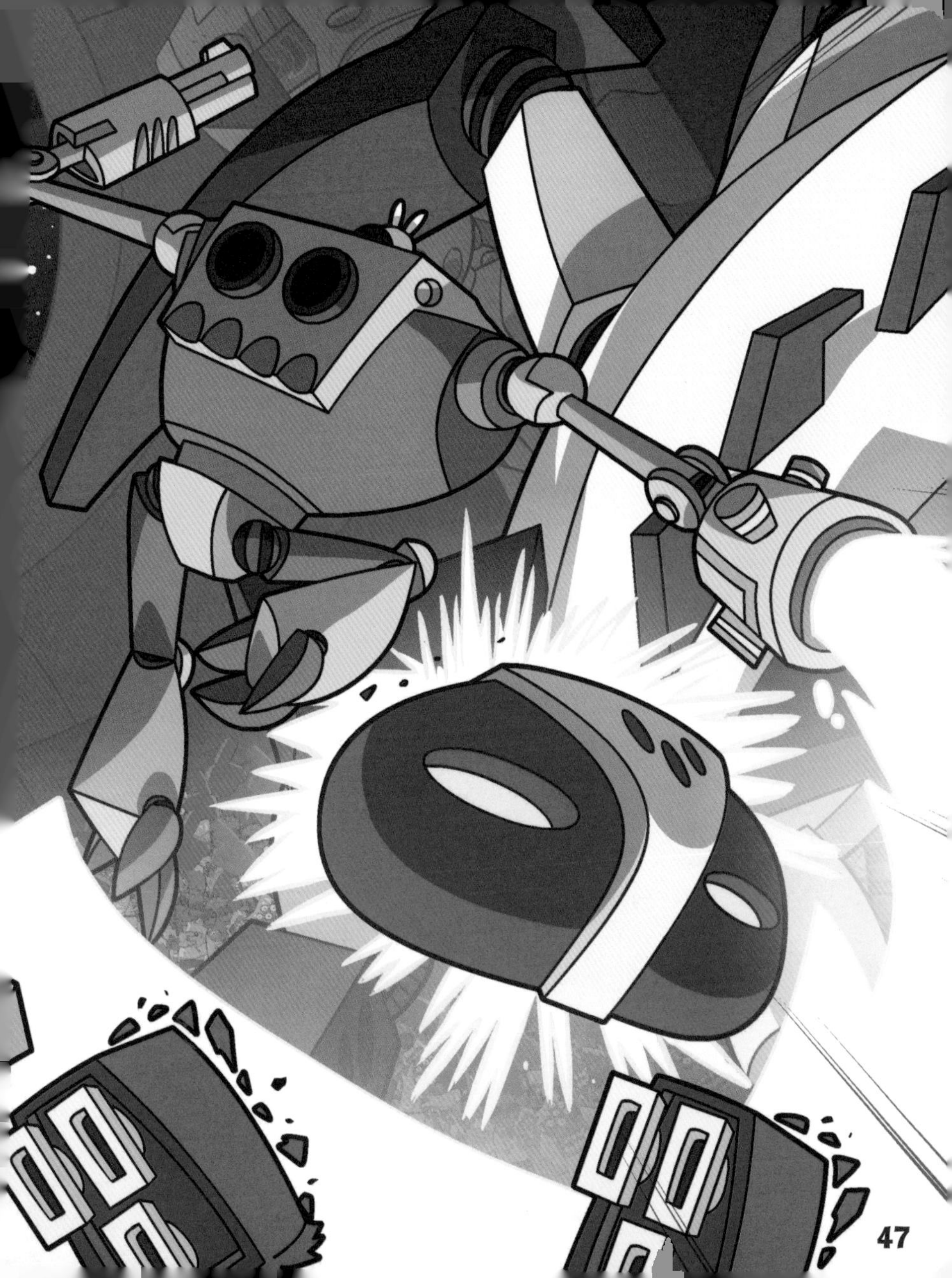

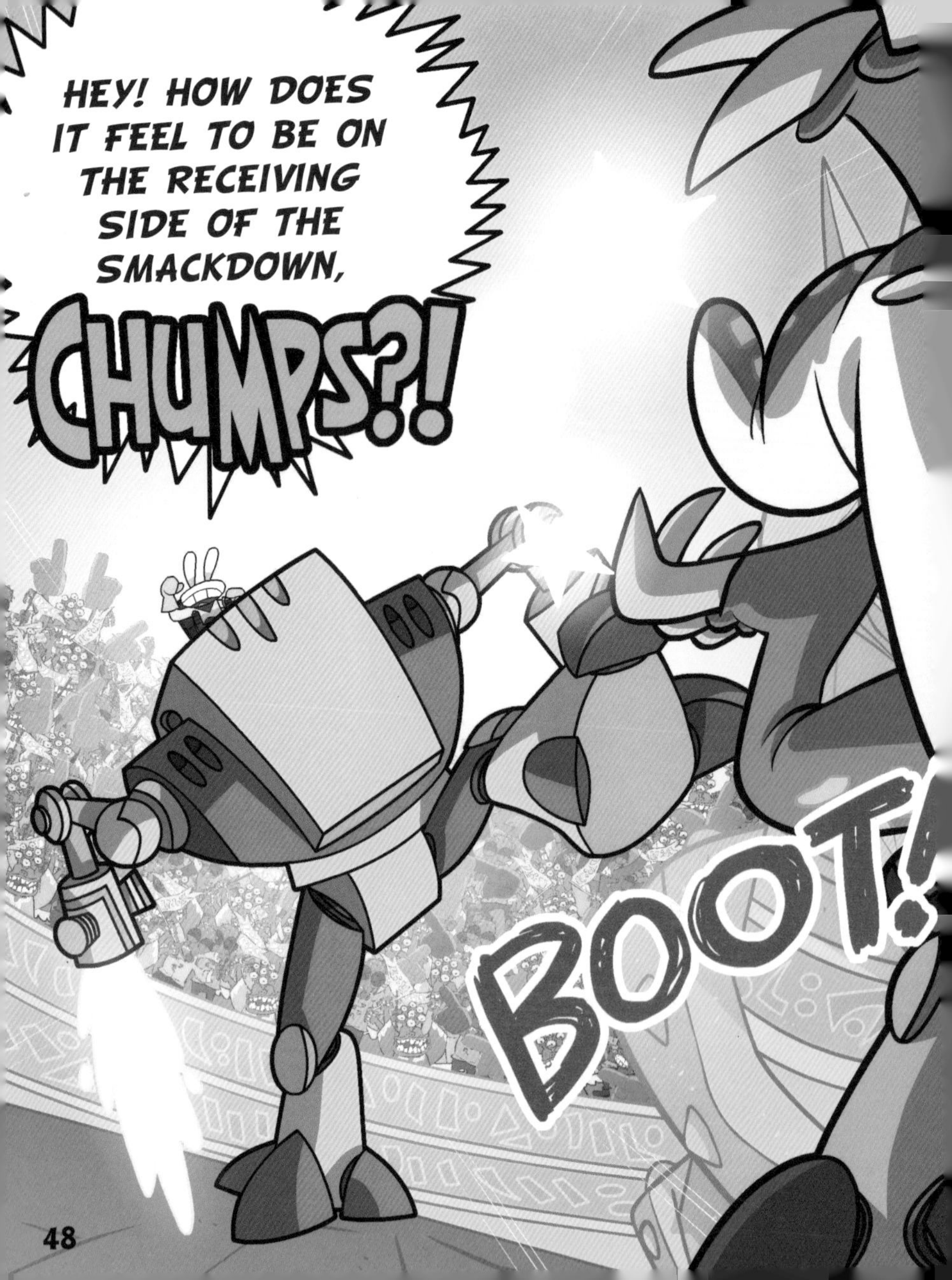
HEY! HOW DOES IT FEEL TO BE ON THE RECEIVING SIDE OF THE SMACKDOWN,
CHUMPS?!
BOOT!

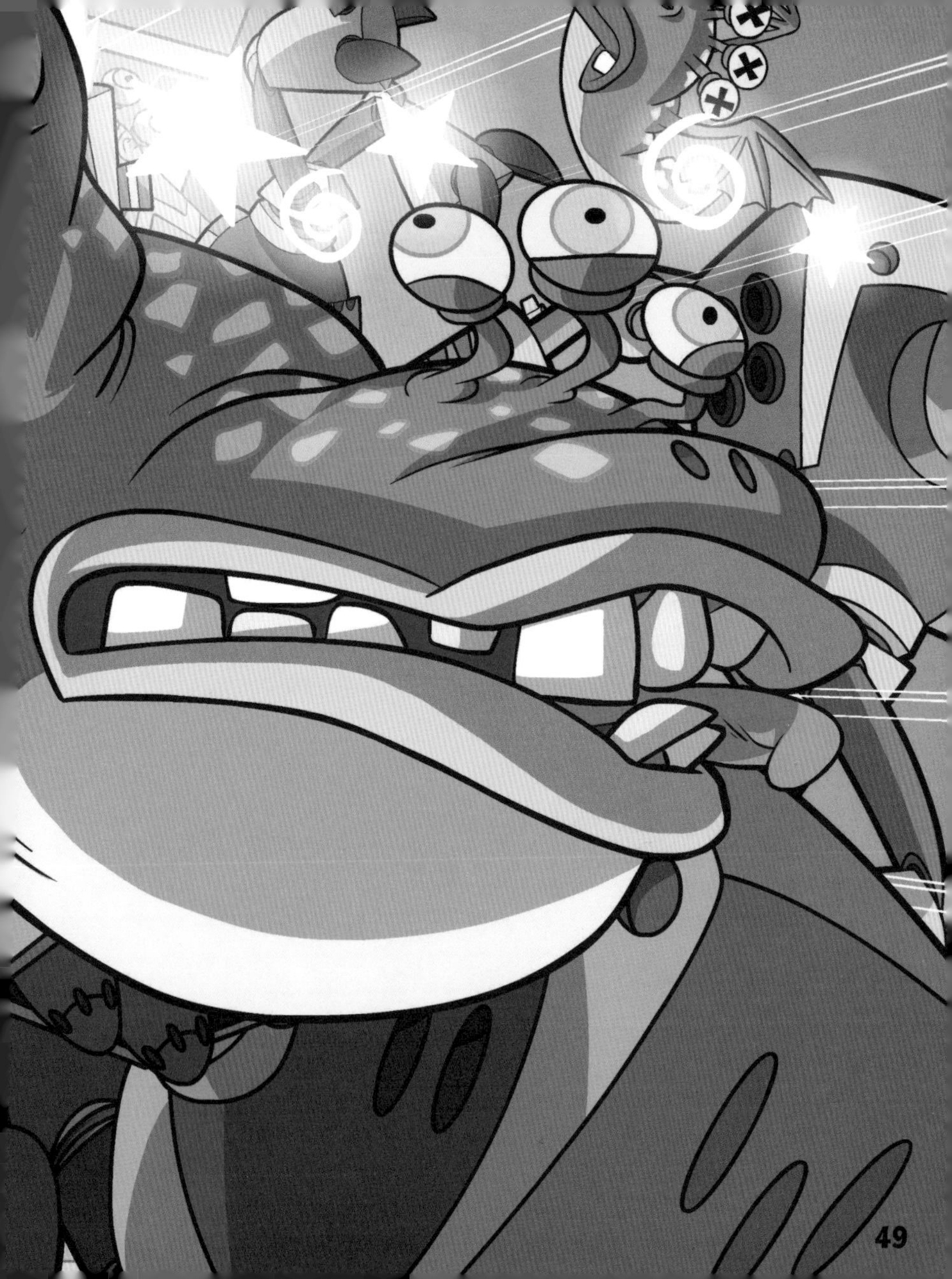

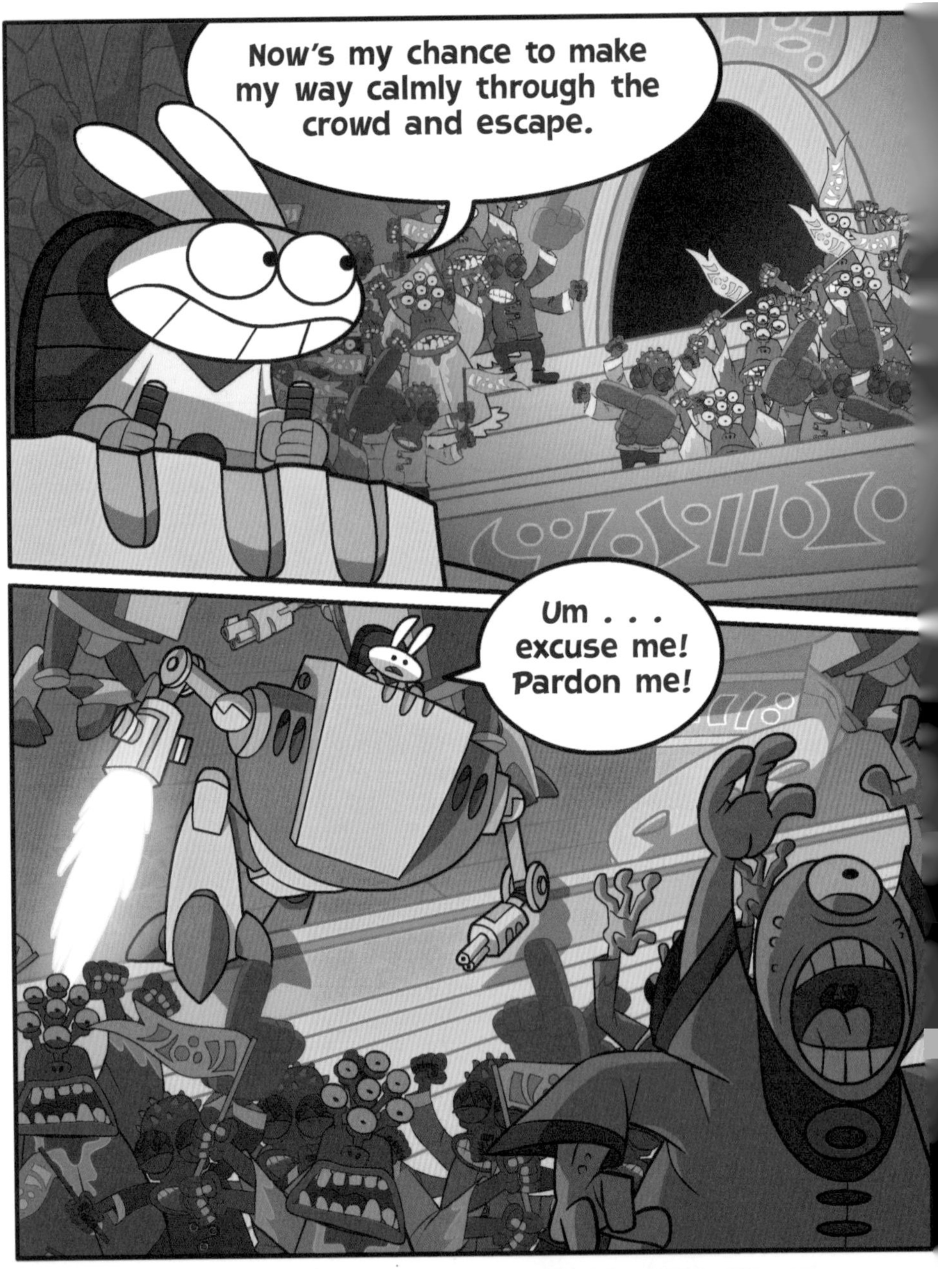
Now's my chance to make my way calmly through the crowd and escape.
Um . . . excuse me! Pardon me!

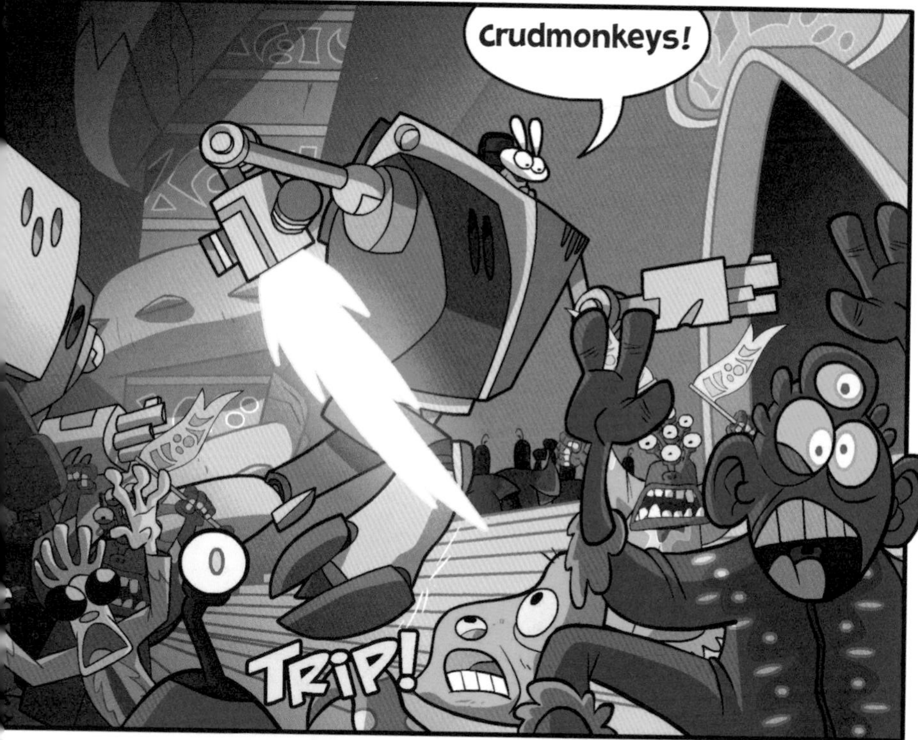
Crudmonkeys!
TRIP!
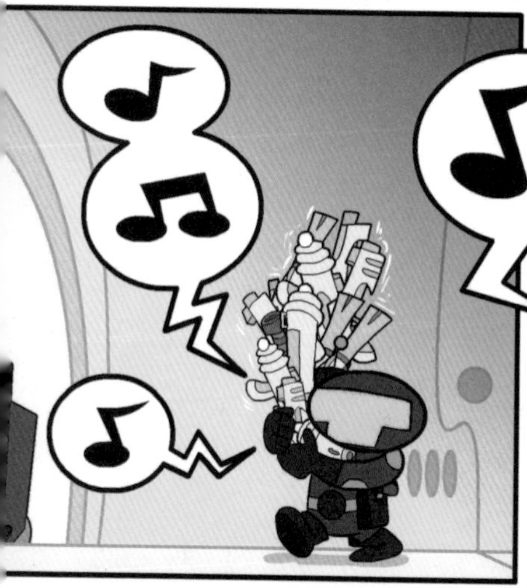
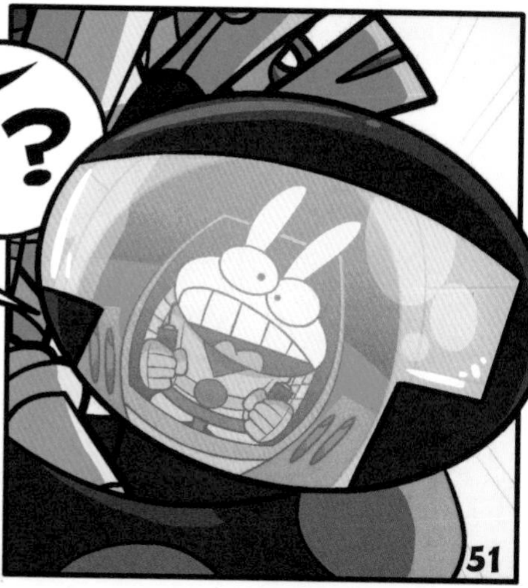
?

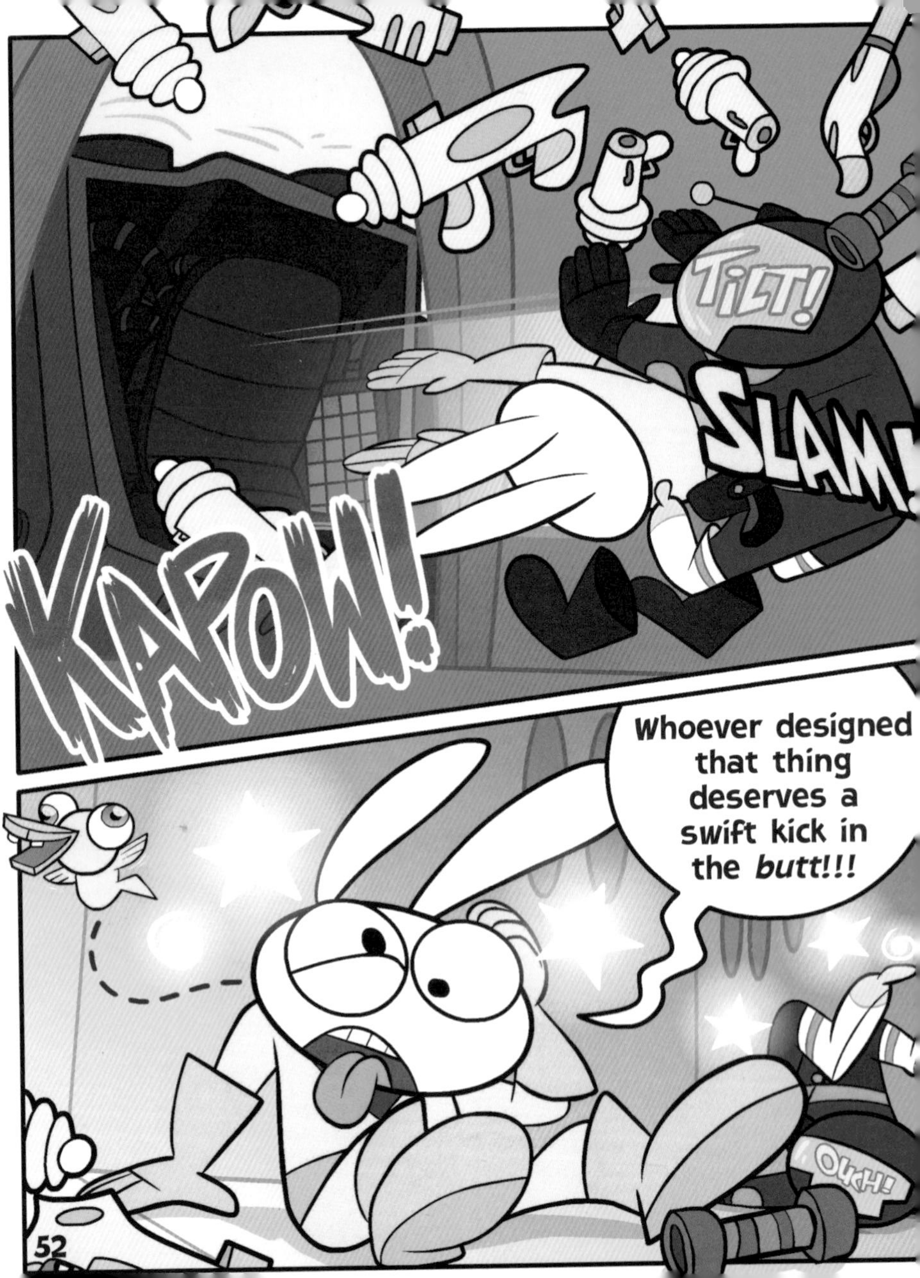
TILT!
SLAM!
KAPOW!
Whoever designed that thing deserves a swift kick in the *butt*!!!
OUCH!

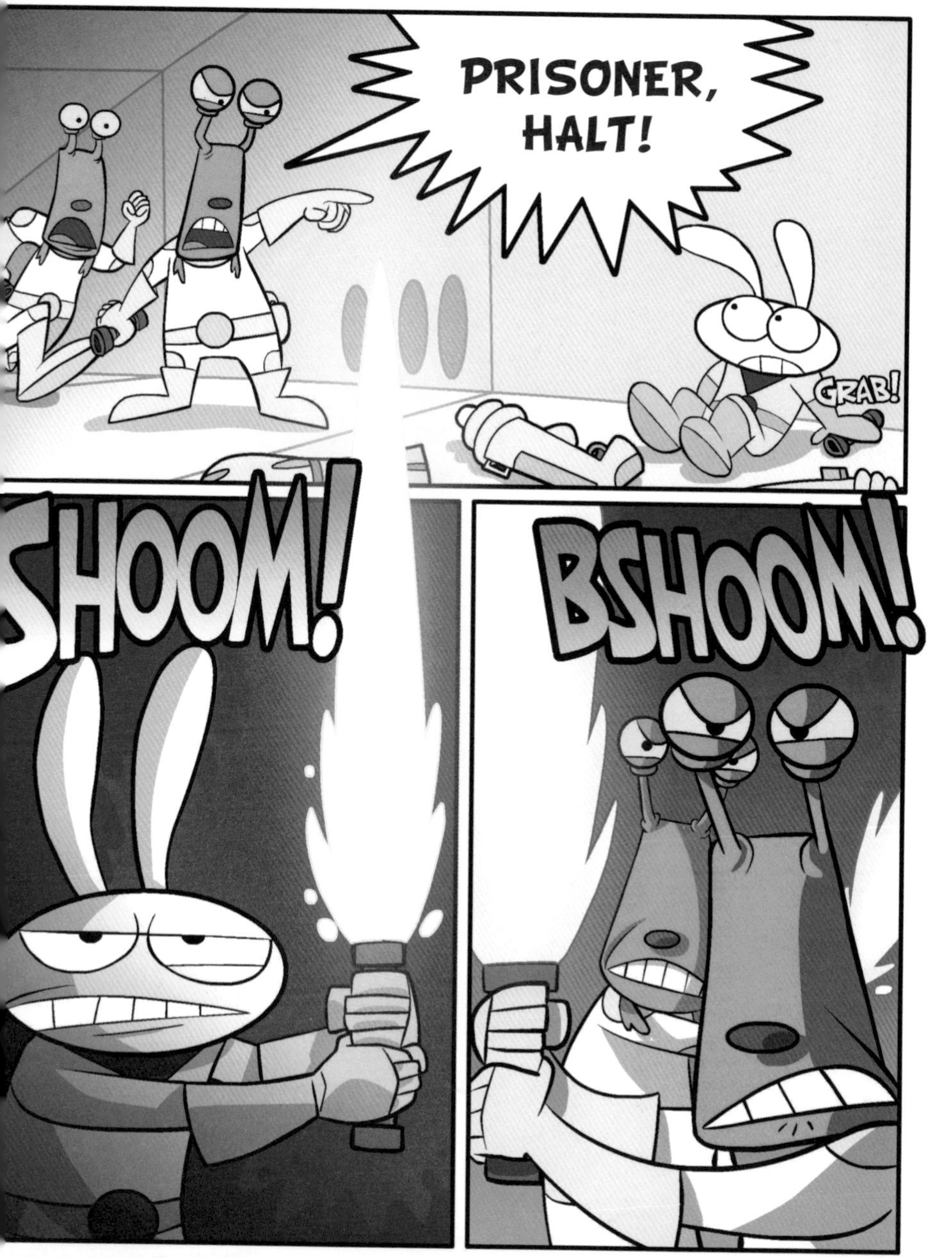

PRISONER, HALT!
GRAB!
SHOOM!
BSHOOM!

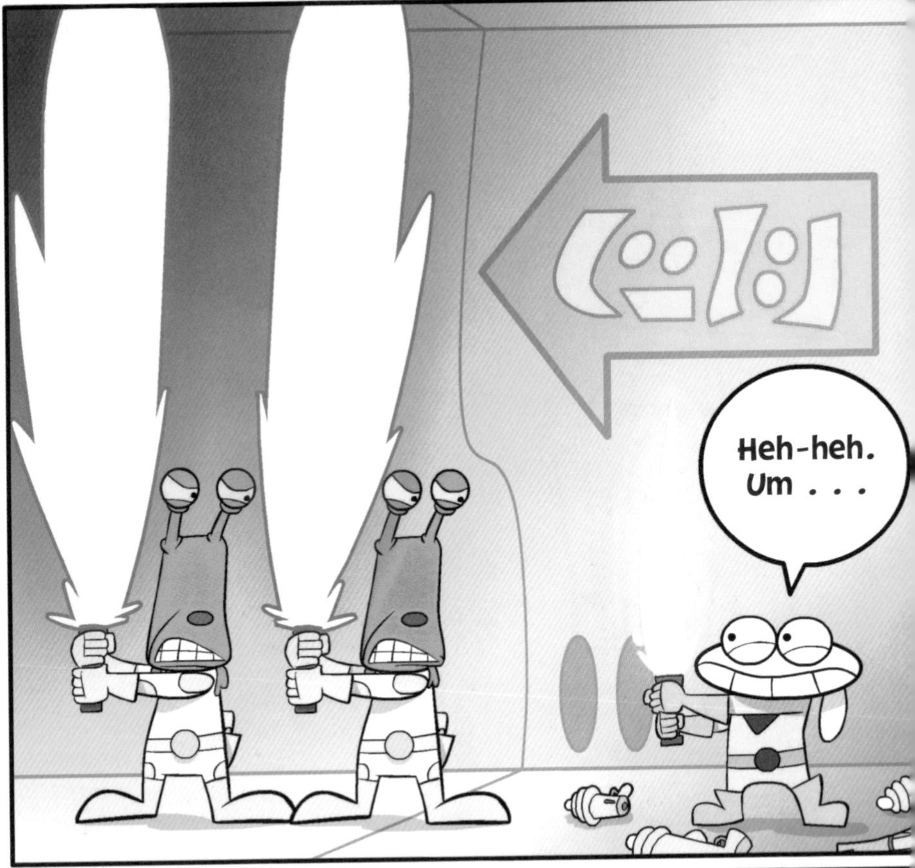
Heh-heh.
Um . . .

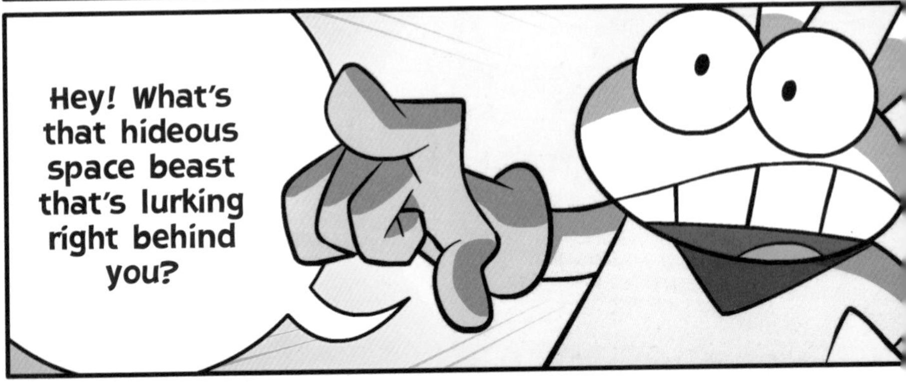
Hey! What's that hideous space beast that's lurking right behind you?

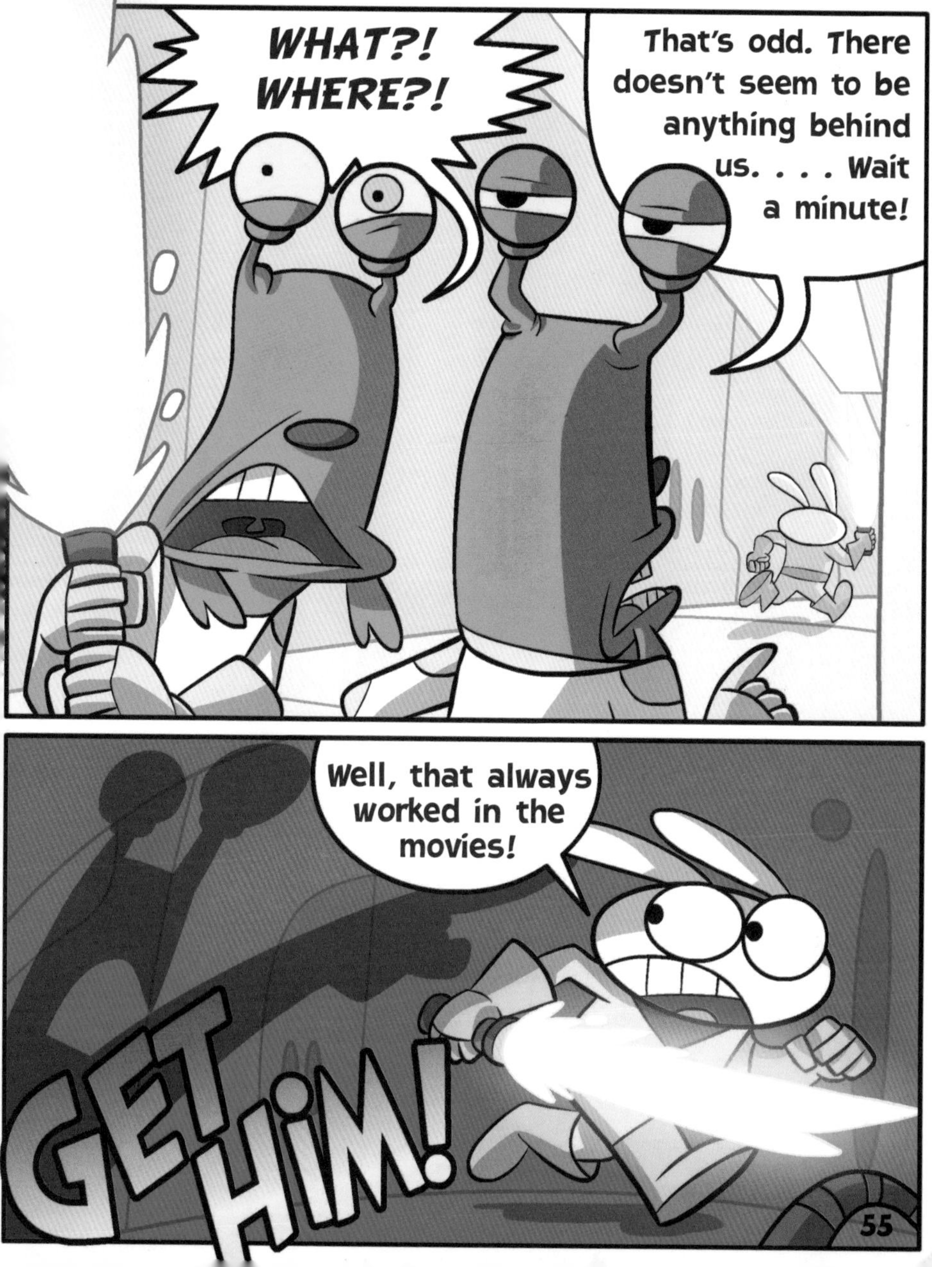

WHAT?! WHERE?!
That's odd. There doesn't seem to be anything behind us. . . . Wait a minute!
Well, that always worked in the movies!
GET HIM!

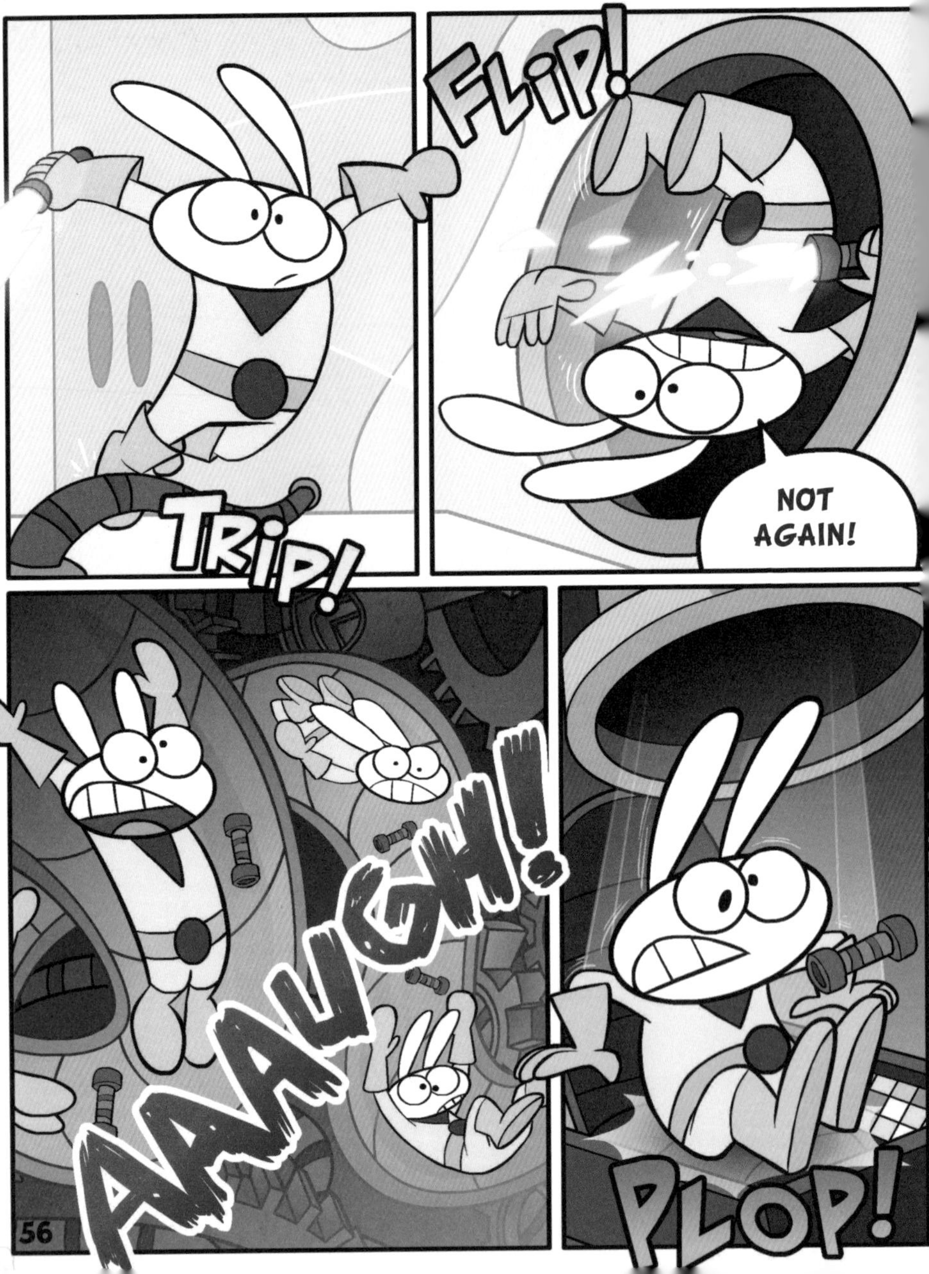

TRIP!
FLIP!
NOT AGAIN!
AAAUGH!
PLOP!

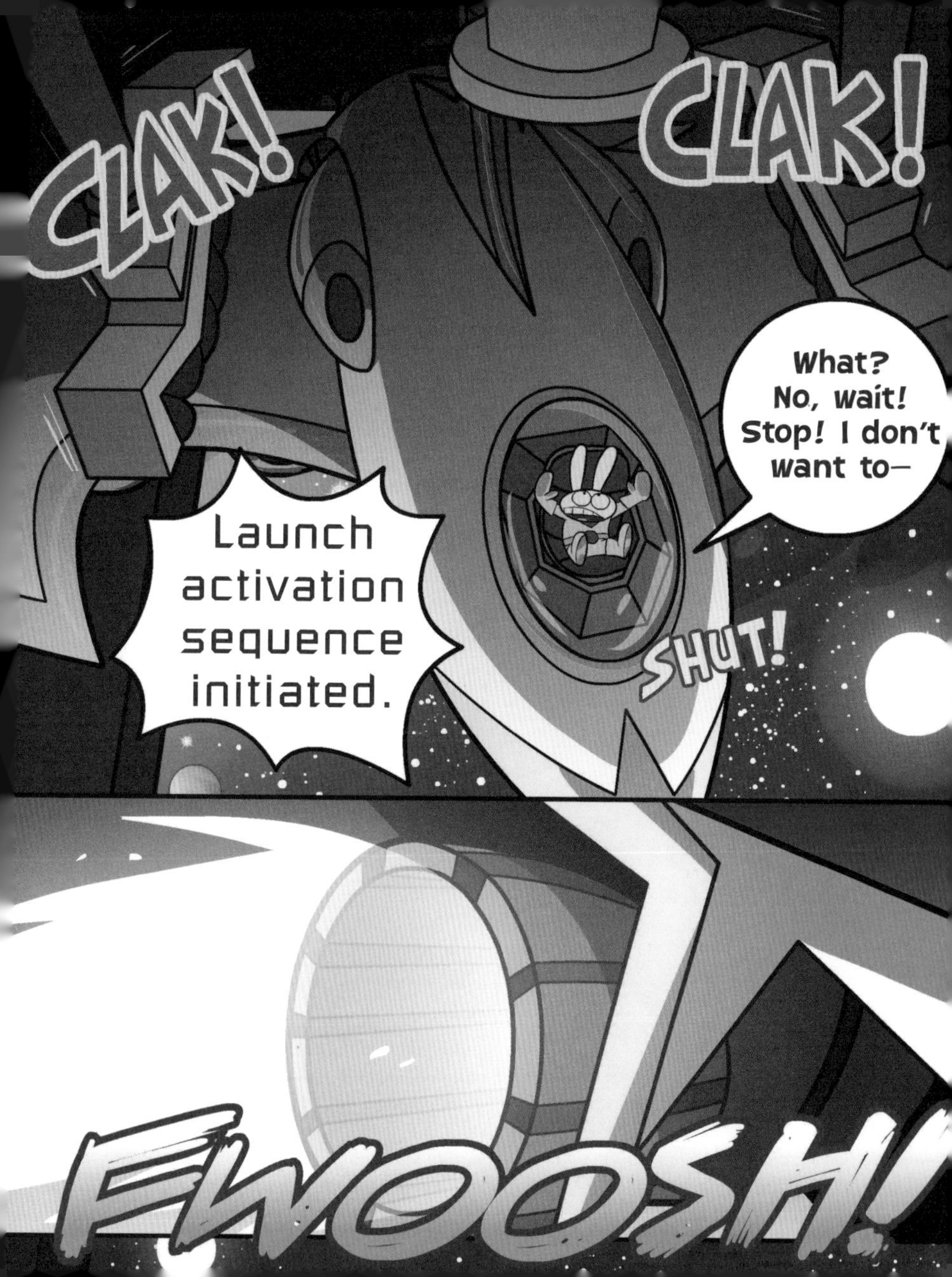
CLAK!
CLAK!
What? No, wait! Stop! I don't want to—
Launch activation sequence initiated.
SHUT!
FWOOSH!

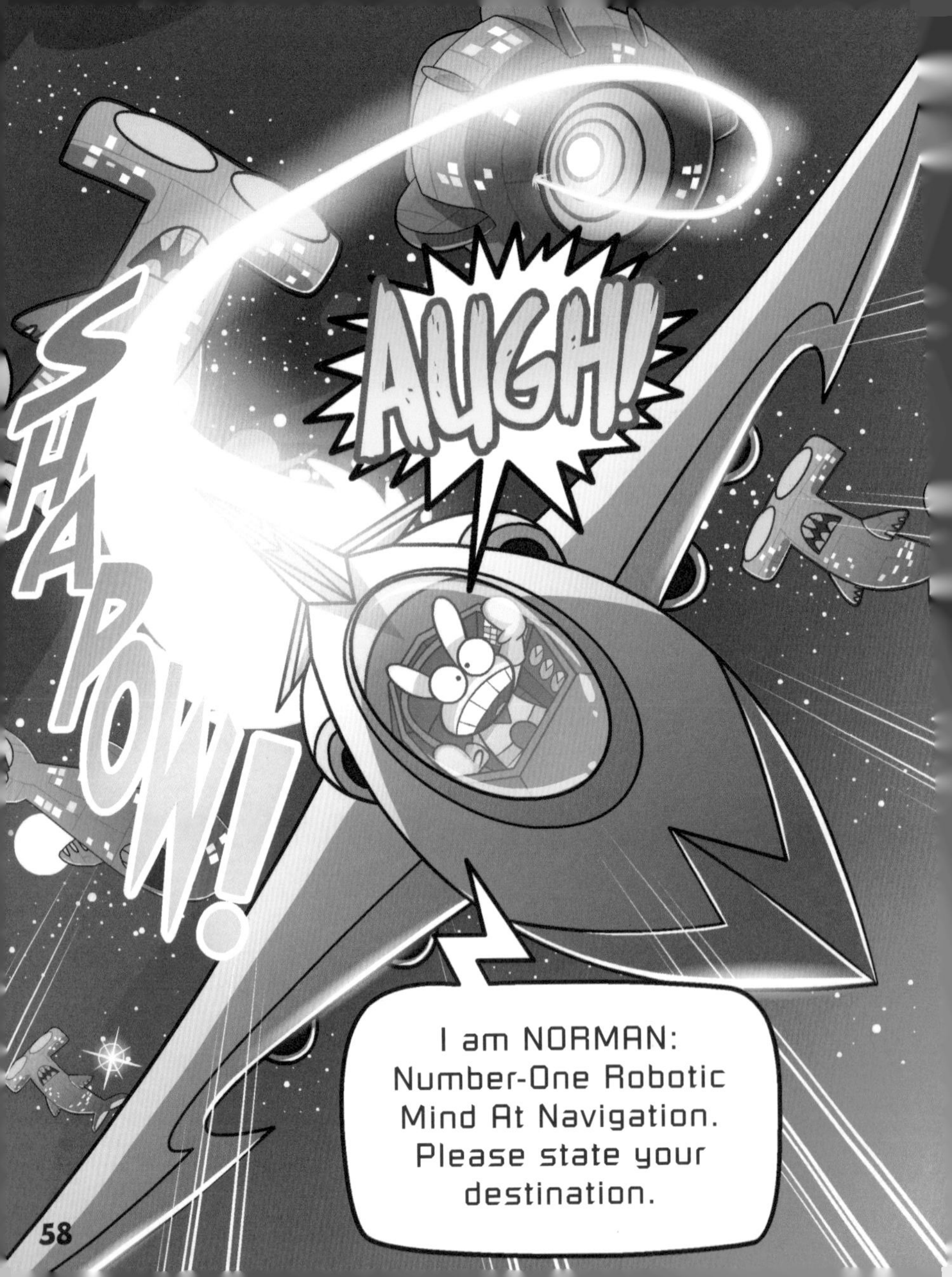
SHAPOW!
AUGH!
I am NORMAN: Number-One Robotic Mind At Navigation. Please state your destination.

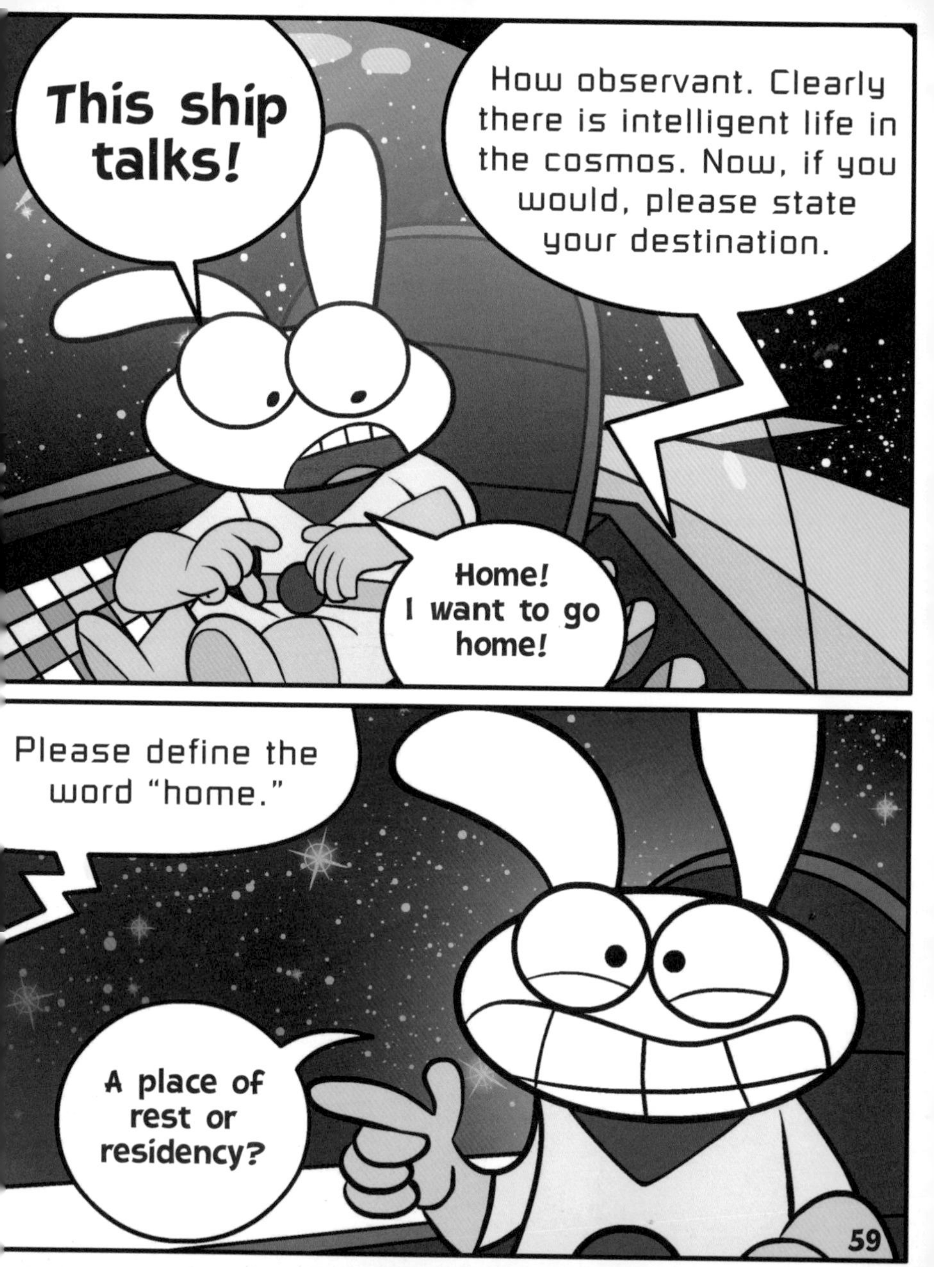
This ship talks!
How observant. Clearly there is intelligent life in the cosmos. Now, if you would, please state your destination.
Home! I want to go home!
Please define the word "home."
A place of rest or residency?

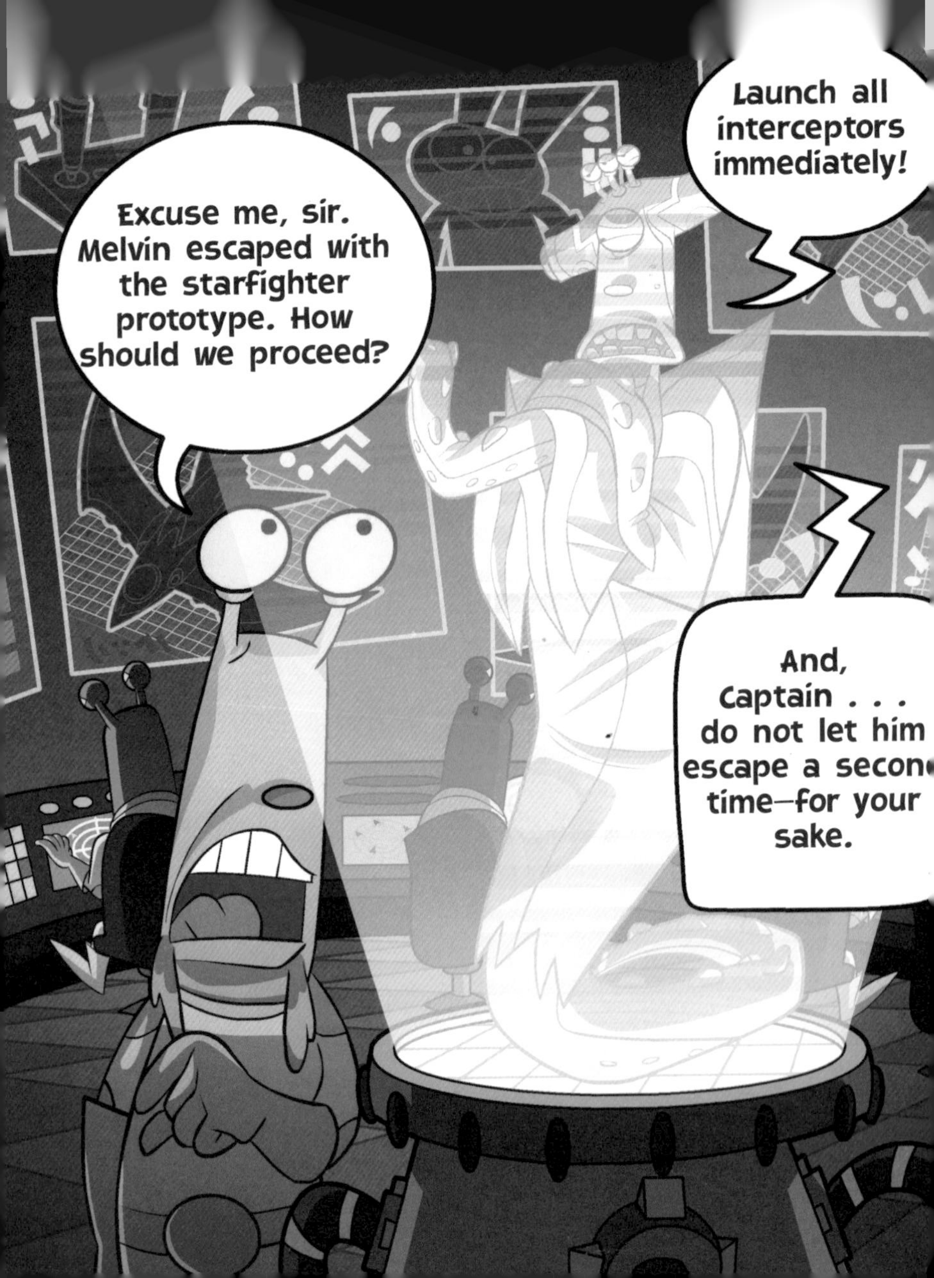
Excuse me, sir. Melvin escaped with the starfighter prototype. How should we proceed?
Launch all interceptors immediately!
And, Captain . . . do not let him escape a secon time—for your sake.

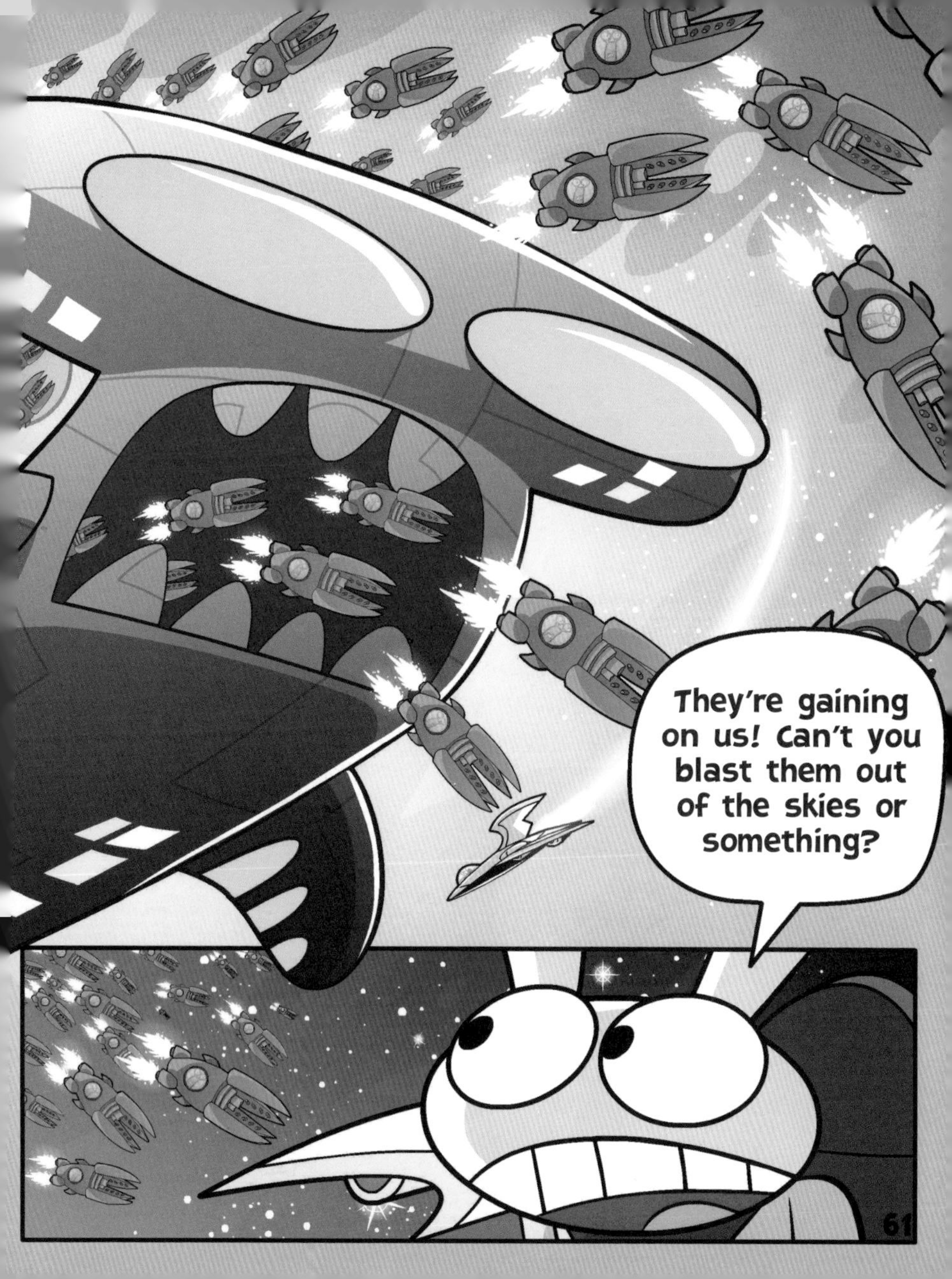
They're gaining on us! Can't you blast them out of the skies or something?

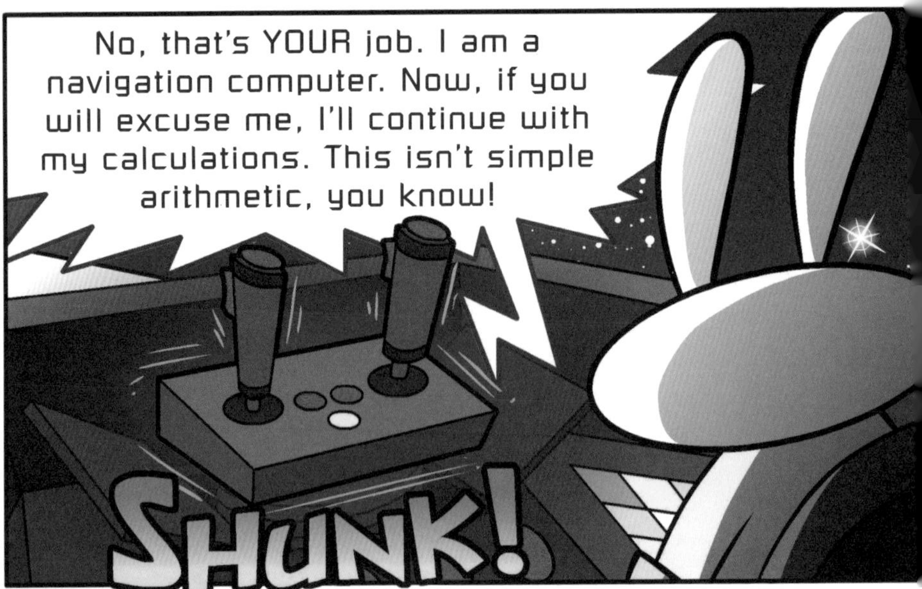
No, that's YOUR job. I am a navigation computer. Now, if you will excuse me, I'll continue with my calculations. This isn't simple arithmetic, you know!
SHUNK!

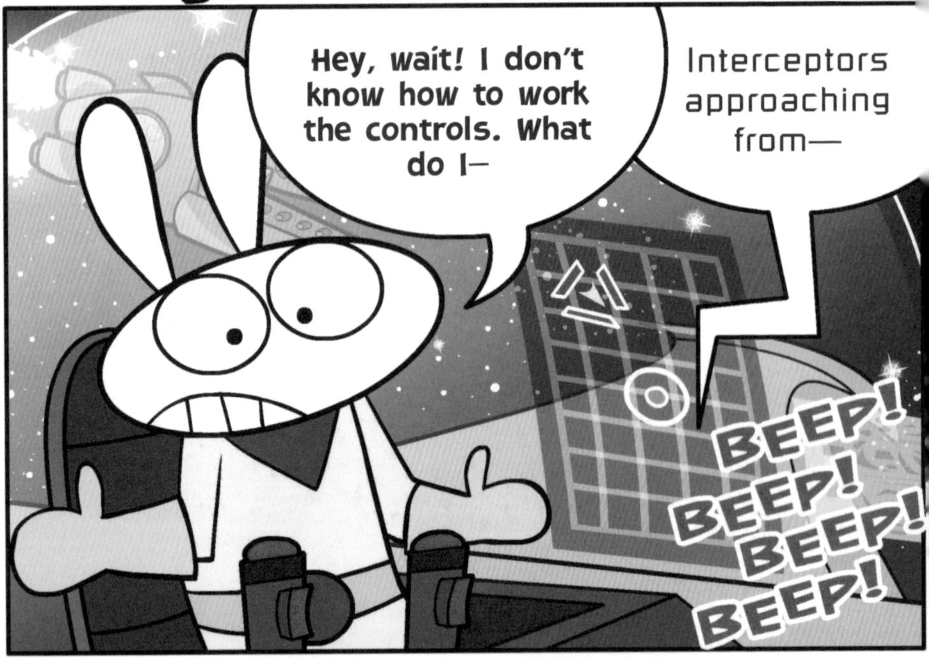
Hey, wait! I don't know how to work the controls. What do I–
Interceptors approaching from—
BEEP! BEEP! BEEP! BEEP!

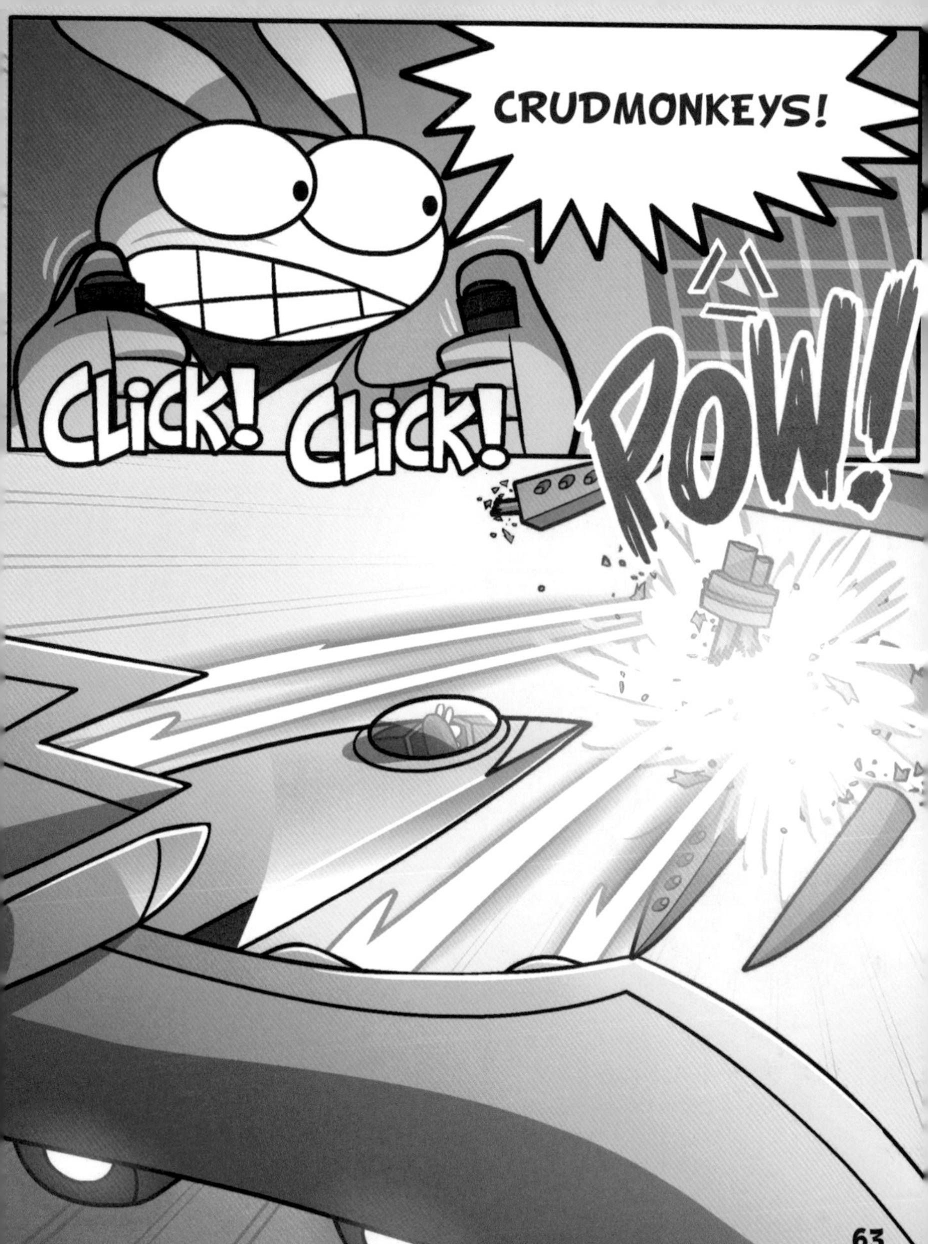
CRUDMONKEYS!
CLICK! CLICK!
POW!!

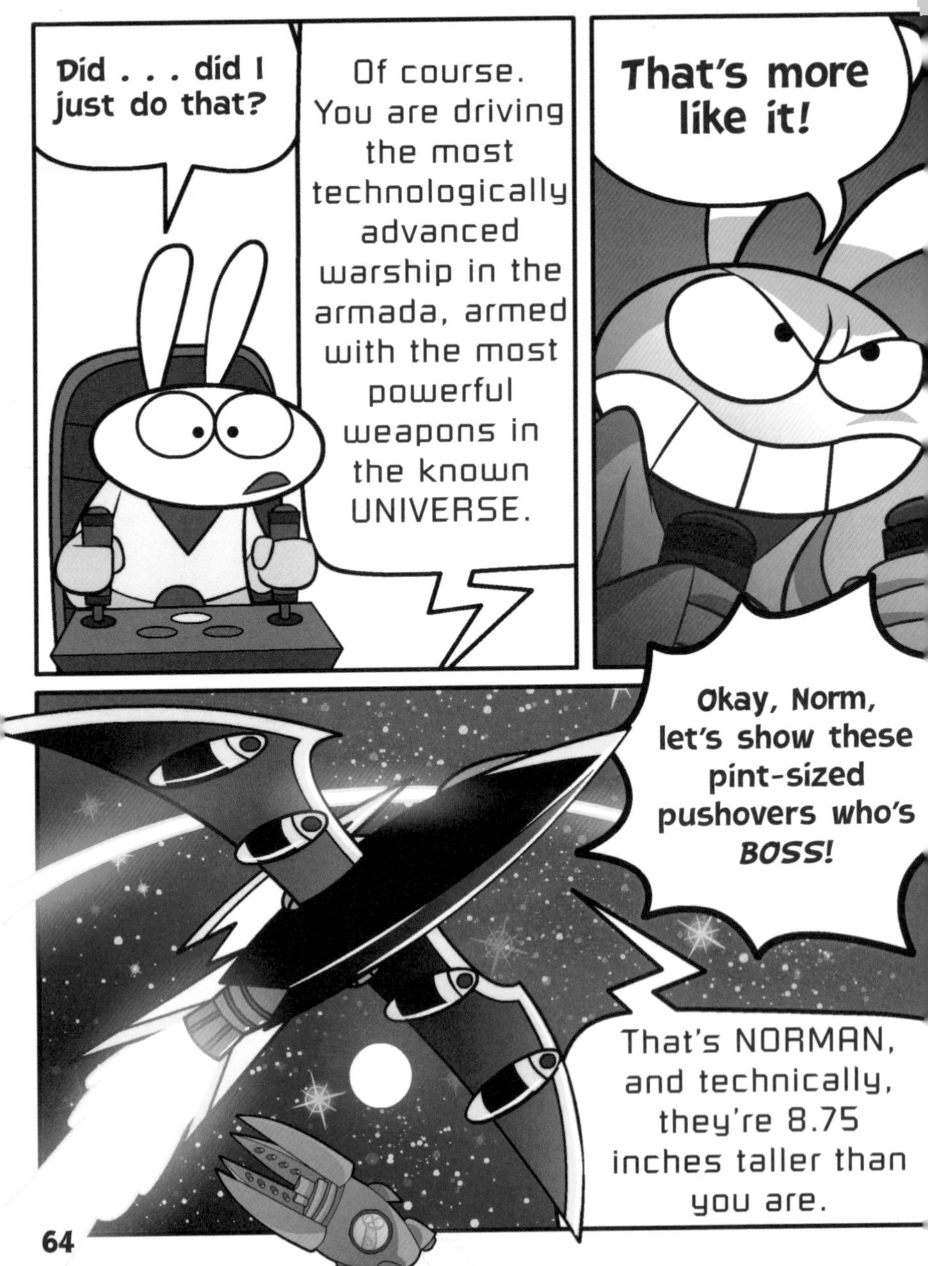
Did . . . did I just do that?
Of course. You are driving the most technologically advanced warship in the armada, armed with the most powerful weapons in the known UNIVERSE.
That's more like it!
Okay, Norm, let's show these pint-sized pushovers who's *BOSS!*
That's NORMAN, and technically, they're 8.75 inches taller than you are.

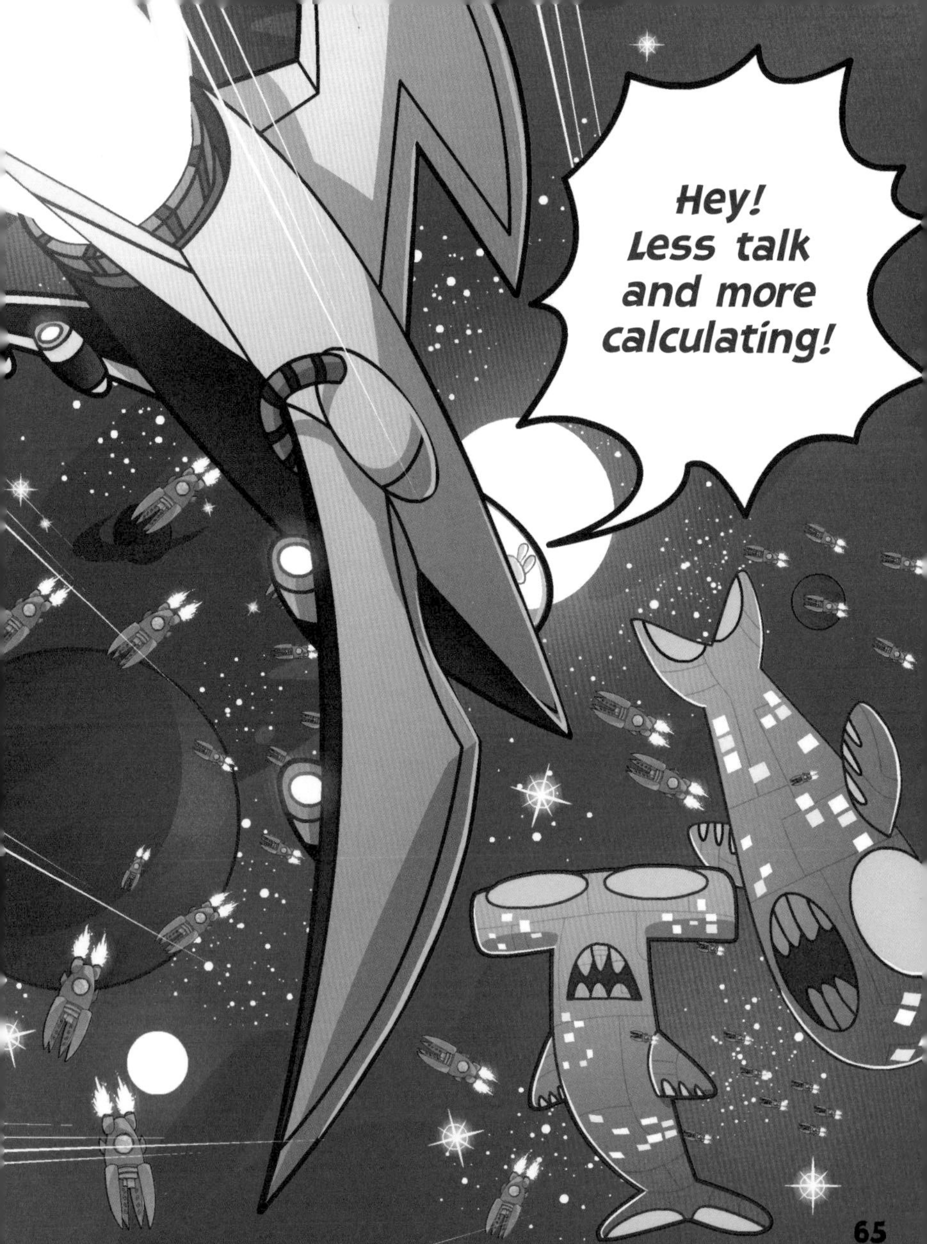
Hey! Less talk and more calculating!

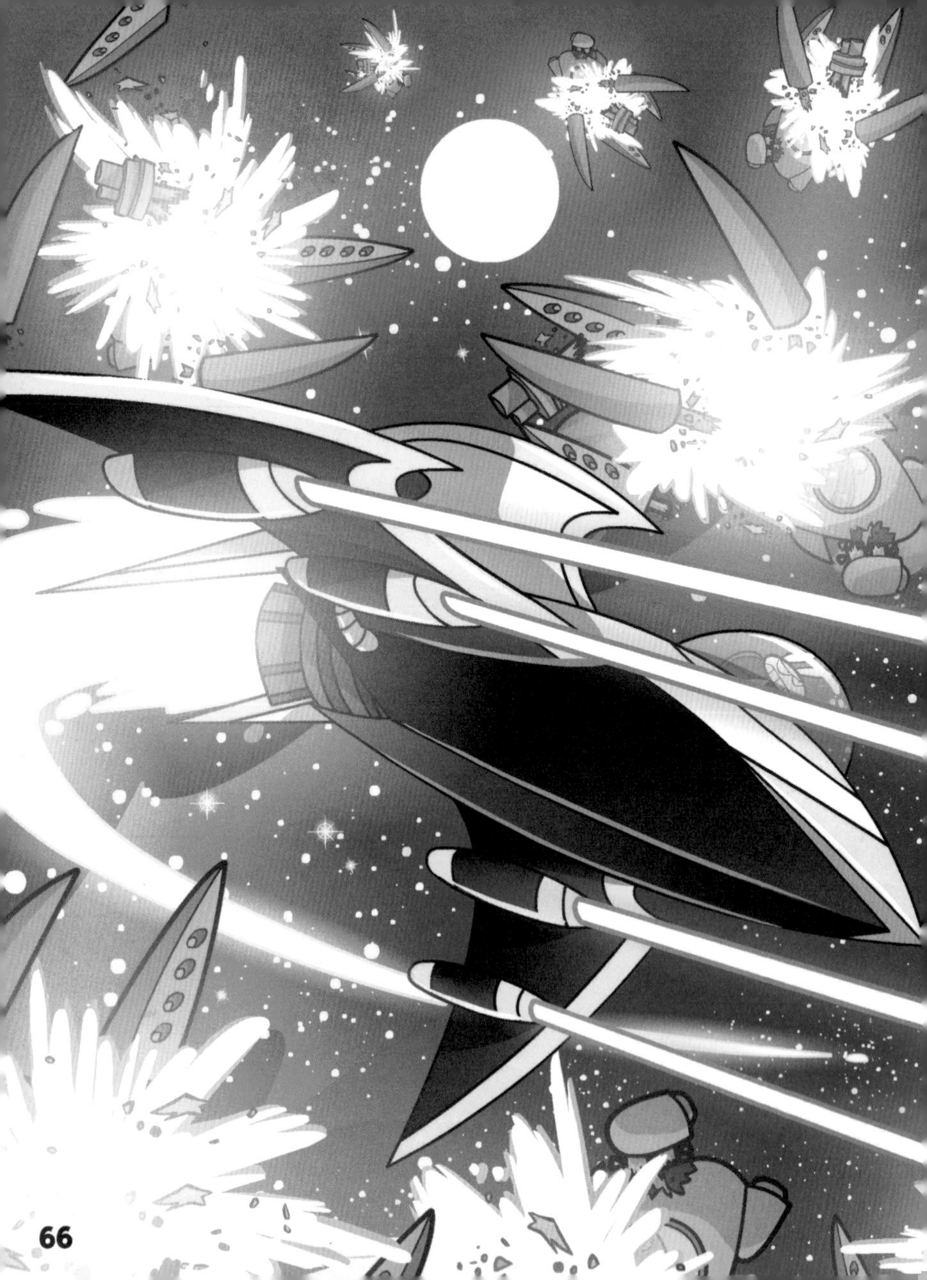

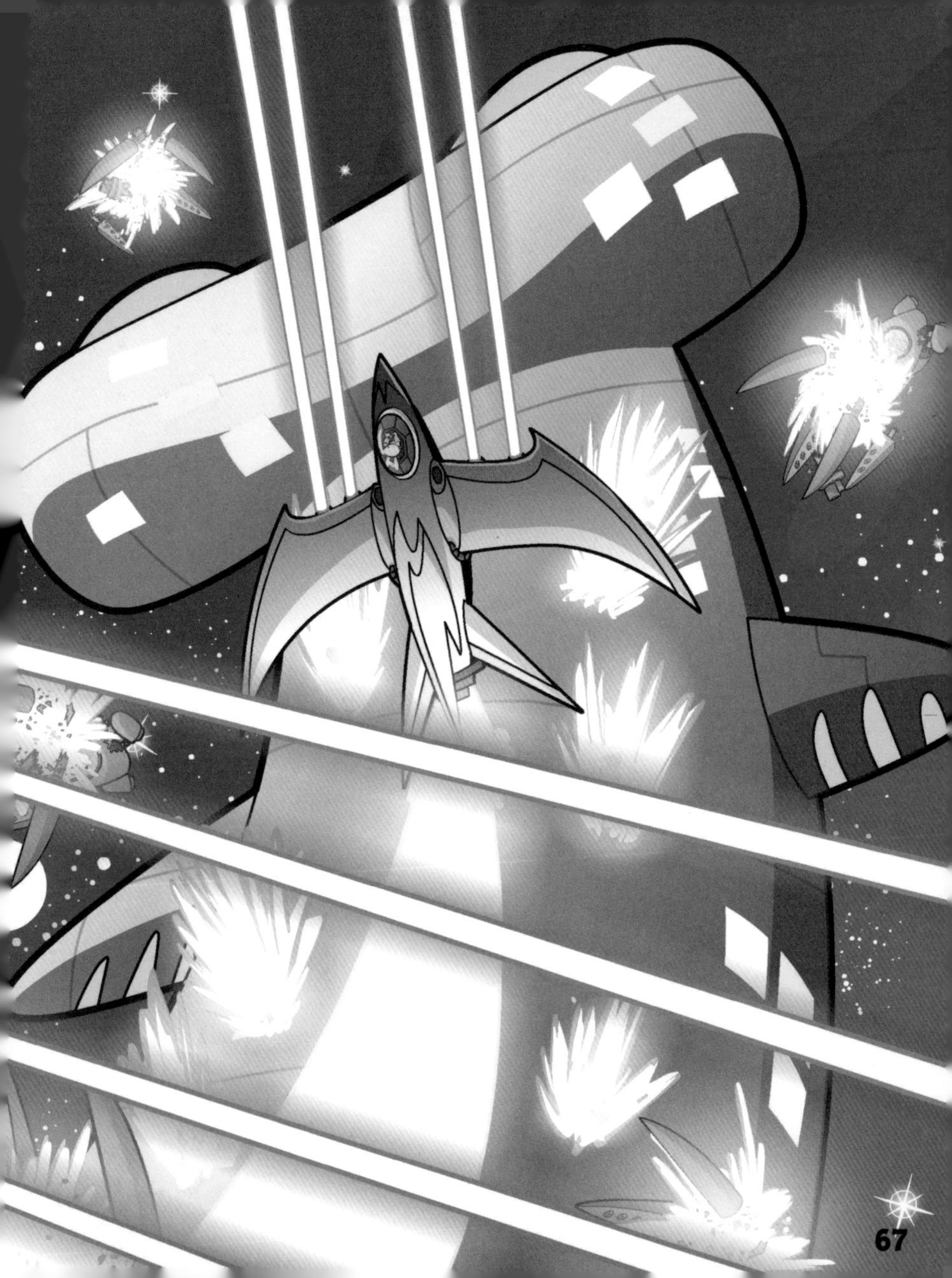

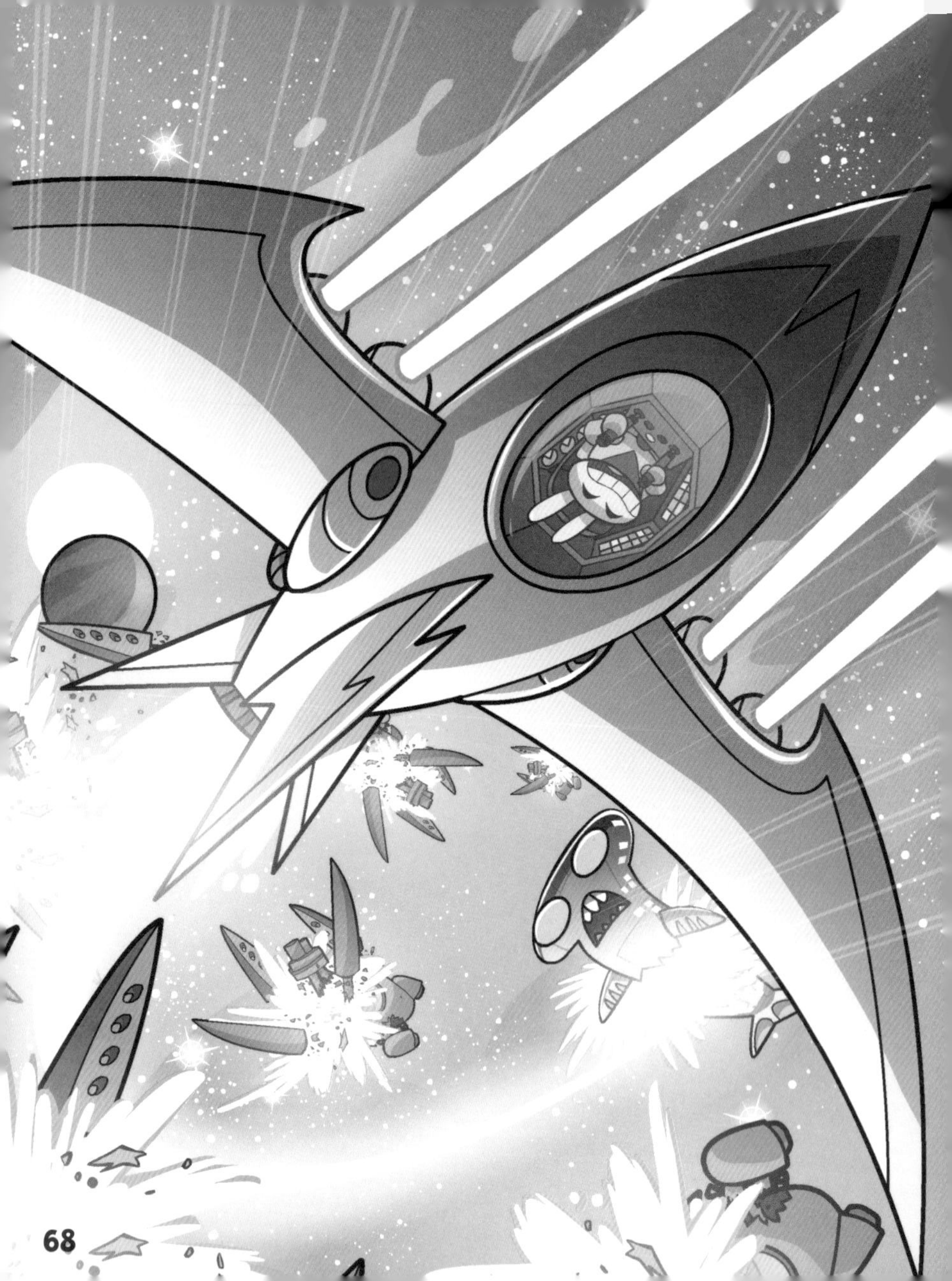

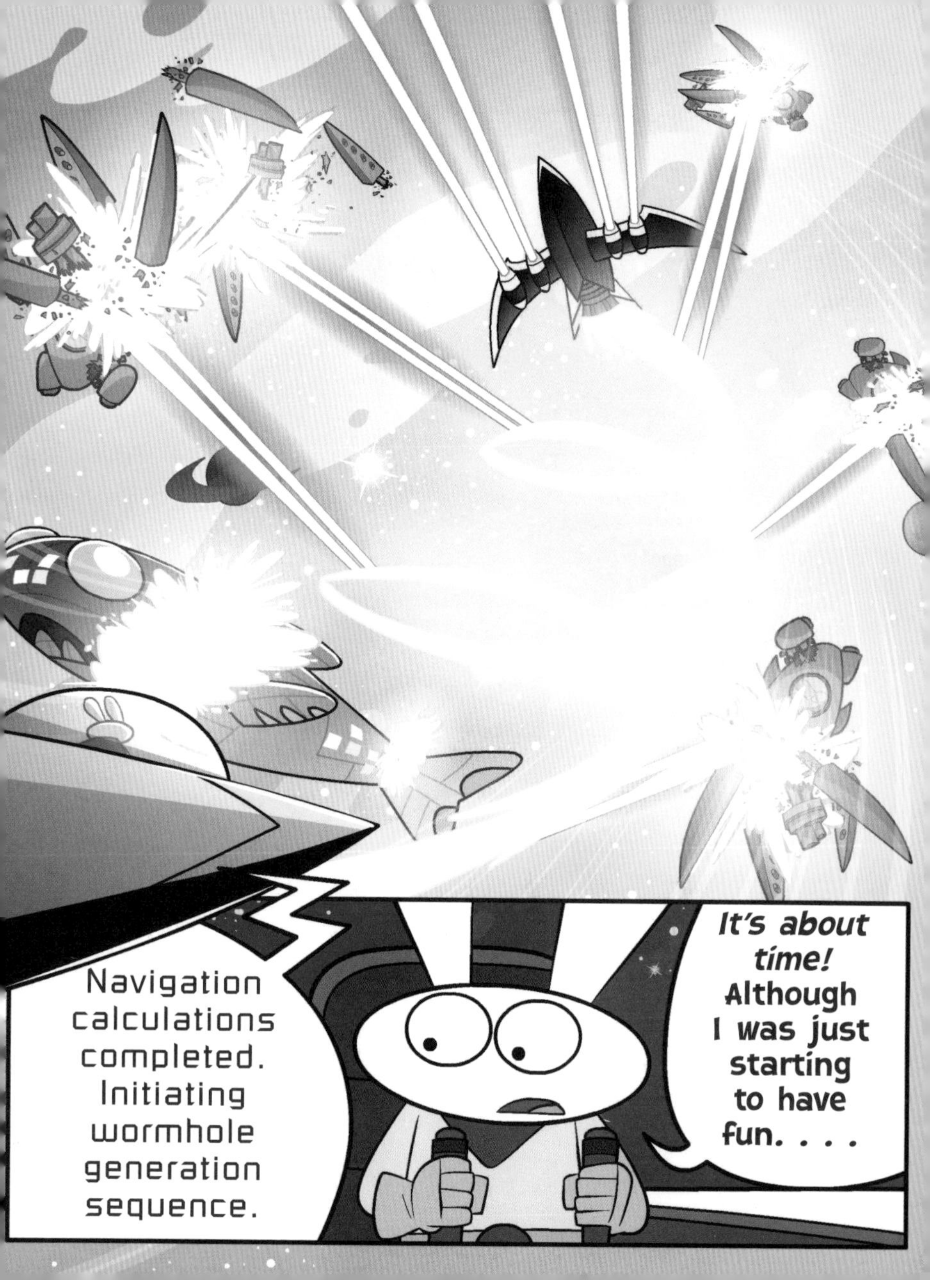
Navigation calculations completed. Initiating wormhole generation sequence.
It's about time! Although I was just starting to have fun. . . .

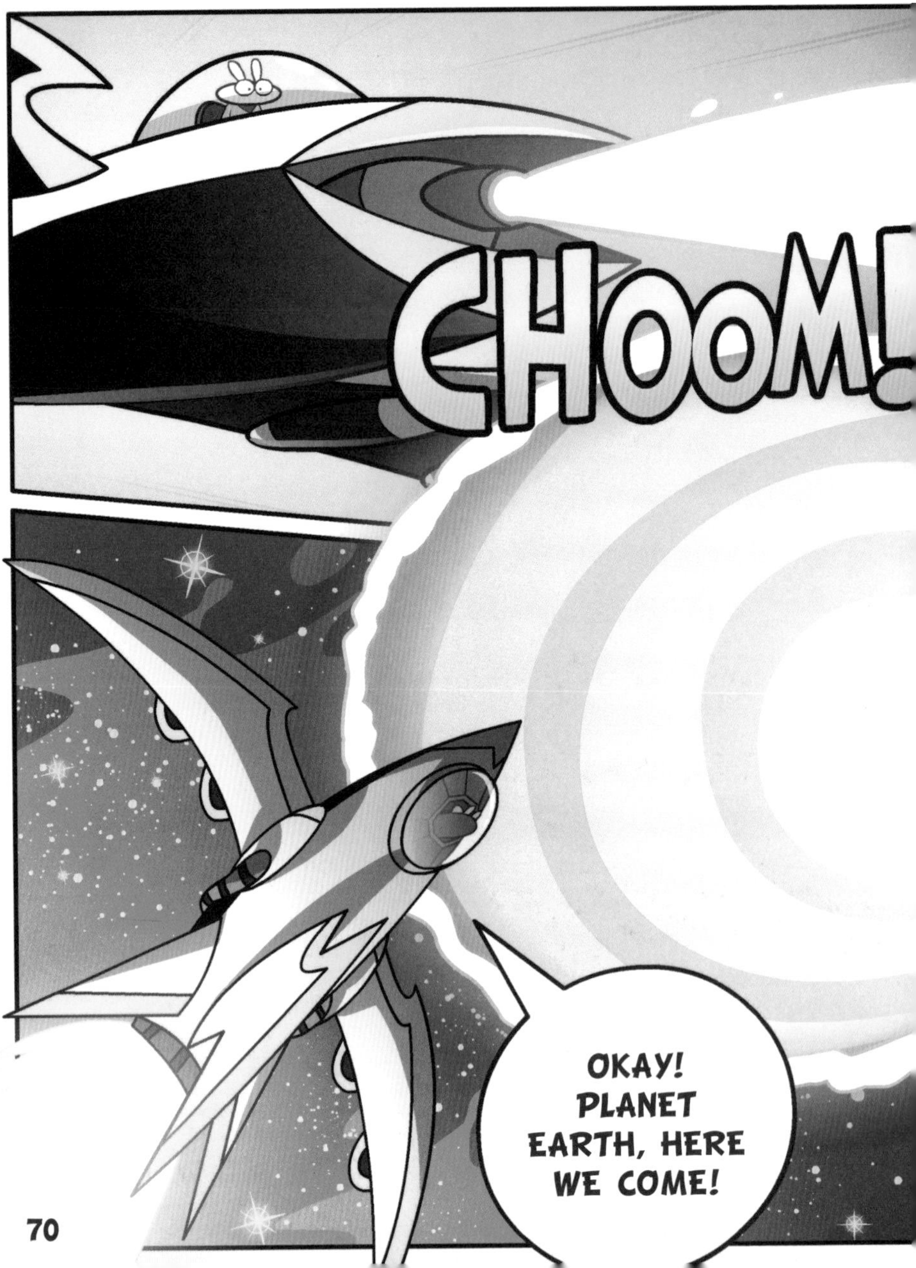
CHOOM!
OKAY! PLANET EARTH, HERE WE COME!

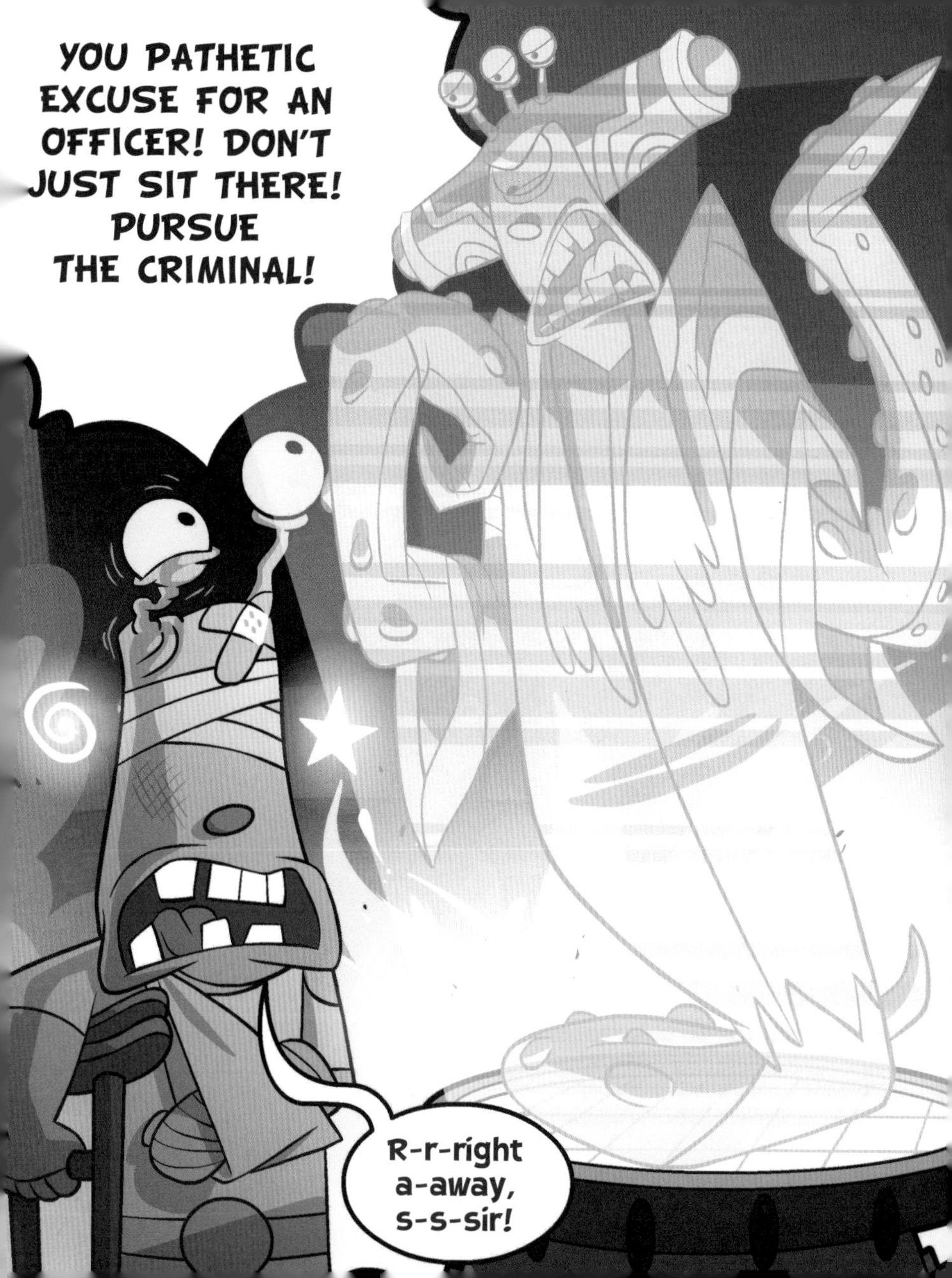
YOU PATHETIC EXCUSE FOR AN OFFICER! DON'T JUST SIT THERE! PURSUE THE CRIMINAL!
R-r-right a-away, s-s-sir!

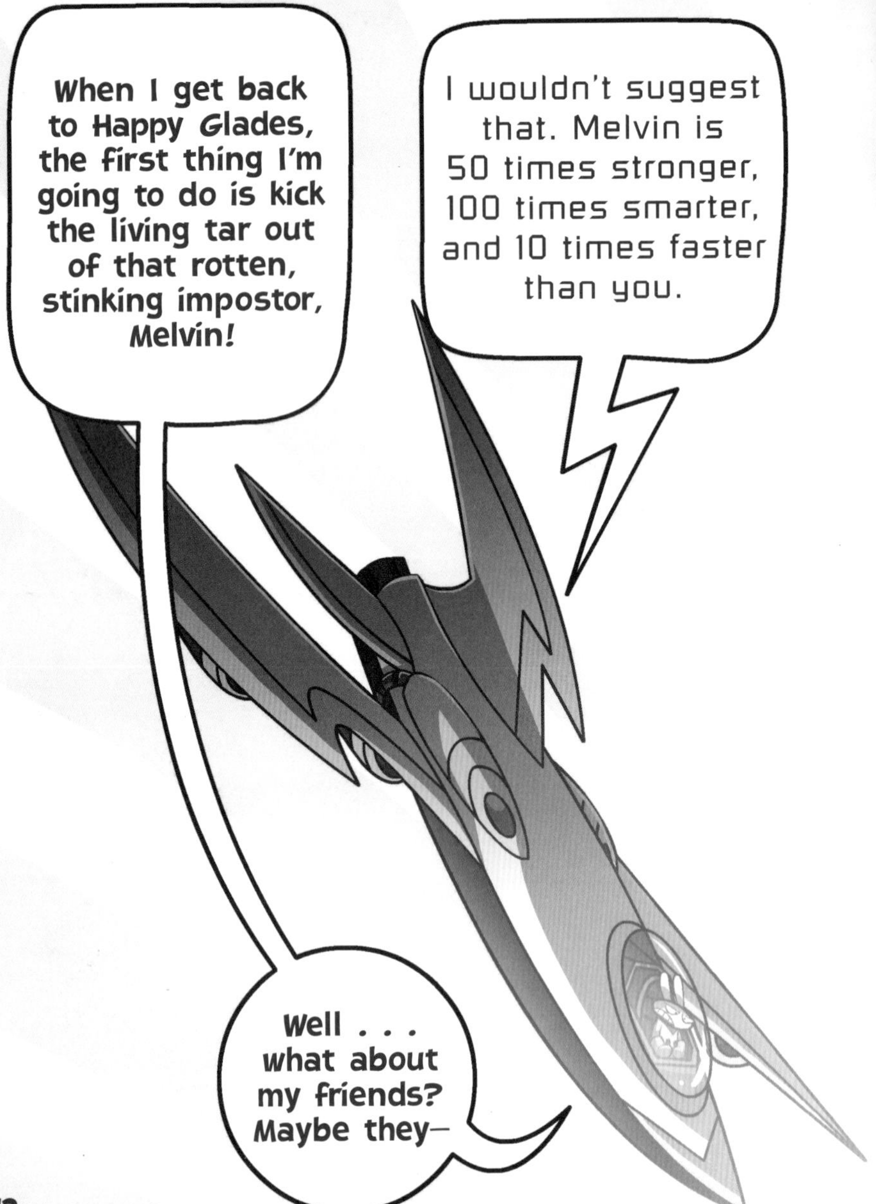
When I get back to Happy Glades, the first thing I'm going to do is kick the living tar out of that rotten, stinking impostor, Melvin!
I wouldn't suggest that. Melvin is 50 times stronger, 100 times smarter, and 10 times faster than you.
Well . . . what about my friends? Maybe they—

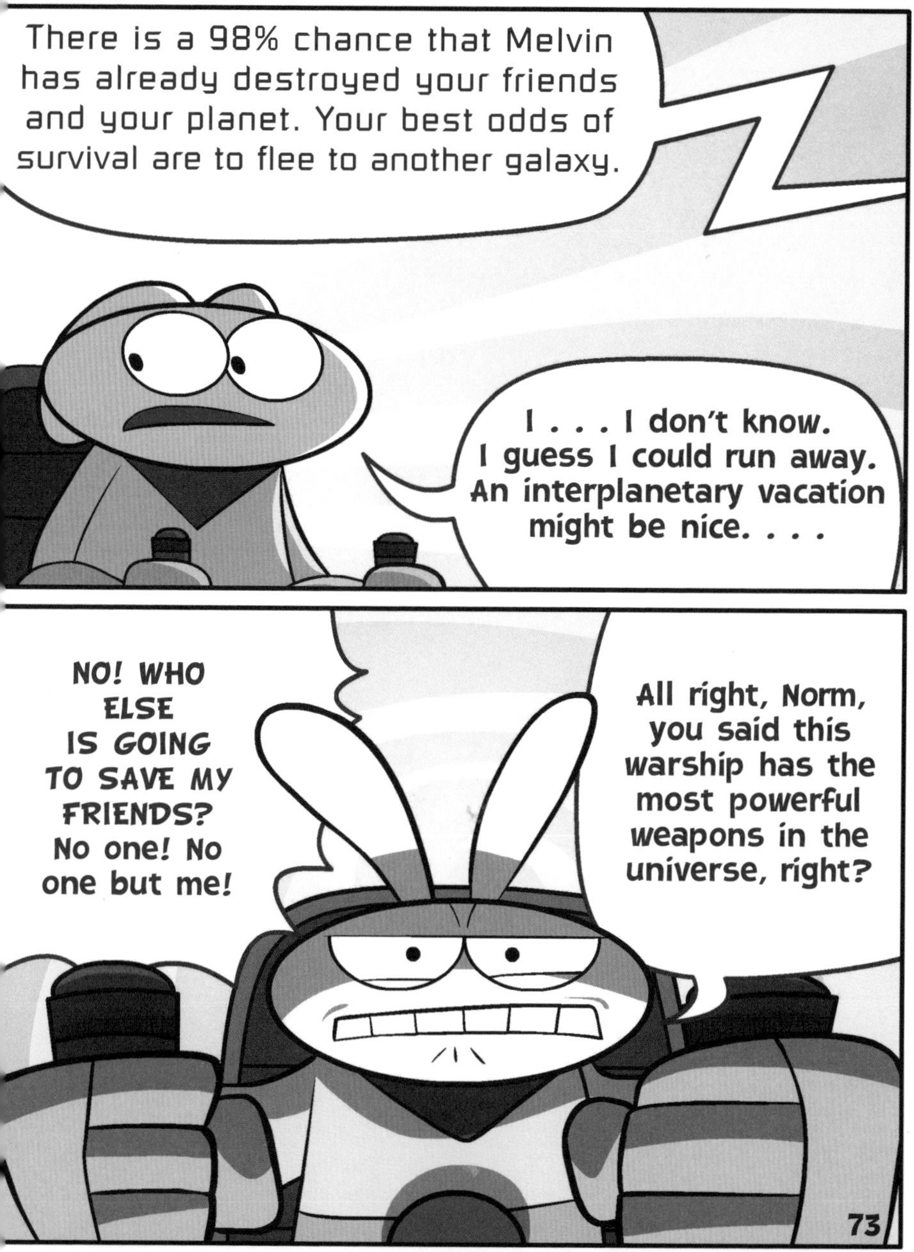
There is a 98% chance that Melvin has already destroyed your friends and your planet. Your best odds of survival are to flee to another galaxy.
I . . . I don't know. I guess I could run away. An interplanetary vacation might be nice. . . .
NO! WHO ELSE IS GOING TO SAVE MY FRIENDS? No one! No one but me!
All right, Norm, you said this warship has the most powerful weapons in the universe, right?

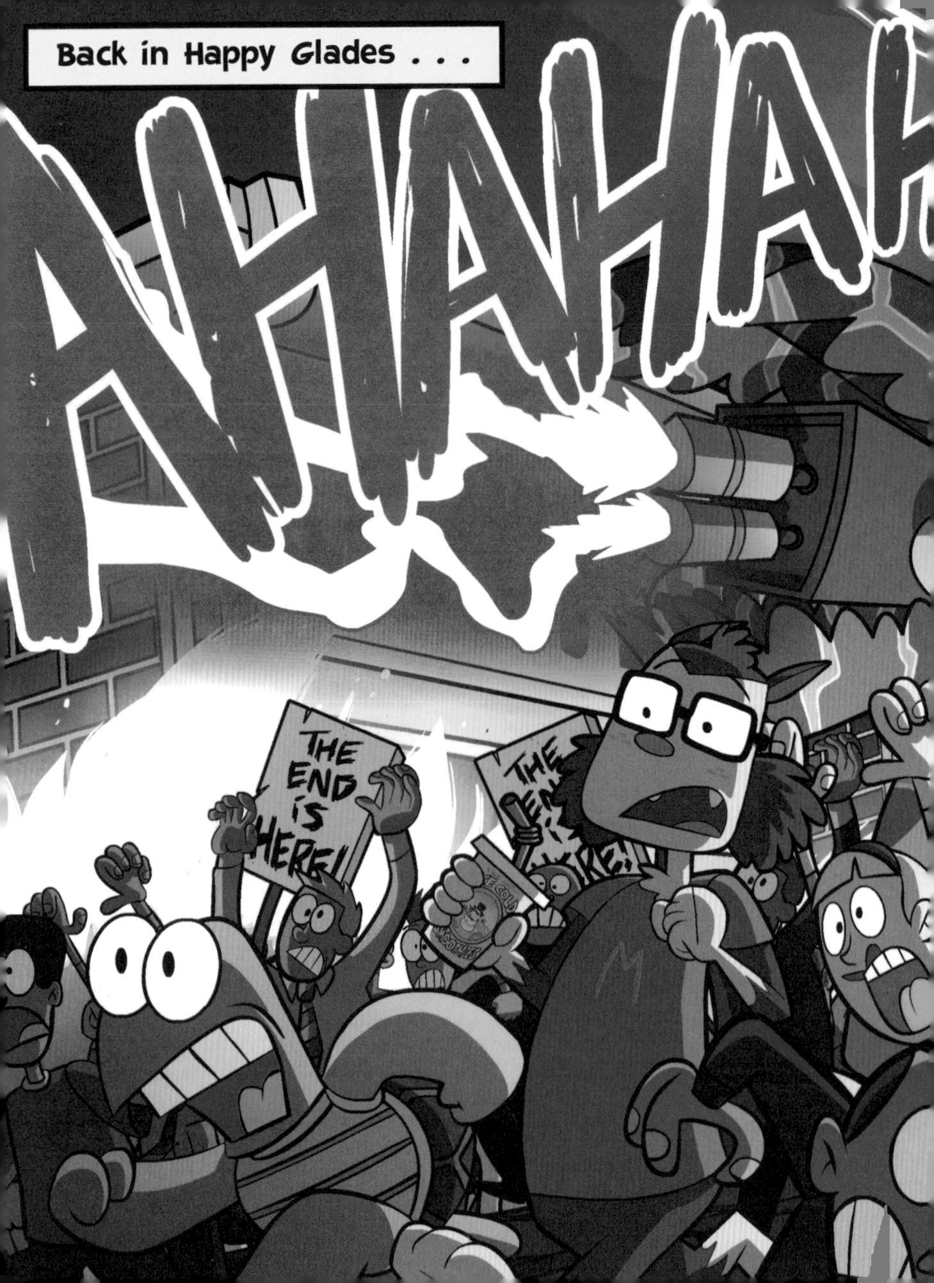
Back in Happy Glades . . .
AHHAHAH
THE END IS HERE!

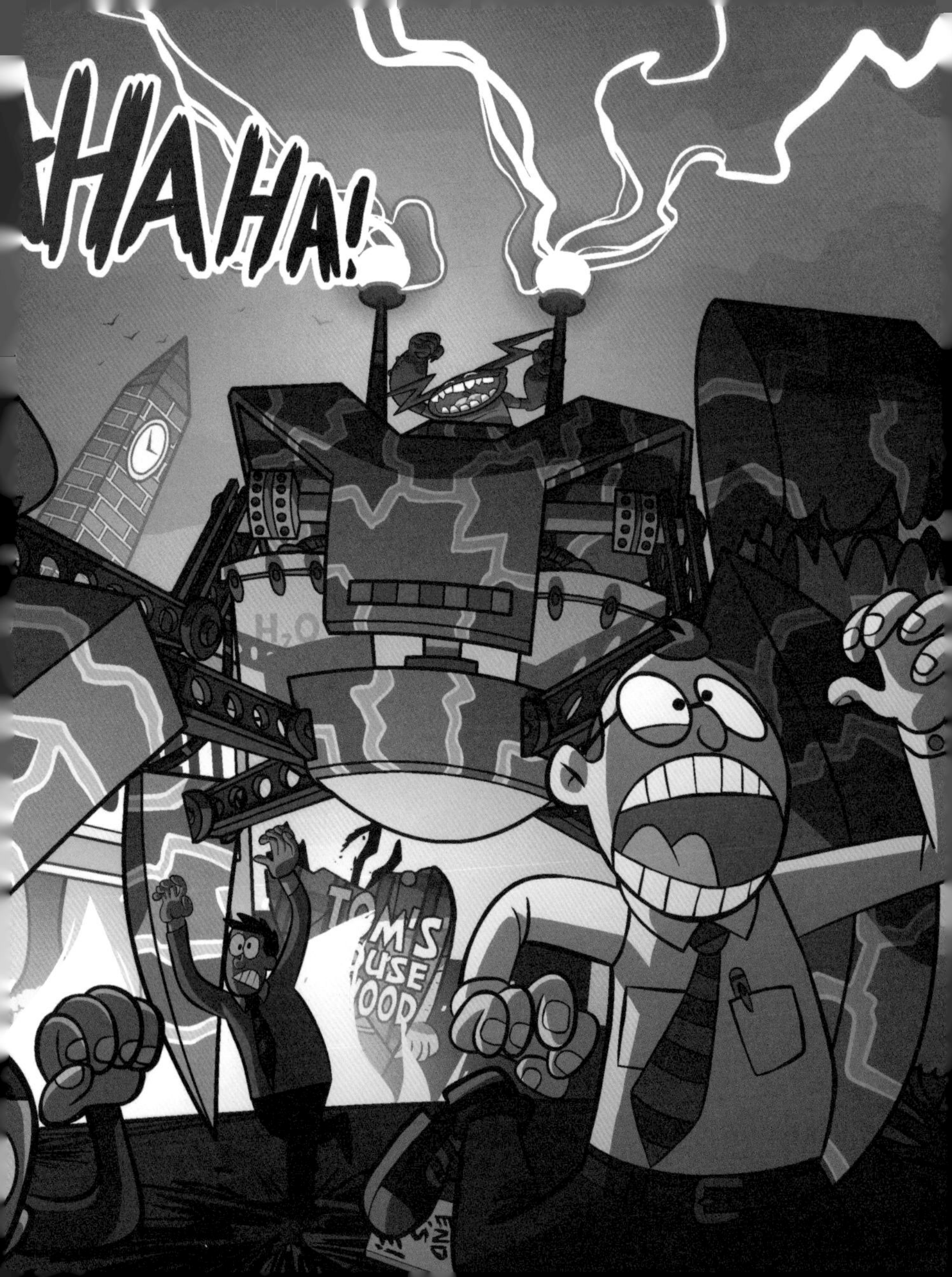
HAHA!
H_2O
TOM'S

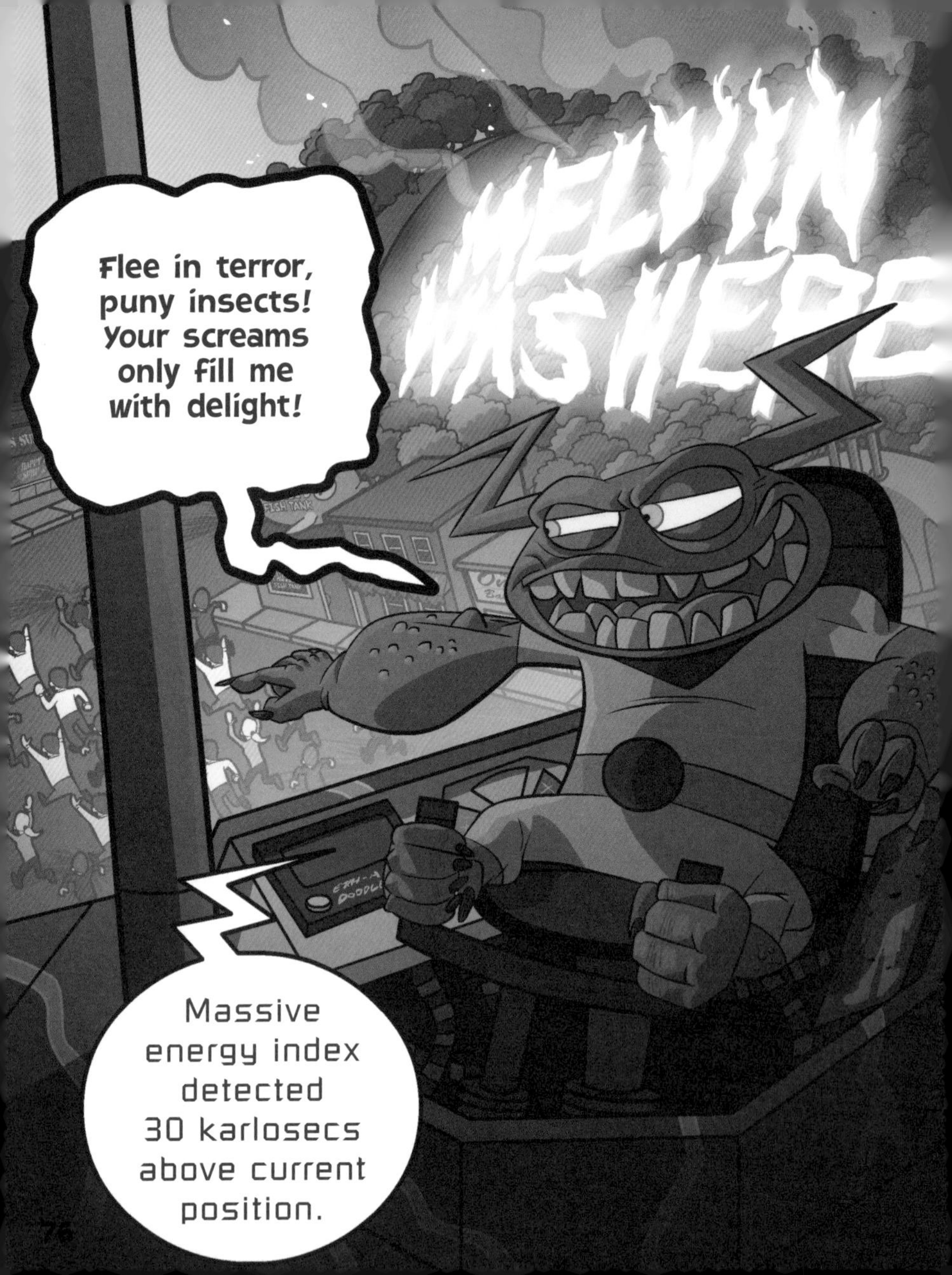
Flee in terror, puny insects! Your screams only fill me with delight!
MELVIN WAS HERE
Massive energy index detected 30 karlosecs above current position.

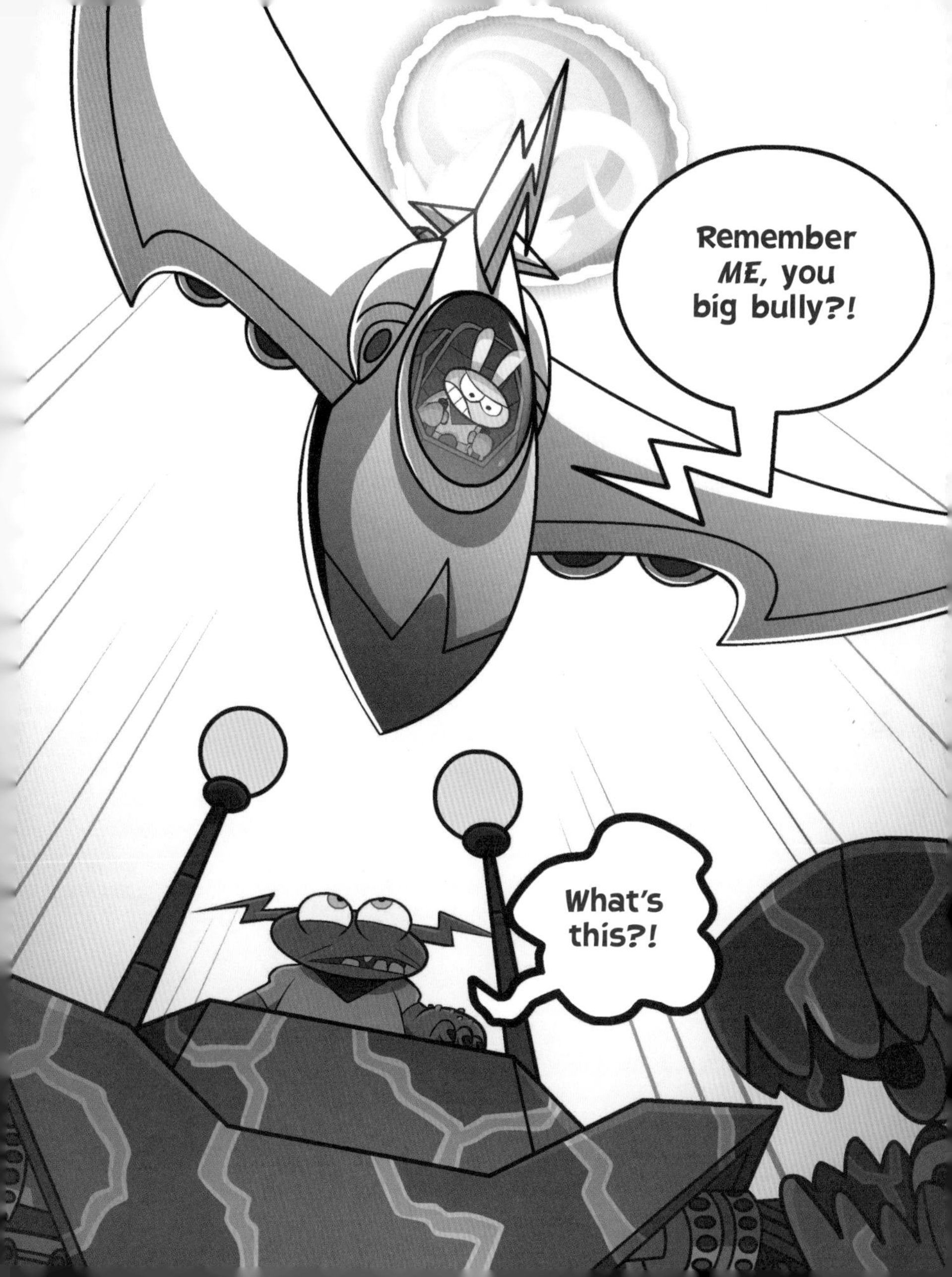
Remember *ME,* you big bully?!
What's this?!

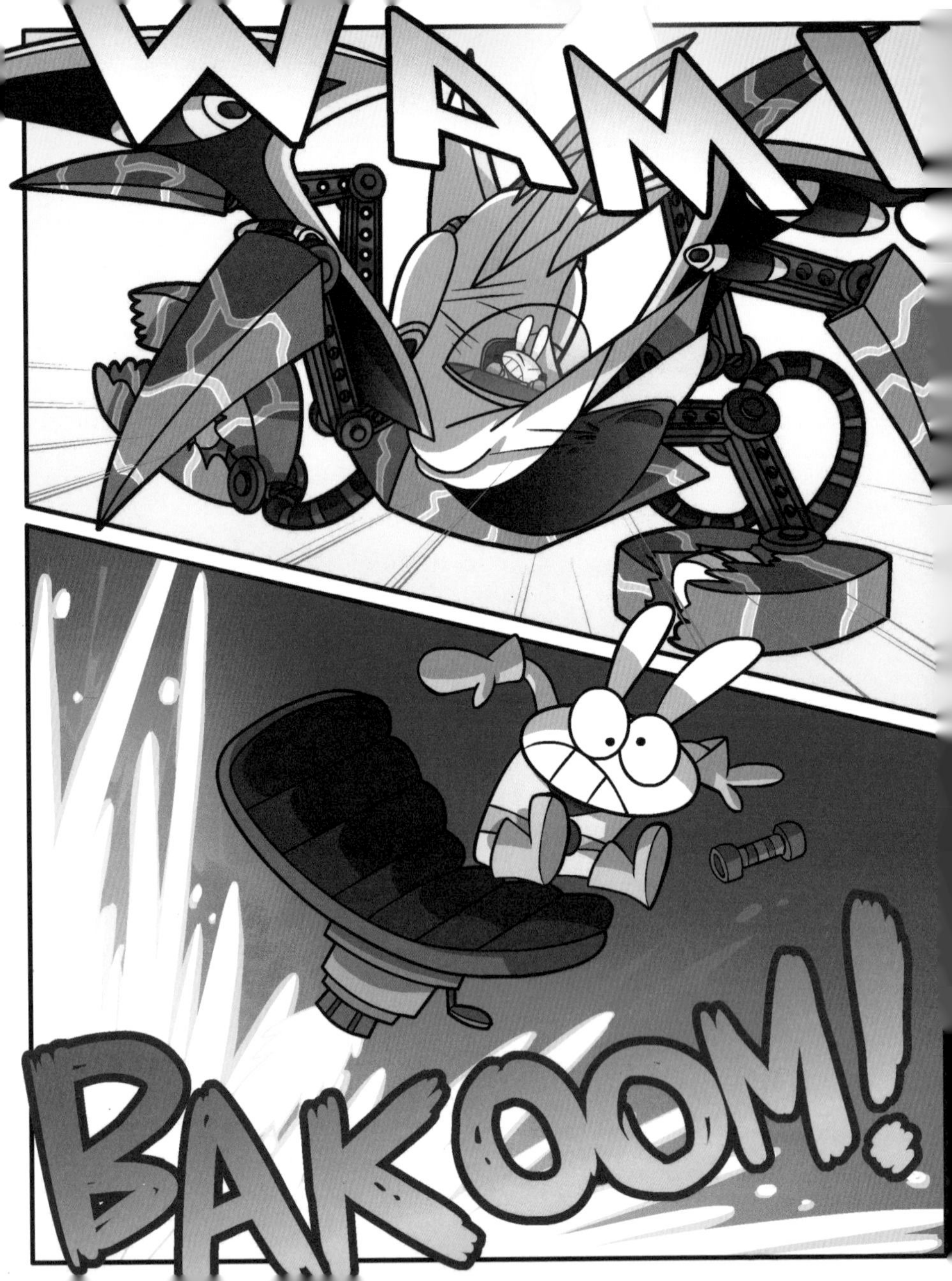
WAM!
BAKOOM!

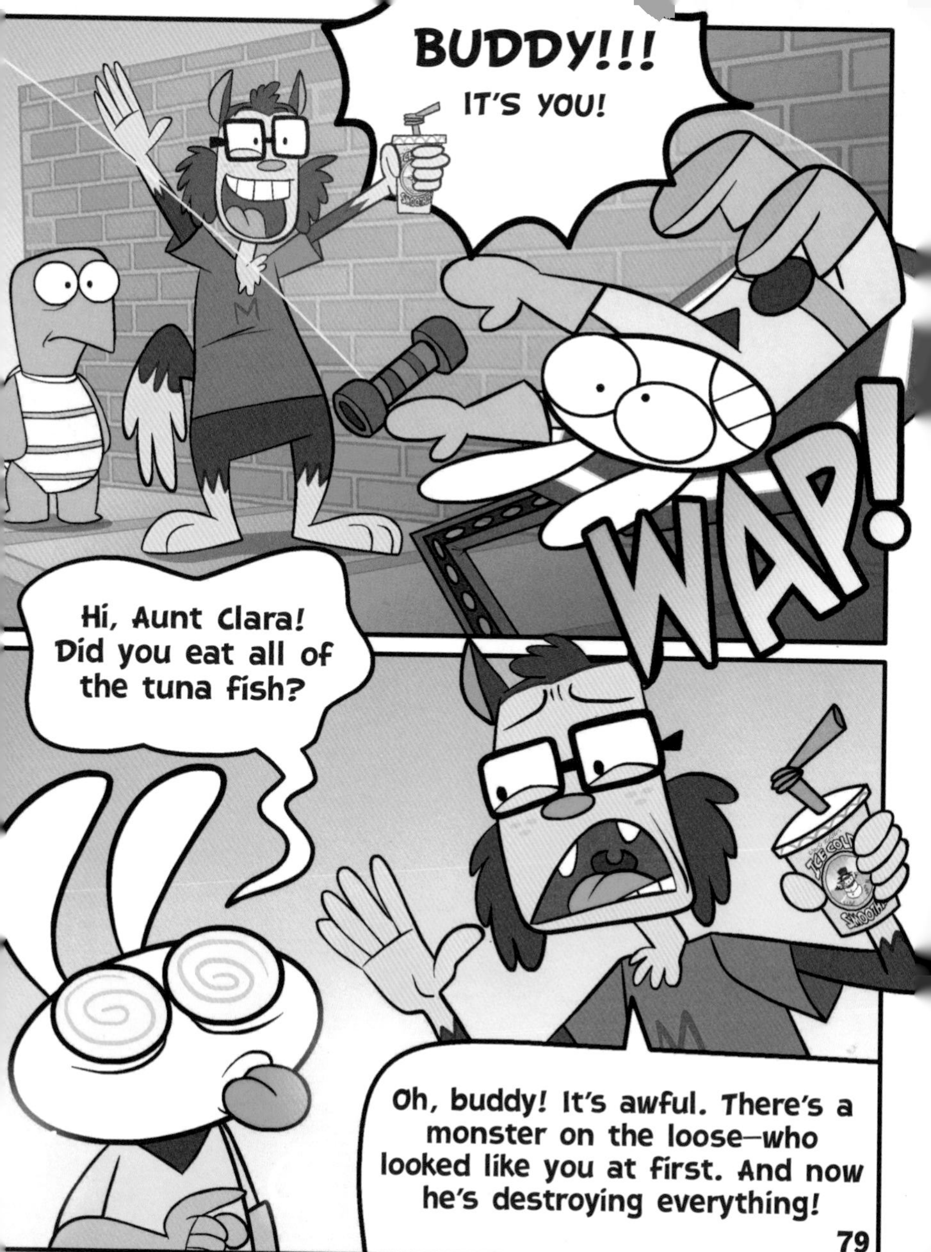
BUDDY!!! IT'S YOU!
WAP!
Hi, Aunt Clara! Did you eat all of the tuna fish?
Oh, buddy! It's awful. There's a monster on the loose—who looked like you at first. And now he's destroying everything!

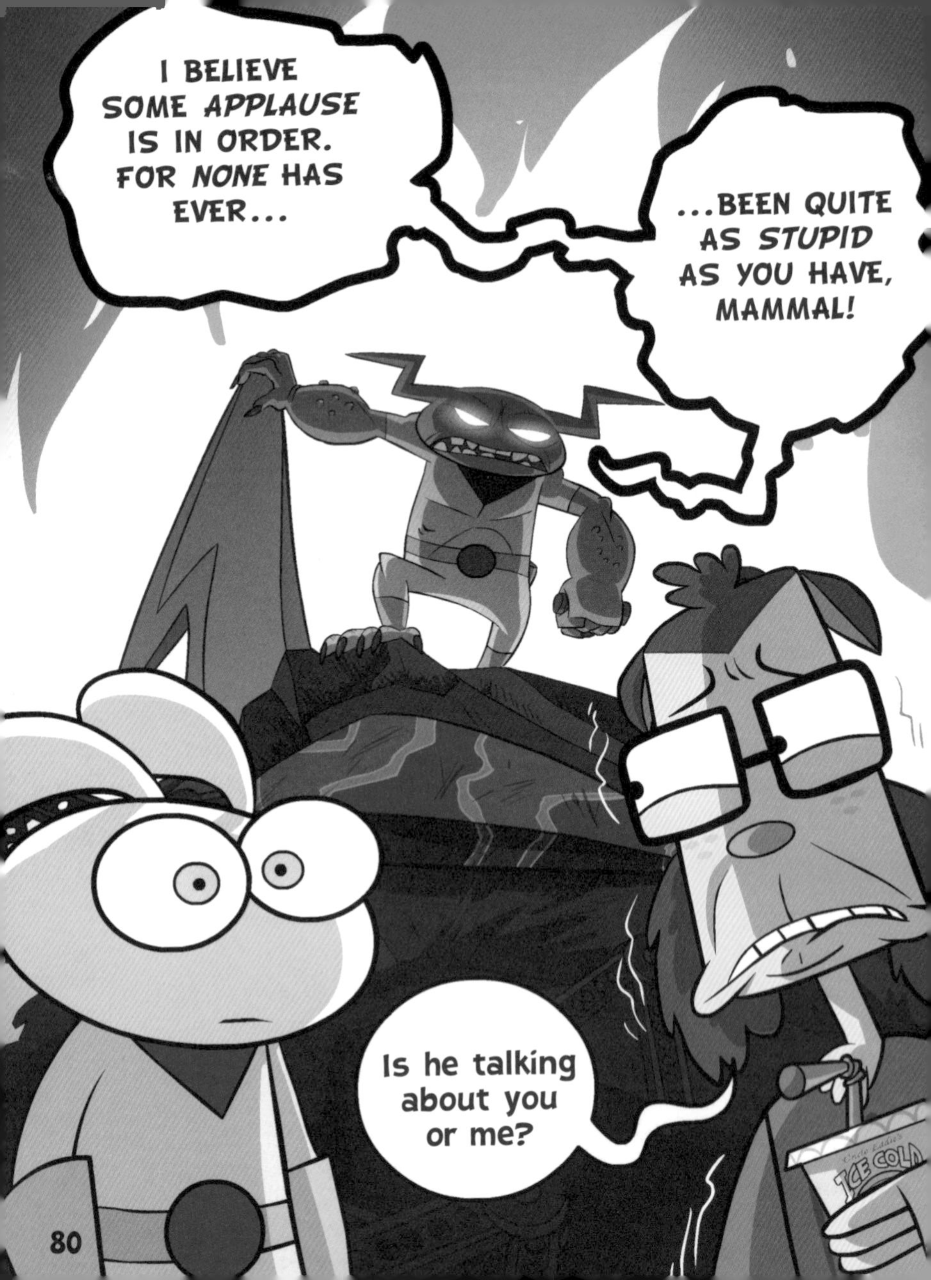
I BELIEVE SOME APPLAUSE IS IN ORDER. FOR NONE HAS EVER...
...BEEN QUITE AS STUPID AS YOU HAVE, MAMMAL!
Is he talking about you or me?
ICE COLD

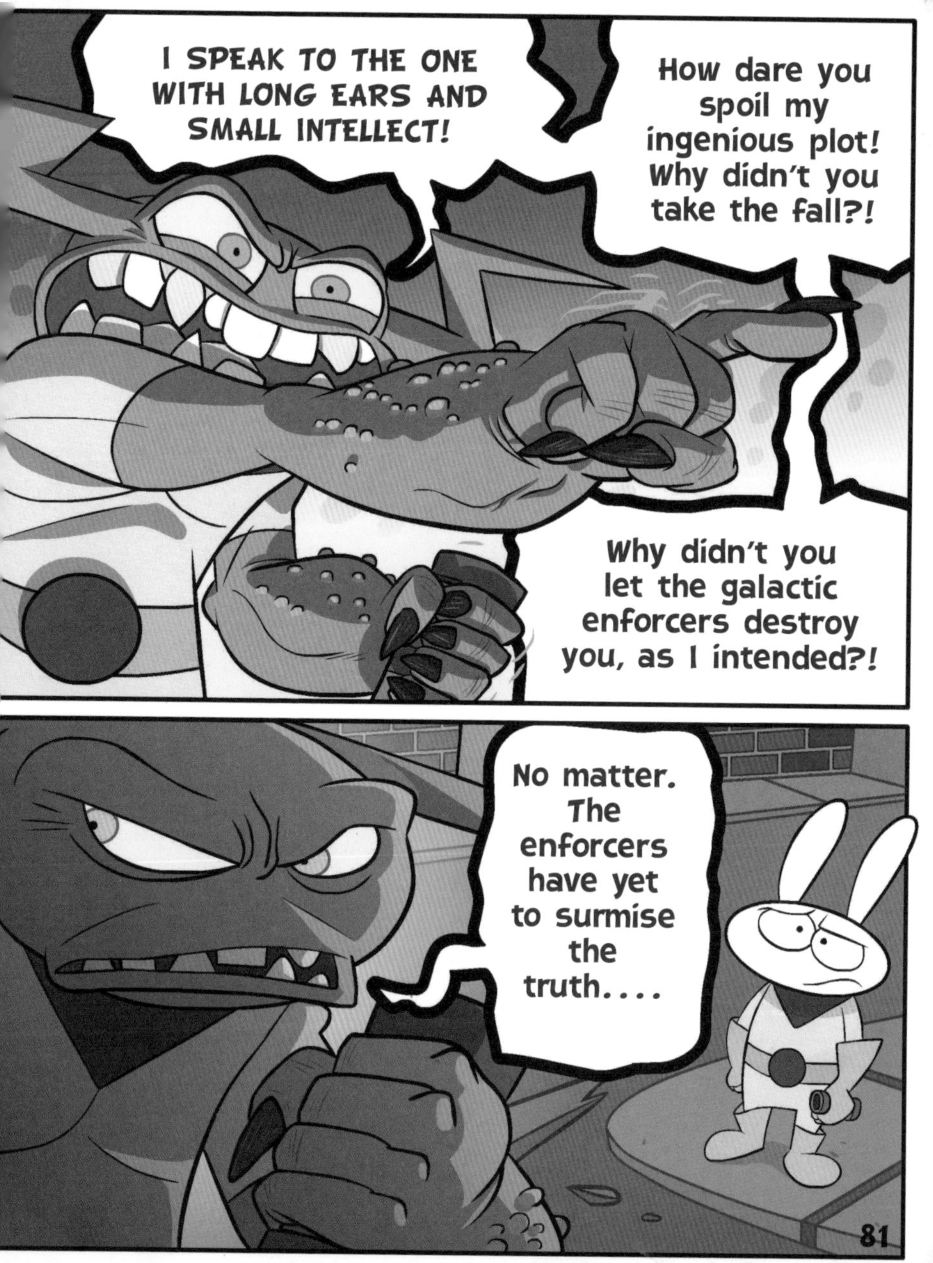
I SPEAK TO THE ONE WITH LONG EARS AND SMALL INTELLECT!
How dare you spoil my ingenious plot! Why didn't you take the fall?!
Why didn't you let the galactic enforcers destroy you, as I intended?!
No matter. The enforcers have yet to surmise the truth....

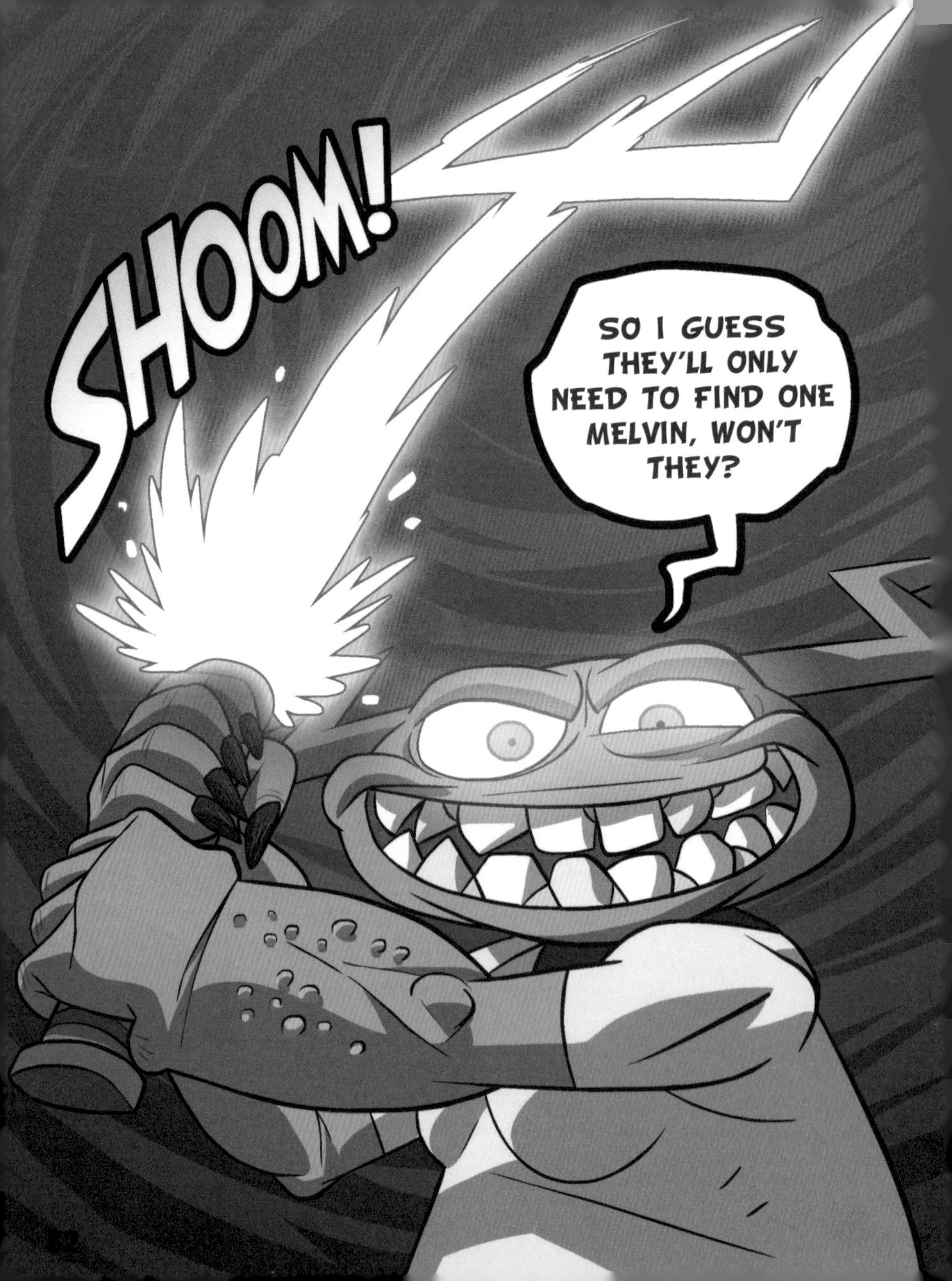
SHOOM!
SO I GUESS THEY'LL ONLY NEED TO FIND ONE MELVIN, WON'T THEY?

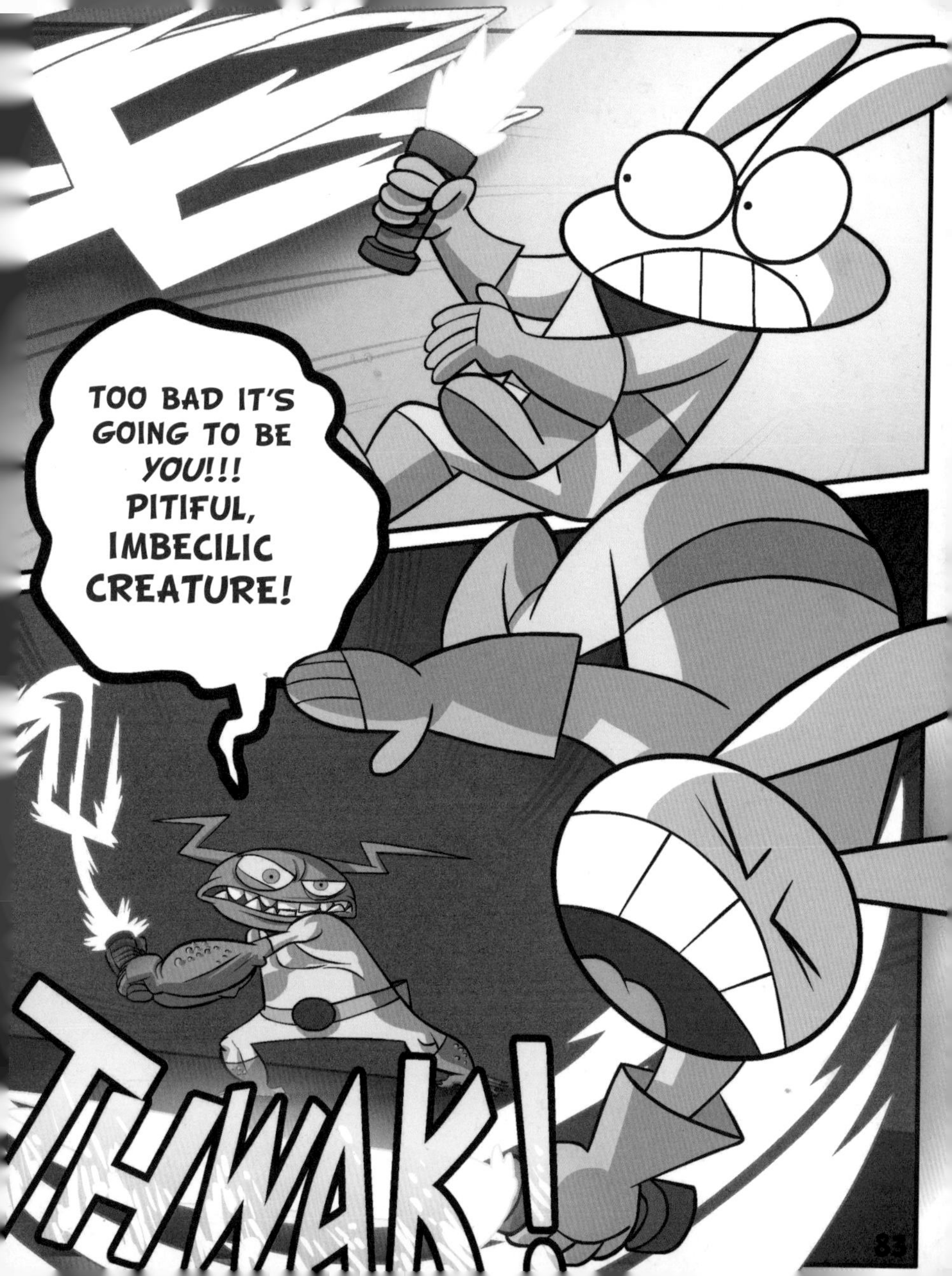
TOO BAD IT'S GOING TO BE *YOU!!!* PITIFUL, IMBECILIC CREATURE!
THWAK!

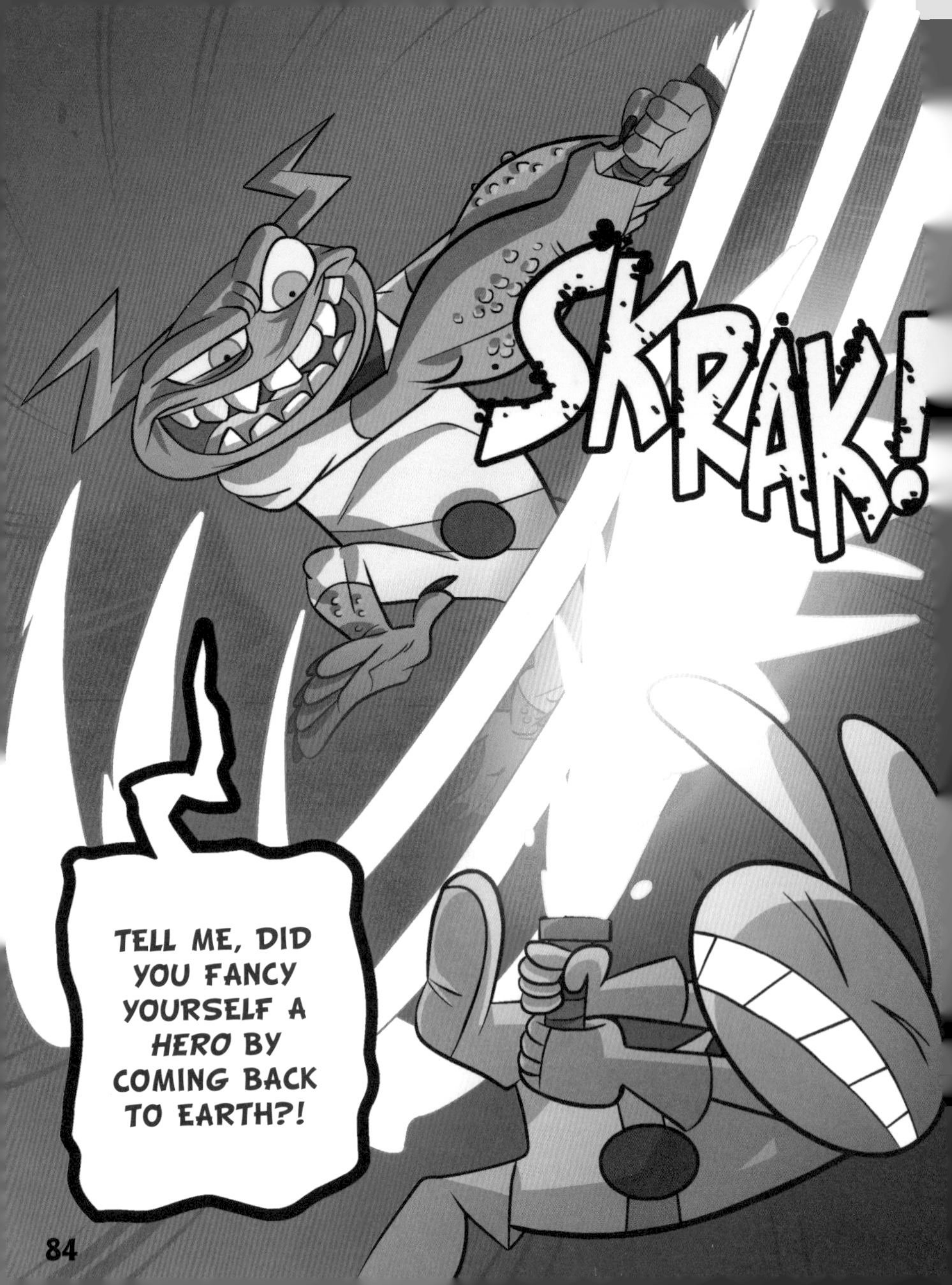
SKRAK!
TELL ME, DID YOU FANCY YOURSELF A *HERO* BY COMING BACK TO EARTH?!

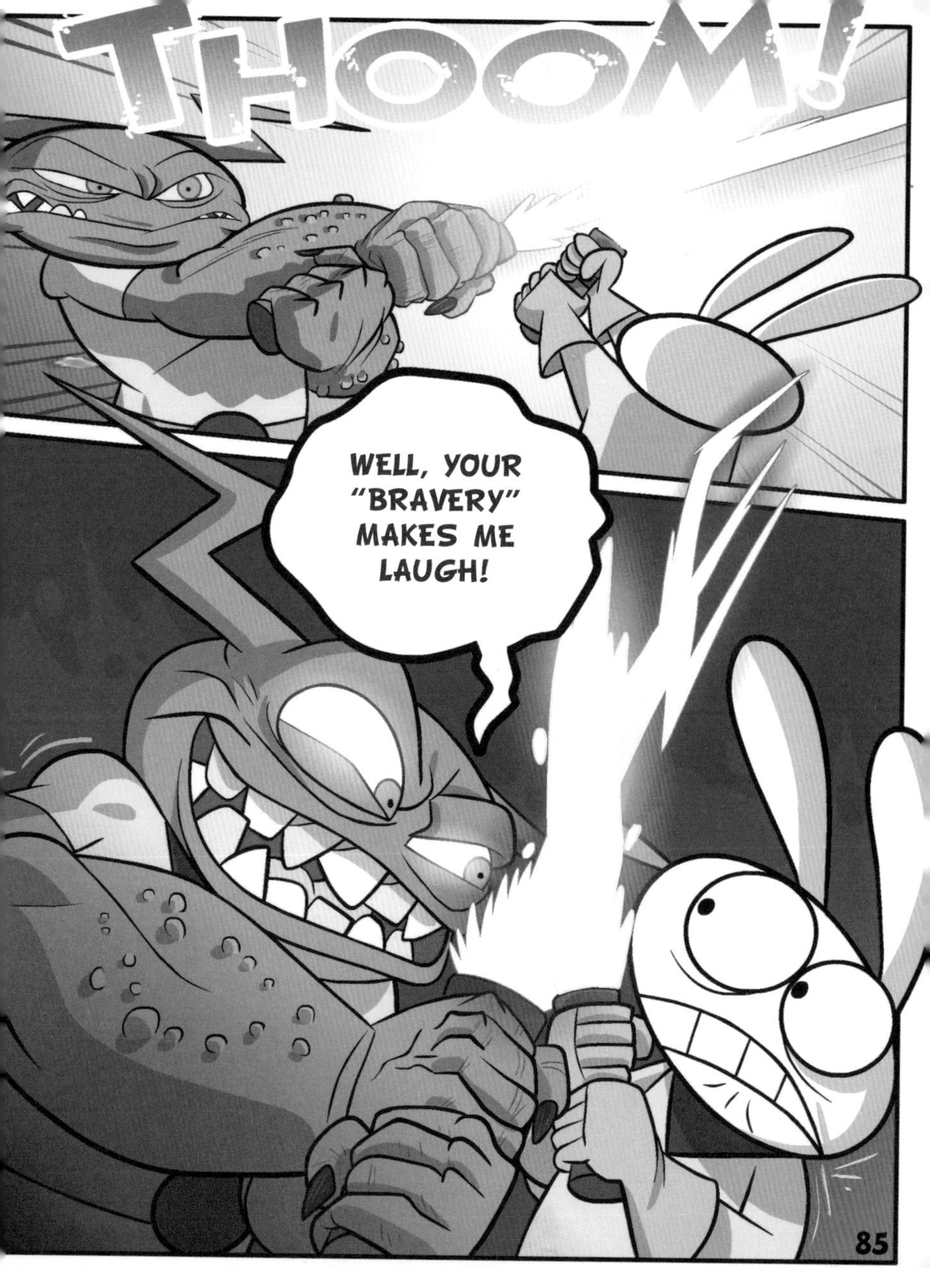
THOOM!
WELL, YOUR "BRAVERY" MAKES ME LAUGH!

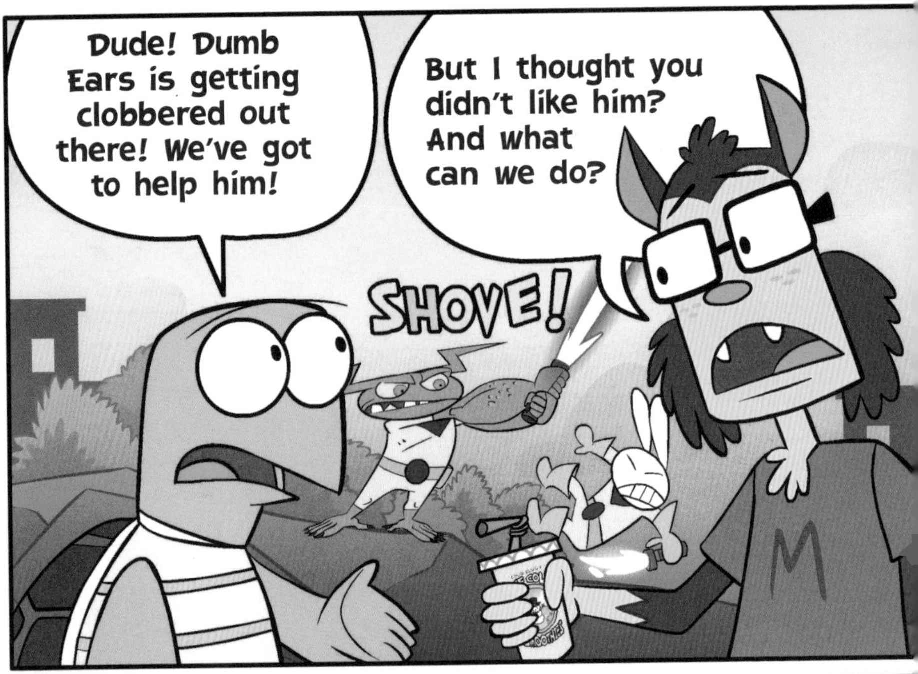
Dude! Dumb Ears is getting clobbered out there! We've got to help him!
But I thought you didn't like him? And what can we do?
SHOVE!

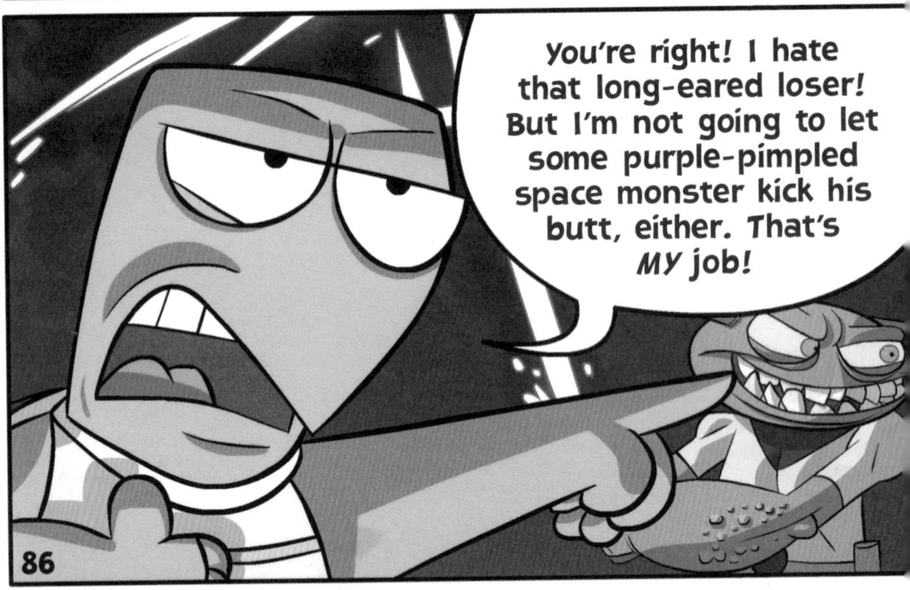
You're right! I hate that long-eared loser! But I'm not going to let some purple-pimpled space monster kick his butt, either. That's *MY* job!

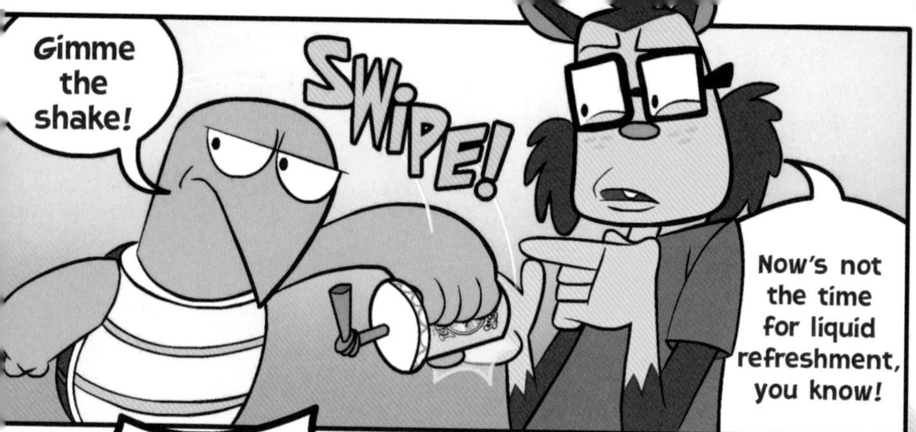
Gimme the shake!
SWIPE!
Now's not the time for liquid refreshment, you know!

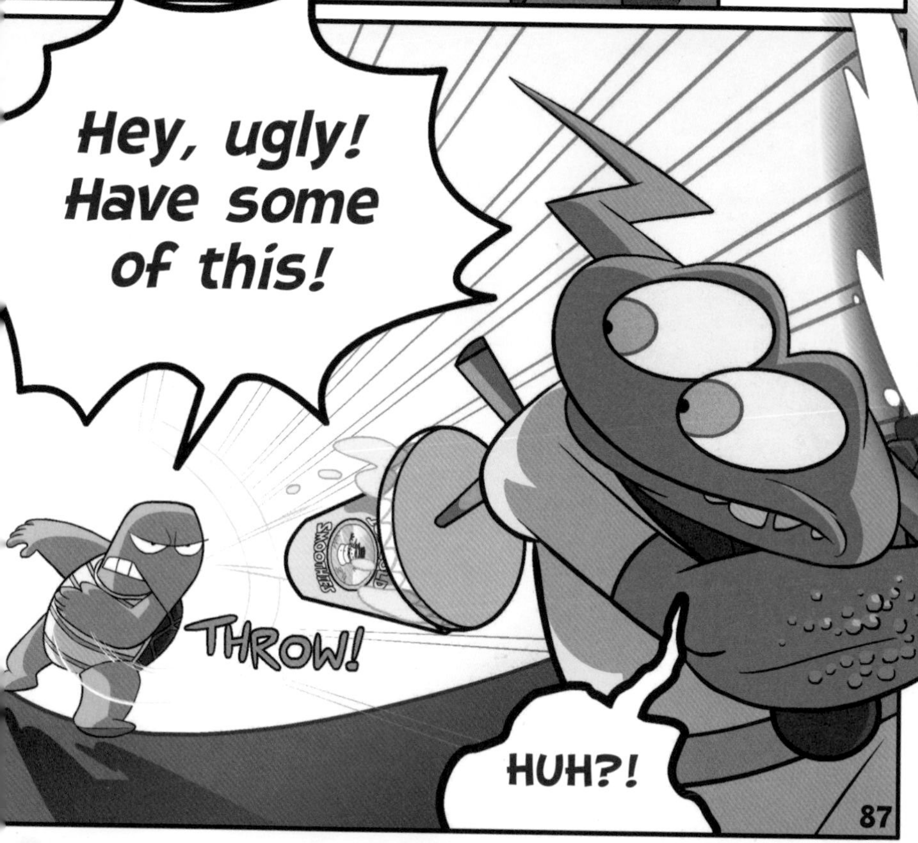
Hey, ugly! Have some of this!
THROW!
SMOOTHIES
HUH?!

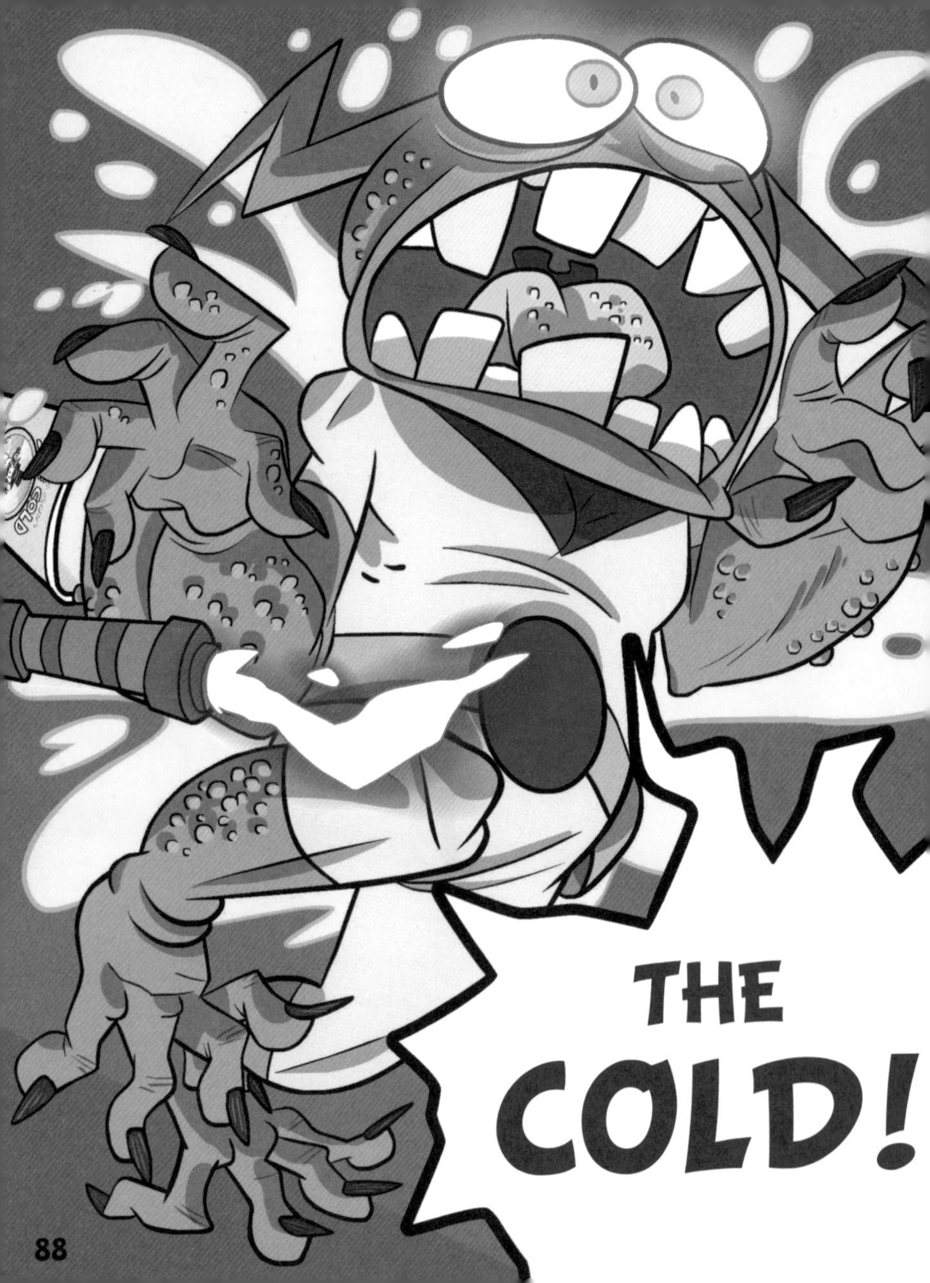
THE
COLD!

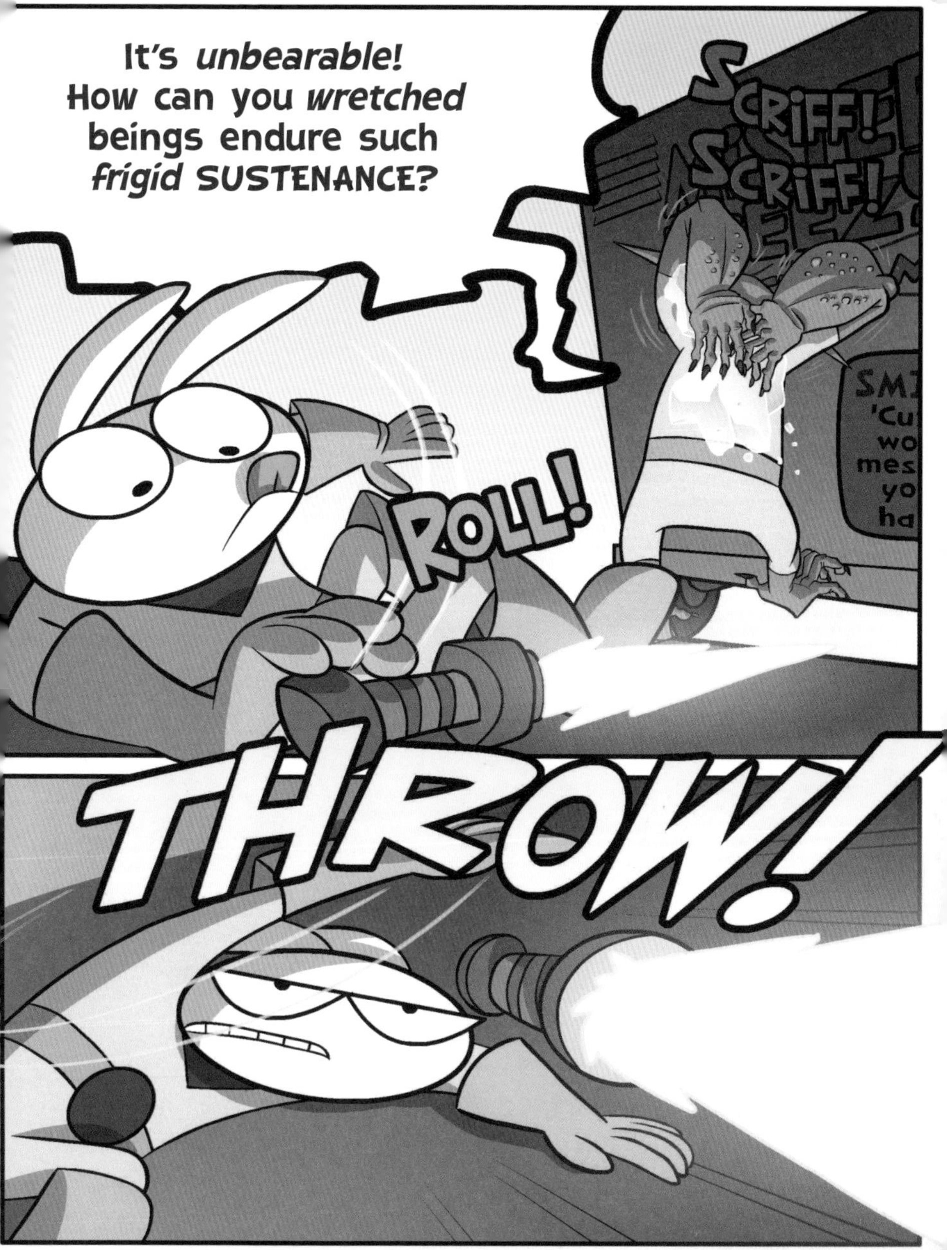
It's *unbearable!* How can you *wretched* beings endure such *frigid* SUSTENANCE?
SCRIFF! SCRIFF!
ROLL!
THROW!

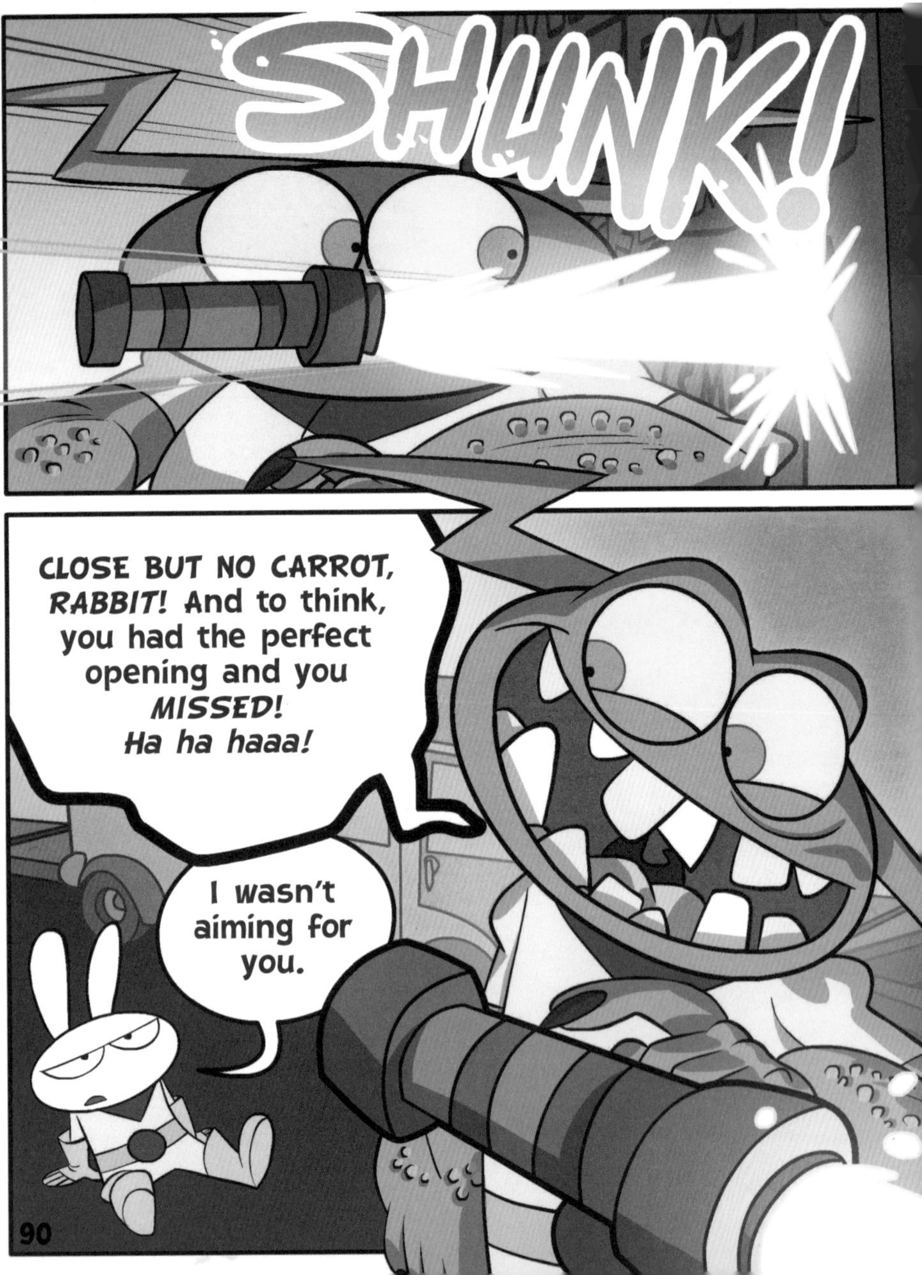
SHUNK!
CLOSE BUT NO CARROT, RABBIT! And to think, you had the perfect opening and you MISSED! Ha ha haaa!
I wasn't aiming for you.

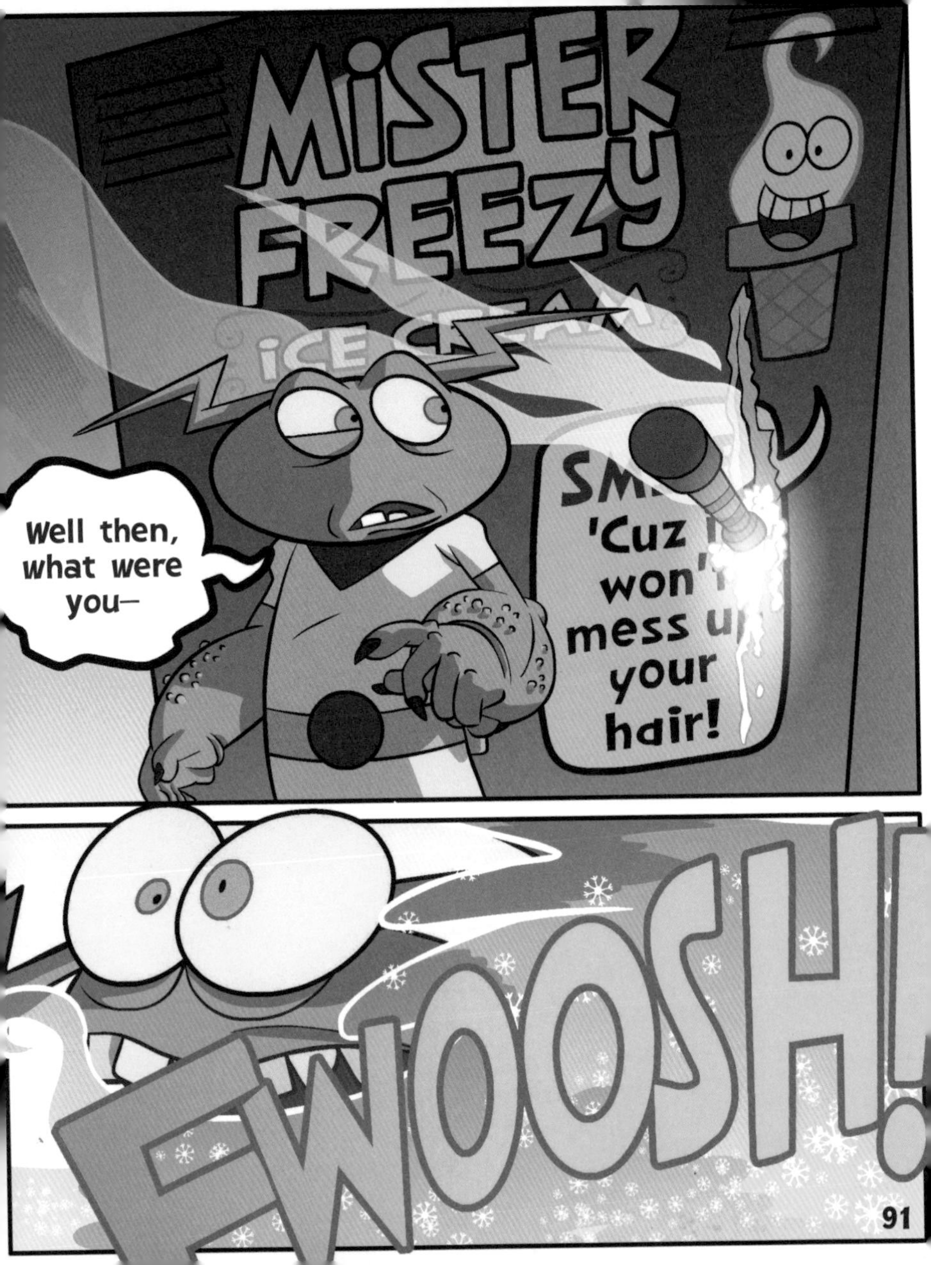
MISTER FREEZY
ICE
'Cuz
your
hair!
Well then, what were you—
FWOOSH!

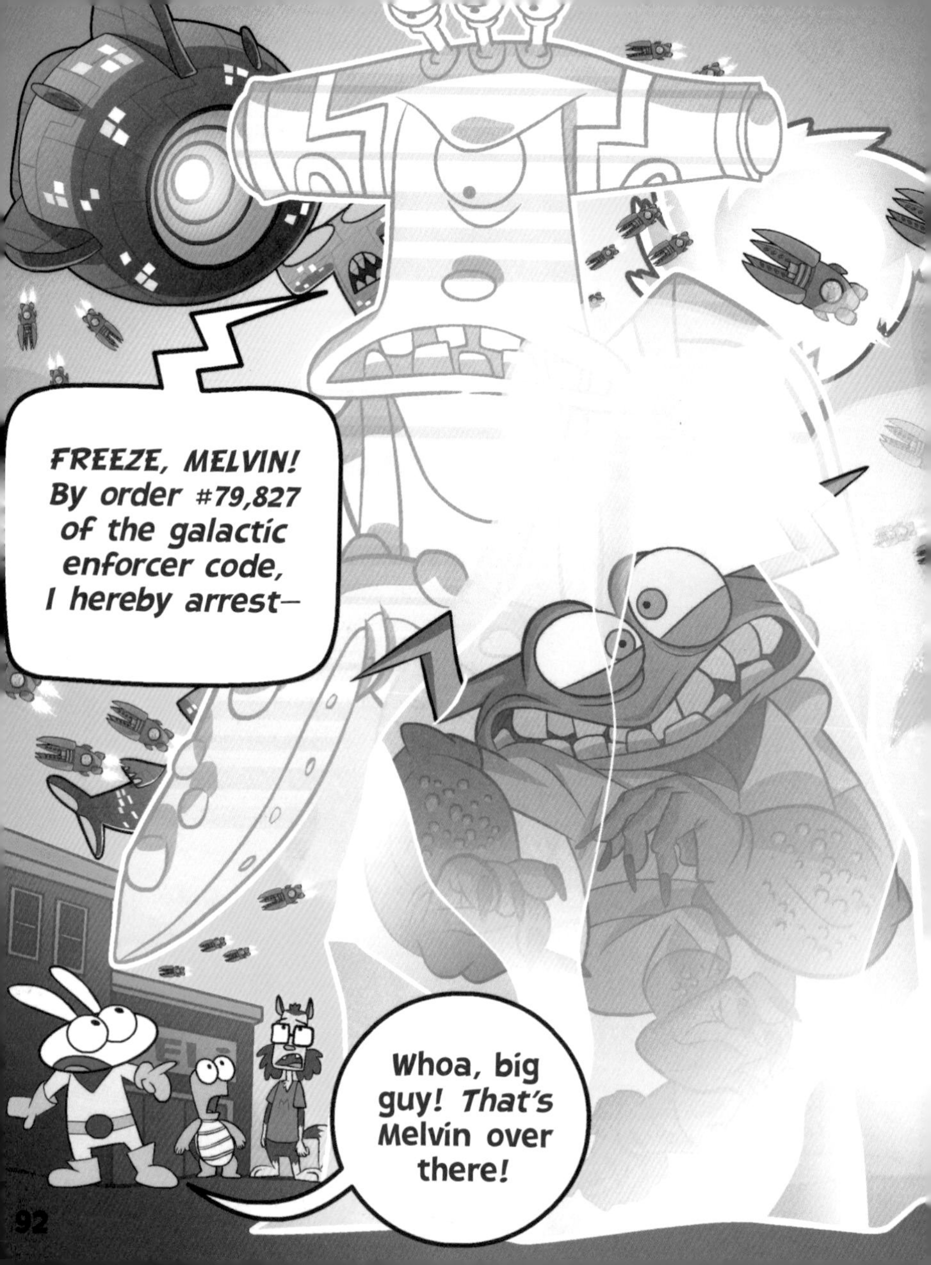
FREEZE, MELVIN! By order #79,827 of the galactic enforcer code, I hereby arrest—
Whoa, big guy! *That's* Melvin over there!

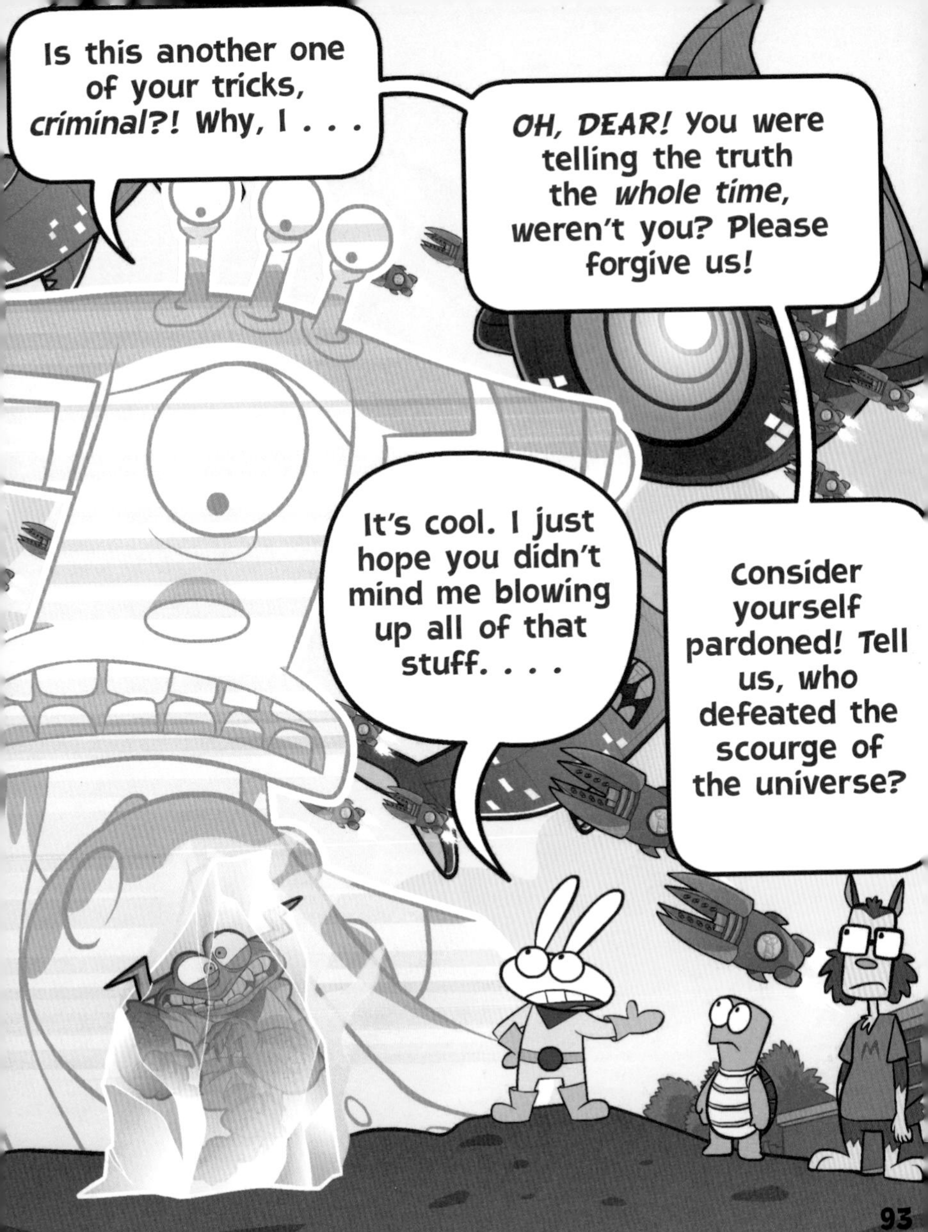

Is this another one of your tricks, *criminal?!* Why, I . . .
OH, DEAR! You were telling the truth the *whole time,* weren't you? Please forgive us!
It's cool. I just hope you didn't mind me blowing up all of that stuff. . . .
Consider yourself pardoned! Tell us, who defeated the scourge of the universe?

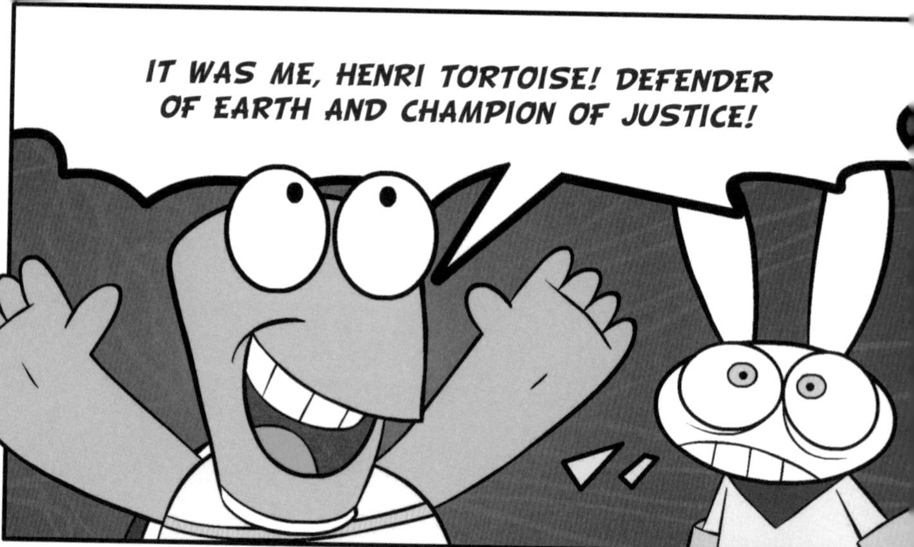
IT WAS ME, HENRI TORTOISE! DEFENDER OF EARTH AND CHAMPION OF JUSTICE!

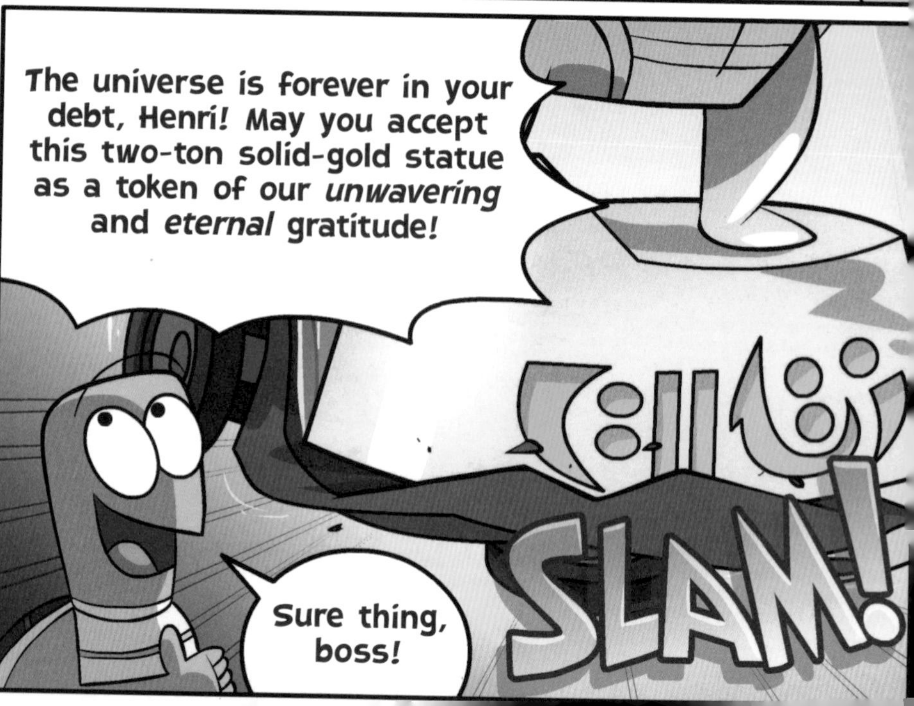
The universe is forever in your debt, Henri! May you accept this two-ton solid-gold statue as a token of our *unwavering* and *eternal* gratitude!
Sure thing, boss!
SLAM!

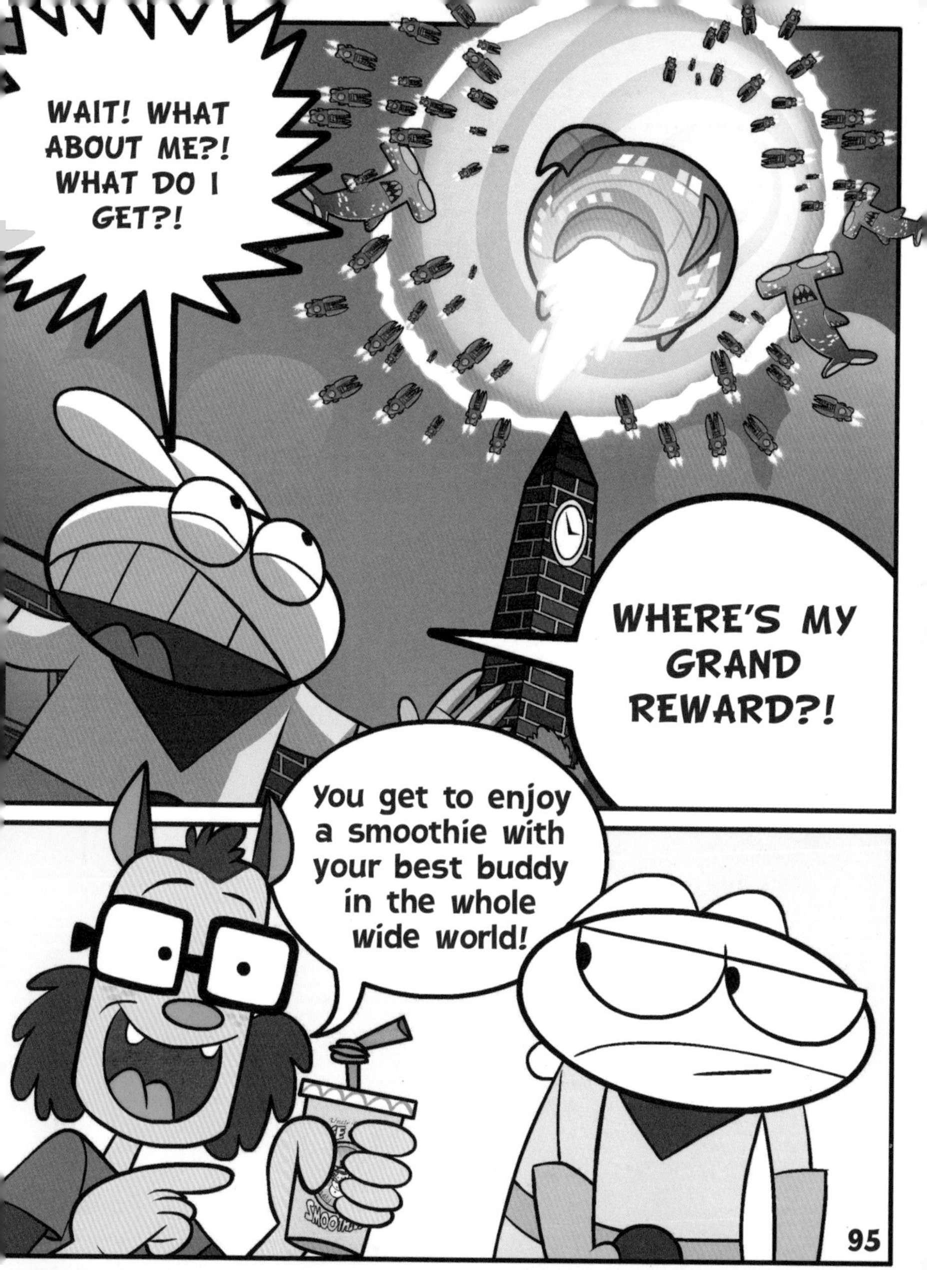

WAIT! WHAT ABOUT ME?! WHAT DO I GET?!
WHERE'S MY GRAND REWARD?!
You get to enjoy a smoothie with your best buddy in the whole wide world!

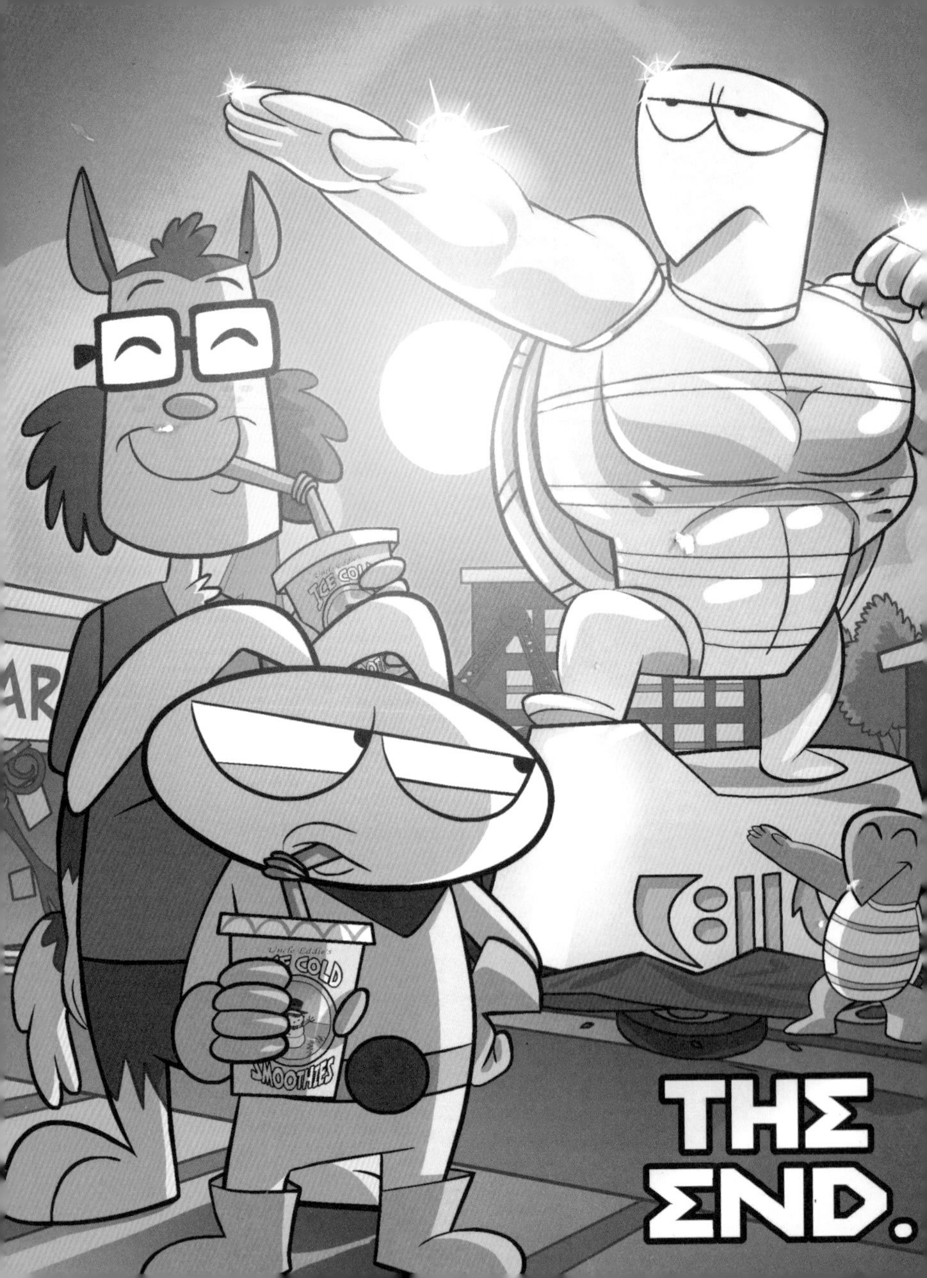
Uncle Eddie's
COLD
SMOOTHIES
THE END.